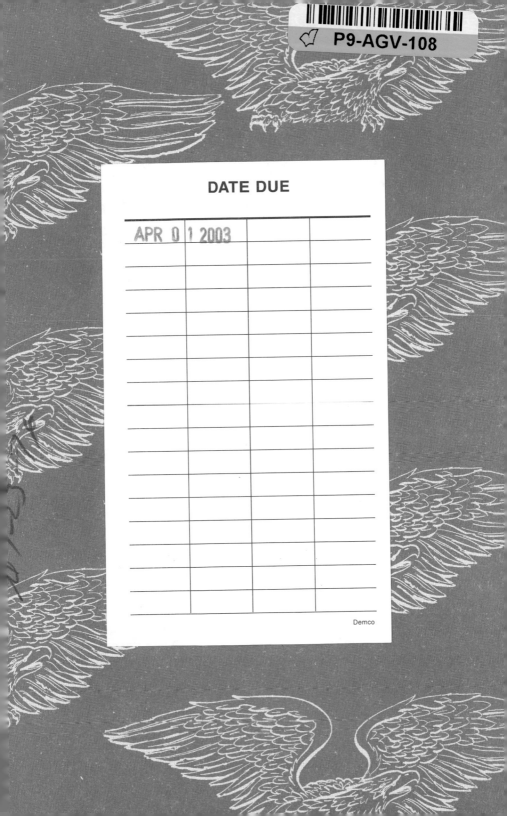

OUT OF PRISON

OUT OF PRISON

By
Mrs. Mary (Andrews) Dension

American Fiction Reprint Series

 BOOKS FOR LIBRARIES PRESS
FREEPORT, NEW YORK
1971

First published in 1864
(Item #732; Wright's AMERICAN FICTION 1851-1875)

Reprinted 1971 in *American Fiction Reprint Series*
from the Henry A. Young & Co. edition

INTERNATIONAL STANDARD BOOK NUMBER:
0-8369-7034-9

LIBRARY OF CONGRESS CATALOG CARD NUMBER:
74-164558

PRINTED IN THE UNITED STATES OF AMERICA

OUT OF PRISON.

"I AM A MAN; AND NOTHING THAT RELATES TO MAN IS INDIFFERENT TO ME."

———

BOSTON:
HENRY A. YOUNG & CO.,
24 CORNHILL.

CONTENTS.

iv

CONTENTS.

OUT OF PRISON.

CHAPTER I.

THE LITTLE OLD MAN.

WHICH to say, 'ee's a muff, John 'Arris."

"I do n't allow it," said the second speaker, revolving a showy yellow pipe in his fingers, and viewing it admiringly as he knocked the ashes from its brim.

It had been blustering weather for several days. Now the wind sprang up lightly from the westward. The sun glorified the great blue waste of waters. Far away stretched its splendors, blending in gold and silver against the horizon. On every crescent-curling wave the foam seemed dusted with diamonds. It was heaven to look, to breathe—to drink in all this calm of beauty and a certain spiritual peace born of the harmony of the elements. Perhaps, unconsciously, the two "hands" of the good ship Laura felt this as they cast quiet glances ever and anon over sea and sky. Attired in the inevitable monkey-jacket and tarpaulin hat, with bronzed, bearded faces that gave an air of travel and experience, they chatted at their leisure. The ship's decks were admirably clean. A nor-easter had served the office of washerwoman, and performed its duties admirably. Not a splinter, not a speck could be seen. The pale translucent colors of the far swells that pulsed along the great bosom of the deep, seemed not more bright than the newly cleansed, clear sea-green of the painted lines of the ship wherever they occurred. The sails nearly blinded one when the sun struck them, they were so icily white. Every thing was in trim, just as good sailors like to have it, from stem to stern.

"Which to say, I did n't like him," exclaimed the first speaker, a blunt little Englishman, whom his messmates dubbed "Which to say," on account of his often reiteration of the words.

"That may be. I do n't 'spose it would trouble his head if he knew it. But I tell you what, we took a little cabin boy to Barbadoes—a regular little good one, he was—used to talk right up like a bit of a man when we big ones ripped an oath out now and then. He and the little old fellow in the cabin there, were jolly together, I can tell you. Well, we run into the jaws of death, that time. Plague was there—could n't get out of course till

our cargo did, and was n't well hands enough to
work. 'Taint pleasant in harbor, such a time.
Water do n't look good—sky do n't look good.
The flies grow fat, and feel cold and blistery on your
flesh. There's a clammy smell on the air that
makes you long for snow and ice in the harbor.
Looked very bad on the cliff—plenty of coffins
packed up, ready for the long-shore men. News
came down every morning that hundreds had died
in the night; sometimes p'lecemen went in a house
and found every soul dead. Fact is, people dropped
in the streets; old death did n't wait to give cards;
just poked his finger at 'em and down they went.
'Twas the cholera; cholera's good deal worse than
yeller Jack; *he* gives a feller time to think if he
did n't get in the head too soon. I felt bad for the
captain; captain's wife, as nice a little lady as ever
brought a blessing on a ship. She looked scared
and pale at first a little, but it did n't last long.
Instead of that she brightened up after an hour or
two, and made us all feel comfortable to see her
smiling. Between you and me, Jim, I guess she'd
been and got a bit of faith from aloft. It looked
so.

"Well, we'd managed along comfortable. Captain, he was particular; captain's wife made us yarb
teas, red hot with pepper, that kept us lively. We
did n't whistle for the fust few days, but pretty

soon we got over that. Little Steevie, bless his heart! was jolly as ever—nice little curly headed lad he was, as will be a great loss to his widowed mother, provided she is a widow, which I believe she isn't, being as I heard the captain say something about his father; but any way, there'll be wet eyes when the tidings reaches 'em."

"Which to say is as the boy died," remarked Jim, doggedly, noticing that his mate's eyelashes glistened suspiciously.

"That's just it, in so many words," replied Harris; " you couldn't have said it more to the pint. He was took of a Sunday, when we'd all done expecting to be sick any way. And the little old man tended him like a reg'lar doctor. 'T was mighty hard to see him suffer so, but my heart warmed to that little old Australie fellow as it never did to no person before. And the boy, why, he died cuddled up in his arms. His last words was, 'take care of poor mother.' Yes, we didn't keep him long, be sure; 't was hard, too, to see him rolled up like a dog, bless his blue eyes! and thrown over. It took all the starch out of us old coveys. I don't know as I've had such a reg'lar cry since the time I was a youngster in shorts, when mammy died. Seemed like a funeral every day after that, we'd been so used to Steevie's bright eyes and merry laugh. Don't like to see such ones cut off, don't seem right, no way. The mis'a'blest dog on the ship took sick, not long after, but he got well. Long and short of it is, I did n't see into it, no how. The lad would have done good if he 'd grown up — old Bunkers jest lives to cuss and drink grog, and be in people's way generally. He 'll go home now, and some day get taken up for beating his wife."

"Which to say is, he 's a hard cove," remarked the short son of Britain.

"Yes, a harder one never lived. And he promised all sorts o' promises too, and broke 'em all the very fust day he got on deck. But look alive, man, we 're coming to Cape Cod light-house — and the wind begins to blow stiff. There 's the mate — forward 's the word."

"Which to say," muttered Jim; and the rest was lost, for just then an order being sharply given, the men went to work.

A bright little affair was the cabin of the Laura. The carpets had been put down, covers taken off, gilding uncovered, and furniture polished. At the farther end, the door opened into a luxurious stateroom, out of which the soft west wind blew the lace curtains of the bed, that had a tinge of pink in them, reflected from the crimson hangings. The captain's wife, a fair and slender woman, reclined under the canopy, reading, while the captain trimmed his whiskers and hummed to himself.

At the table, in the cabin, sat the little old man whom the Englishman had denominated a "muff." A well worn pack of cards laid on the baize cloth. These he shuffled, deliberately dealt them out to three imaginary characters, making a curt, positive bow to each. Then beginning to play, he picked and threw the cards successively, indulging in odd ejaculations after the manner of card players.

"A very good card, A," he would mutter; "ah! you have me there, B. I see I must play sharper. Now match that if you can." And thus, good naturedly smiling and chatting with his invisibles, he played the game through to the musical accompaniment of the waves, as they curled and dashed against the keel of the vessel.

Before he had quite finished, Captain Gurney came out of his state-room. A sailor every inch, he walked quietly forward and stopped before the little old man, buttoning his coat preparatory to going on deck — his keen eye sparkling — a quizical smile curving the firmly outlined lips. He watched the singular proceedings of his solitary passenger.

"You must find it rather quiet, Mr. Lyons — did you always play alone?"

"Alone! So you thought me alone, did you? O, no! I'm never alone, Captain Gurney. I have three friends, but unfortunately they are not visible to human ken." The sunlight at that moment shone on his blue goggles, giving a spectral hue to the old man's face.

"Ah!" said the captain, humoring his mood, "then these three I presume were comrades of yours once."

"Yes, captain, and three finer fellows never lived. Carol and Archer were killed while prospecting, and Billy had a stroke. It was a sudden death with each, and I expect it will be a sudden death with me. Very well, I am ready;" and the little man gathered his cards up.

"Then you can say more than many can, Mr. Lyons; death is generally something to be dreaded."

"Not at all, sir; not at all," returned the old man in a lively way. "I've no fear of the thing in the least, sir, because I've come to the conclusion long ago, that death makes no difference in a man's state, captain. I am firmly convinced there is nothing of us after the worms have finished us. You do not digest my confession comfortably, captain."

"I confess, such principles always strike me with horror," replied the latter.

"Sorry for you, captain, but I never talk of this thing; never go into argument for argument's sake. It's enough for me that I hold and enjoy the conviction. I wish to make no proselytes, captain."

"Heaven forbid; and you are an old man," said the captain, with something of pity in his voice.

"O! as to that, not so very old," was the lively rejoinder, "not so old as I look. I was always old looking. Were you going on deck, captain?"

"Yes, as soon as my wife is ready. We shall be in the dock in half an hour, and she is anxious to see the shores of our native city. But, sir, one word more; surely your declaration a few moments ago, disproves your last assertion. You are never alone, you say; and the three who are gone sit with you at your games."

"All a pleasant little hallucination, my dear captain; an effort of memory. My brain retains the impression of their individual faces and characteristics, and there they live sir, till I am gone. I wonder who I shall stamp my personality upon?"

By this time he had returned the cards to their case and stood upright: a queer, small figure, that provoked a smile by its odd accoutrements, as well as its shrivelled proportions. The white hat which he lifted from its nail must have seen the service of years. It was bell-crowned, and suggested thoughts of ancient garrets filled with furniture no longer used. It was the same with his narrow-skirted, swallow-tailed coat, and unaccountably spare pantaloons. His face was keen, indicating caution and benevolence. The twinkle of his eye denoted a relish for humor, (and he could tell a story capitally) while his lips, thin, yet mobile, worked con-

stantly, showing that he was always absorbed in
thought, when not talking. His forehead was fair —
ample in the regions of benevolence; his hair was
white and silky, and his disposition so thoroughly
amiable that during the whole voyage, though exposed to sundry vexations, he was never known to
lose his temper in the slightest degree.

His baggage consisted of two boxes, one of which
was marked in large letters, " NAILS ;" the other
had only the initials of his name, clumsily knocked
in with brass-headed tacks. These boxes he kept
always with him, neither of them being very large;
and every day as he went round singing under his
voice—this also being a peculiarity of his—he
would methodically open and inspect them thoroughly, though no one else ever saw their contents.

"Laura," called the captain; and presently his
wife came out shawled and bonneted, and went on
deck with him.

"I'm completely mystified about that man," said
Captain Gurney, half whispering in her ear.

" Why, dear?"

" He's an enigma; professes himself entirely destitute of religious principles; alone in the world ;
for he must be a stranger to this part of the country :
without resources, apparently, and yet he's as
happy as a king."

"I think he's a delightful old gentleman," said

Laura, smiling and nodding as she caught his eye;
"but look, Philip, there's the old wharf—the dear
old wharf—and I should n't wonder if that is
Colonel Willerton's carriage. But oh, Philip, how
I dread meeting poor Mrs. Franklin! What will
she do when she learns that her beautiful boy is
dead? She'll be so sorry she let him go!"

"What sort of a person is this Mrs. Franklin,
madam?" asked Mr. Lyons, readjusting his spectacles, and looking across to the crowd that was just
leaving the wharf, yet at a considerable distance.

"A very lady-like, pretty little woman," replied
Laura; "and so devoted to her children; I dread
to meet her. She is an old friend of mine."

"And their circumstances," said the old gentleman, quietly; shaking out his handkerchief, a
bright pink and yellow Madras silk.

"O! poor, very poor; or she never would have
parted with Steevie. They have been particularly
unfortunate in their children. Little Steevie was
the youngest."

"How many children?" queried the old man.

"There *were* four. One of the girls works out;
the other is an invalid."

"That makes three," said her listener, promptly.

"There was an elder son; I should say, there *is*
an elder son," she flushed painfully, "but, I am
sorry to say—"

' Eh! some sort of disgrace, I see. Don't be afraid to tell me, madam. One of my peculiarities is, making allowances for people. The worst are not as bad as they seem; I found that out long ago. I have been among convicts, ma'm. Perhaps the youngster is a rogue by constitution;" and he shook out the folds of his handkerchief again.

"Which to say is, there's landsharks coming in that 'ere boat," said a voice in the distance.

"O, no, no!" cried Laura, earnestly, the quick blush paling out. "In a moment of temptation he committed a crime that consigned him to State Prison. But for all that, Mr. Lyons, he's a thoroughly reformed and noble fellow. In the very depths of his suffering he has found a hope that sustains him and makes him happy."

"Hum—glad to hear it," said Mr. Lyons, pursing his lips; "but what did the boy do?" he queried, as the cynical smile faded away; "put his hand in the money drawer, eh?"

"He did what was as bad, sir; he forged a check."

"The thoughtless rascal!" muttered the old man in a low voice. "So, he has plunged an honest family in disgrace—ruined himself for life," he added in a lower tone; "and that's the end of *him*."

"O, no, sir; not so bad as that!" Laura spoke

up, cheerfully; "though he did break the law, he is penitent, and thoroughly reformed. We all feel that he was led away by evil companions, and we shall stand by him," laying peculiar emphasis on the we.

"Pray, who are we?" queried the old gentleman, his eyes sparkling as they lingered on the fresh, sweet face, now daintily touched by the tremulous curls dancing in the sea-breeze.

"Colonel Willerton, my husband, and several others," said Laura. "O! we're not going to desert the poor fellow, I assure you; he has a host in the colonel, himself."

"Colonels and captains, and convicts—dear, dear," muttered the old man, as they now came close in to shore; "I must seem an insignificant personage beside them—very insignificant indeed. But I'll go down and attend to my boxes."

CHAPTER II.

SHE was a poor woman, with a pale, pinched face, in a decent gown and shawl. By the hand she held a young girl, who, in countenance and expression, was as fair, as pure and heavenly as an angel.

You and I, reader, may have seen such but once in our lives — an undying memory. The face was framed in masses of golden hair. It floated against the delicate cheek in curls so thick and wondrously gleaming, that they seemed mould-ed in the very matrice of celestial beauty. The dark blue eyes of the child were dreamy in their depth and motion; only in moments of excitement the iris grew large and radiant, deepening the soft color that always flushed her face. There was a sensation of airiness in the mind of the beholder who gazed long upon this exquisite creature, such as one feels who sees the rich hues of the rainbow floating down a transverse sunbeam. The tender lips that never opened save for some sweet speech of gratitude or consolation, or trembled with un-

17

spoken love or pity, were the fitting portals for
her pure heart.   The very sight of this almost
guileless creature commanded an instantaneous
reverence.   Her presence elevated and refined,
and the bold eyes of grosser natures fell before the
pure light of her glance.   Whence come these
beautiful creations who know by some sweet intui-
tion how to master every weakness and overcome
every obstacle to a lofty spiritual progression that
concerns the thoughts of others only when it is
time for them to die?

For such, is there, in truth, any death?   Live
they not on the borders of the unseen world, in the
immediate care of angels, who wait almost with
impatience for their companionship?

It was not strange that her mother often felt the
spirit of these words :

> " *Come to me, darling, thy wings for a while*
> *Folded though shining;*
> *Look in my face—oh ! that beautiul smile*
> *All sad thoughts lining.*
> *Art thou to stay but a limited season ?*
> *For heaven to use thee?*
> *If thou art earthly, then what is the reason*
> *I so fear to lose thee?* "

Surely, if ever there was a temple of the Holy
Ghost, that slight, misshapen form was that human
temple.

Misshapen, I said.   After the perfection of finely

moulded brows, glorious eyes and stainless lips, there all perfect beauty ceased. The limbs that should have been more than mortal fair to fitly match the glory of the upper visage, were marred, though not to deformity. The hands were infantile, the arms shrunken, the body bowed in a scarcely perceptible curvature. She was not what is vulgarly called hump-backed, yet her stature was small, so that at the age of sixteen she looked several years younger. She was dressed in plain, dark garments, very neat, yet bearing evidence, in whitened seam, and worn fold, of poverty and age.

"Are you cold, mother?" she asked, throwing the light of her gentle eyes in the worn, sad face at her side. "The wind is fresh, let me stand a little this way; there, now you will not feel it so much."

It was as if the warmth of another sun had suddenly shone upon the anxious woman, yet she smiled, as if at sudden thought of the frailty of her protector, and thanked her for her little gift of sweetness.

"I wonder if Steevie will be much grown, mother; it is six months, you know."

"Perhaps, darling; strange that your dream haunts me."

"I dreamed that he was with the angels of God," said the child, softly; "and I was just thinking of it, mother. If he *should* be gone up there, do you suppose he sees us waiting in the cold?"

A sharp cry, low, and ending in a wail, broke from the mother's heart.

"O, Bernie! how *can* you always speak of it so?"

"It"—the child looked thoughtfully forward— "how can I help it?" she asked. Then added in a soft musical voice, "it seems so beautiful! so beautiful, mother! If you dreamed of heaven as I do, you'd almost want to fly there. Why, it's pure crystal and gold. Do you see that?" She caught her mother's hand breathlessly and pointed to where the waves, ruffled by a keener wind, leaped in small ripples, each ripple a lambent fire; "it is like that; oh! how I love that shining, beautiful color! It is like the shore we sing about. There, that is the vessel; I should know it. We shall see Steevie soon. Why, mother, are you crying?"

"No, dear," and the woman swallowed her tears, "but I have such a strange foreboding."

"Take comfort, mother; be sure God loves. us through all. When Steevie was getting ready to go to that foreign land, though you wept some, you smiled also to think of the new experience he would have. If he should, in reality, be gone to *another* land — a more beautiful country—" she went on slowly exploring her mother's soul as it were by her searching gaze, "ought we not, after all, to be more glad than sorry? For, if there *is* a foreign land that we have not seen, there is as surely a heavenly one in which, if he is there, he is safe, you know, safe from every earthly sorrow."

Mrs. Franklin drew her not over warm shawl more closely, as she listened with a far off look. The wind had grown cooler. On every side of them, boxes and bales of ponderous size stood ready to be conveyed to their floating castles. Great warehouses, whose faded windows and grimmy doors were never brightened by the flickering fire-light of home, shut heaven out by their dull uniformity of height. Off in the stream wheezed and puffed the great steamers, skimmed the light sail-boat, or with soberer motion the down east schooner, deeply loaded, drifted along. A Portuguese brig, not far away, displayed her national colors, and lines on lines of wet shirts, for it was washing day. Farther off loomed up the hull of a man-of-war, its cannon pouting their iron lips, as if in the sulks at having nothing to do. All the picturesque life of wharf and ocean seemed to dispose itself in groups, while ponderous cart-loads of goods were rearing walls of merchandise from the verge of the landing to the busy street. Over these the glorious sun shone redly, lighting sky and water, and white canvas.

To catch a nearer view of the coming ship, now much larger than the mere speck it had at first

appeared, little Bernice, or Bernie, as she was most
lovingly called at home, had moved far in advance
of her mother, till now she stood quite near the
edge of the wharf.   The coping there was not very
high, and the bales shut her in.   Her mother stood
nearer the space left for the gangway of the vessel
when she should come up to the wharf.   Furiously
busy were the porters and packers in their bright
red and blue shirts ; some of them standing upright
upon topmost bales shouting their orders.   Suddenly a powerful horse became restive and commenced backing.   All their endeavors to hold him
were fruitless ; still, with his strong haunches, he
pushed cart, bales, everything.

"Take care there, madam ! " shouted the almost
gigantic figure on one of the highest bales.   " For
God's sake, men, stop that horse ; there's a woman
there."

Mrs. Franklin was almost paralyzed.

"Bernie ! " she cried, extending her arms, then
grew dumb with terror.

" I'm coming, mother," chirruped the sweet
voice.   A scream, wild, sharp, brief ; a plash, dull
and heavy ; a parting of the dark waters, sullenly
beating against iron and wood.

" My child ! my child ! save my child ! " shrieked
the woman in tones of the most passionate agony
and entreaty ; and lifting her arms, she would have

thrown herself struggling in the inky depth, but a ponderous hand was laid upon her shoulder. A hoarse voice cried, "hold back, madam, hold back!" and before she could think, breathe, or speak, he was in the water.

Tattered, dirty, huge, uncouth, what he was could hardly have been told, but by the almost superhuman exertions that he was now putting forth, and that proved him to be a man. On pressed others, springing over every obstruction; fathers with pale faces, brothers, breathless and dumb; all actuated by the common impulse of humanity that leaps up to sorrow or danger.

"He's got her; don't worry ma'm. There ain't such another swimmer in Boston as the Duke. Why, where could the rascal have been?"

"Coiled up somewhere here; it's his time for retiracy from public life."

The mother heard nothing. Eyes, senses, heart, soul, were all in those darkling depths. Her hands were clasped with a rigidity that nothing but death could rival; her large eyes fastened down there; never a sigh, never a motion, never a glance elsewhere. The world might have been blazing at her back without touching the tension of her strained faculties.

"Good heaven," said a voice, "what a beautiful face!"

"O! Bernie, Bernie!" groaned the pale mother, her hands falling a little; "oh, my angel, to meet death thus!"

"She ain't dead, ma'm; at least we hopes so," said a rough fellow, who might have sworn, if told that the tears were running down his cheeks.

"The Duke's a trump!" shouted another, as the matted hair, unshaven chin, and bold black eyes of the man appeared now above the tide mark. "I say, boys, give the Duke a collection. He isn't over and above flush, I'll warrant ye."

"O, bless you! bless you!" cried Mrs. Franklin, as the lovely face, upturned, gave by the lips signs of coming consciousness. "How shall I thank you?" she cried, her voice drowned in tears, as she turned first to the savior of her child, then back to the pale form in her arms.

"Spare yourself, madam; I am glad I was near enough to render you this slight service."

Even in the whirl of her excited feelings, the grateful woman started at sound of that voice. Deep, ringing, rich — it was formed, one might fancy, to hold listening senates in thrall; and the language above the average in its well chosen words and fit delivery. It was only for a second. The state of Bernie called for prompt action. A gentlemanly man, the same who had been struck with the exceeding beauty of little Bernie's face as it uprose from the water, came forward.

"Let me take her, madam, there's a carriage here;" and as the burden was transferred, he said again, with a glance almost of awe, "what an exquisite face! Heaven surely never held anything more perfect."

And thus one sorrow being balanced by another, the pale mother was in some measure prepared to hear the ill tidings that by nightfall were to reach and overwhelm her poor heart. Up the wharf she followed the man and his precious burden, while the "Duke" remained to receive the congratulations and hand-shakings of the men who both admired and despised him. A strange and striking object he was, towering in their midst. Scowling a defiant hate, yet, perforce, receiving their money through which he might for a few days live on the verge of delirious ecstacy.

The man had once been a grand image of his Creator. Even now, with shrunk muscles and contracted nerves, there was something about him that made one say, "he would honor the arts." He looked like one worth saving. Struck down by the gauntleted hand of vice while in the full possession of every vigorous manly attribute; cut off from all hopes of happy domestic life, or the less attractive ambition of intellectual society, it was indeed a pitible existence that he led — half human half beastial; employing the splendid gifts with

which he had been originally endowed for the perverted amusement of men who knew not, cared
not what they heard, provided the "Duke's" splendid gesticulation and powerful voice made it attractive to them.

Here then was a man in which the animal clearly
predominated. A menace or a curse roused his
passions to a frightful degree. Pat him and speak
to him softly, he purred and listened ; blame, or try
to shame him with words of blame, and he flew at his
accusers with a hand tingling for their throats. To
all intents and purposes the man was lost. Under
the thick scales of his indifference and hatred of
all things good, where was the single spot that a
pitying hand might probe? Only one thing on
earth did he seem to care for now, and that was
drink. How, with his native violence of temper,
he had managed to keep beyond the bounds of a
jail, it was impossible to tell. He had at one time
been an actor, but his increasing love for drink
caused him to be expelled from even the lowest
theatres, and other occupation he had none. So,
when he was sober, the thoughtless, heartless
crowds who gathered in bar-rooms, hired him to
personate some of the characters in which, but a
few years before, he had won money and fame.

CHAPTER III.

IN the depth of the great metropolis, in a very obscure street, lived the parents of Harry Franklin, the forger. The house was old and leaned a little. It wore a subdued and careworn look, and seemed always appealing to somebody to prop it up. There were signs of extraordinary neatness, however, in the small, blue-white windows, which, notwithstanding the spatter of paint long ago stamped thereon, and the plashes of mud occasionally deposited on rainy days, were scrupulously bright. The third, or corner window, was furnished with things saleable and otherwise. Tempting to the juvenile gaze were those bright glass cases full of candy, colored as freshly as if the painter's brush were used but yesterday. Inside, a miscellaneous collection smacked of older trade: brooms and pans, and earthen pots, a few half barrels of beans and other commodities; here and there a dried cod defiantly yawning with a perpetual stick in its mouth; sundry samples of comestibles; a can of milk; a box or two of herring.

27

The little store did not draw much custom however. A smaller one, less neat, less respectable,
on another corner, not far off, was full nearly all
the time. That matter was easily explained. The
Franklin's kept no strong drink for thirsty way-
farers, consequently they had less custom.

Mr. Franklin had always considered himself an
unfortunate man. Beginning life with a good
business and fair salary, he had met with various
mishaps, not the least serious of which was a pro-
tracted illness of twelve months, inducing a weakness that unfitted him for his former vocation. His
children were growing up around him, fair and
beautiful, but the strength of his wife was taxed
too severely, and her health began to give way.
Little Bernie met with an accident from the rude-
ness of a playfellow at school, which deformed and
weakened her permanently; and to crown his
misery, his eldest boy, the idol of his heart, brought
upon the humble, but proud family, the first disgrace that had ever blotted its annals. From this
shock, it seemed for a year that he could not recover. Neither could he forgive the poor boy.
Towards him his bitterness seemed to increase day
by day. This feeling was shared by his daughter
Irene, a handsome, stately girl of seventeen, who,
in order to eke out the small means of the family,
had lived some time with a lady, as her seamstress

and companion, but whose spirit chafed at the restraints imposed upon her by poverty.

The room leading from the shop was very comfortable, though low and dark. On this November evening the fire burned cheerily, and Mr. Franklin, a pale, handsome, melancholy man, sat before it, watching the flame leap against the kettle which he had put on the hob. A small boy lounged in the shop, tieing his fingers with a bit of twine, varying the exercises by occasionally dipping them into a box half full of raisins that stood conveniently near.

"I wonder Mrs. Franklin stays so long," muttered her husband to himself. "It's almost tea time, and the night air is bad for Bernie. O! here she is."

Some one opened the door that led from the shop into the little room. He turned in expectation; it was only his old neighbor, Tim Stebbings, the carpenter, in his slouched hat. Tim was a cheerful companion, generally, but now his face was elongated to such a degree, that Mr. Franklin suppressed the impatience that had almost found vent on his tongue.

"Why what's the matter, neighbor?" he asked.

"Then you hain't heered, maybe," said the other, pulling a chair forward with a doleful countenance, and instead of sitting down, folding his arms, and looking straightforward into the fire.

"Heard of what?" queried Mr. Franklin, rising, for he read disaster in the man's face.

Tim Stebbings shook his head and sighed.

"Neighbor, I'm about clean tired of life."

"Why, Tim Stebbings, you're the last man in the world that should say that. I consider you one of the jolliest fellows I know. Why, man, you've not seen a tithe of the trouble I have, and you're older than I am by ten years."

"Then you hain't heard of the fire?"

"The fire, what fire? I hope you're not burnt out?"

"No, but my shop is. Everything gone, stock and flue. Not so much as a second-hand file to bless myself with, and Nancy down with the rheumatiz. I tell you it's a hard thing, any how. I'm ruined."

"Why, Tim, I'm sorry to hear that; indeed I am. When did it happen, and how?"

"Can't tell any more than you can. I went over to Murray's, to do a job on his stairs; and while I was there, I heard the engine go thundering down street. I didn't dream, however, that it was the shop; and when I saw the flames bursting out, I declare to you, I couldn't move."

"Why, I am really sorry. You weren't insured, then?"

"Not a cent. In fact, it never seemed to me tha

old thing was worth insuring; but gracious! what I've lost! for, you see, I'd carried my chest of new tools down there last week, that I've been saving for so long; and now everything's gone. I dares n't tell the old woman;" and taking up the ends of the red woolen comforter he had been twist- ing together, he hid his face in it, and his shoulders shook with a sob or two.

"Well, neighbor, I don't know how to comfort you, I'm sure, except to tell you to bear it like a man and a Christian. You've always paid me fairly, so do n't mind running a reasonable bill, till you can set yourself up again."

"O, no, Franklin, don't say that; I can't be that burden upon you, with your family to support. Betsy and me are only two, and I s'pose I ought n't to be so childish; but it does seem hard, and me getting old. And then, to see the rich growing richer, and them as is n't decent in their morals, nor kind to the needy, going right straight up the track, and we poor folks, strain as we will, losing step after step, till we're e'n amost crushed down and trampled under foot. It do seem, sir, some- times, as if God cares a great deal more for some of his creatures than others."

The boy from the shop came in with a bill. Mr. Franklin looked at it, grew pale, catching his breath.

"I had no idea," he said, "that he would perse-cute me again with that old debt; at least, till I had got my head above water. We all have our troubles, Tim," he added, aloud. "Here's an old debt turned up to haunt me. Two hundred and fifty dollars, think of that; why, that's more than I'm worth, put everything together. This man has found me out, and thinks I'm making a fortune in my shop;" and he laughed bitterly.

"Well, sir, he'll wait, I suppose," said Tim, diverted for a moment from his own trouble.

"He says he wont; and I have reason to know that he would ruin me if he could. He's got an old grudge against me."

The door-way was darkened again. This time it was a woman, hard-featured and poverty-strick-en. Her grayish blue cloak made in an old, old fashion, descended but a little way below her arms; her bonnet, crossed with a faded black ribbon, had been altered and dressed over so many times that it was hard to decide upon its original shape or present style. She came in quickly, and laid her ungloved hand on the grocer's shoulder.

"George," she said in a hard voice, while her features never altered, "will you lend me ten dol-lars?"

"Chrissy, I have n't ten cents in the world of my own money," he said, in a forced and painful voice.

as the woman brought her haggard face more into the fire light.

"Then what are we going to do?" cried the woman, half fiercely. "Joseph is down again, been down two days with that old wound. The very cat is starving. I don't care for that, though; that is, I mean I'd as lief go hungry for a few days as not; but we owe ten dollars for the rent, and Joseph hasn't had work for two months."

"You see there's a stranger here, Chrissy," said Mr. Franklin, his cheek glowing red.

"Beg your pardon, Mr. Franklin, I'll take my-self off," said Tim, rising; but he was arrested by a spectacle that changed even the half ferocious aspect of the woman in the short cloak.

Little Bernie in the arms of a handsome stranger, her long locks, wet and heavy, falling in great masses over his arm, and along his fine broadcloth, rolling and glistening, spite of the damp, while her sweet pale face gleamed out in the deepening gloom with unnatural whiteness.

"Never mind, father, it's all over now, only I'm a little weak," said Bernie, softly, as her father sprang up in an agony of apprehension.

"What's happened? what's happened?" he cried; my darling, where has she been?"

"In the water, George," said Mrs. Franklin, in a voice so calm and cold that Mr. Franklin turned

towards her, struck chill by its strangeness
"Bring her in here, sir," she continued, still in
that icy way; "we carried her to Colonel Willerton's, father, and they undressed her and wrapped
her up. She needs rest." So saying, she went
into the little bed room adjoining, and the gentleman followed her.

Still Tim stood there, thoughtless of intrusion,
yet full of sympathy. Chrissy threw back her
cloak and struck a light, saying as she did so,

"I never saw your wife look so down in the
mouth before. Seems to me ill luck comes all
round."

Then she set the light on the mantel and glanced
about.

"Where do you keep your table-cloth, George?
Oh, I know. I can't stand idle, if there is misery
here and at home. Besides, I'm hungry for a
mouthful myself. I gave Joseph the last bite
there was in the house; it wasn't much, to be
sure. I might as well get one more good meal
before I go to the poor house;" and she ended
with a short, dry laugh.

Presently, amid the clatter of placing cups and
saucers, knives and folks, she said,

"I shouldn't wonder if that girl of yours dies
from this shock."

"There never was anybody better fitted for
heaven," said Mr. Franklin, despondingly.

"Does very well to talk so. You don't know what it is. Stop till you lose a child. I've lost four; kind'r hardened to it. Now where's your tea? Dear Lord! where *ever* am I going to get ten dollars?" She pushed her bonnet back, leaned on the table with both hands and looked at nothing, drearily. Tim had, meantime, backed to the door. The strange gentleman was going out now; he must stand aside for him.

Presently Mrs. Franklin went over softly and stood by her husband's chair. She smiled in a strange way, not like herself.

" George, perhaps you remember Bernie's dream about Steevie?"

"Yes," he said, looking up anxiously.

" It's come true."

This she spoke shortly, almost sharply; then knelt on the hearth, and began piling fresh wood on the blaze.

" You don't mean—" faltered Mr. Franklin in a changed voice.

"I mean what I said, dear," and the tone had softened somewhat. "Bernie's dream has come true; we've got no Steevie now. He died in Barbadoes," she added, with a hard, dry sob; " O, it's bitter, bitter!" and she let her head fall on her husband's knee, her face hidden in both clasped hands.

Chrissy came out of her reverie, and bit her lip hard. The color went from her before almost colorless face.

"Never mind," she said, hoarsely, "you've got three left; I've not one."

Mr. Franklin threw his head back, lifted his eyes heavenward, and a deep, long-drawn heart-broken sigh issued from his pale lips.

"If it's the Lord's will to afflict us in this way, to bring sickness, trouble, humiliation and death," he cried out, after a moment of silence, "I suppose I must bear it."

"That's not the right spirit, dear," said his wife, uncovering her tearless eyes; "I know you felt hard and unchristian then. We *must* bow humbly, dear. It is only another treasure laid up above."

By this time, Tim, somewhat awe-stricken, had left the room.

"It seems strange that I shall never see the dear boy again," said the father, almost sobbingly.

"One good thing," muttered Chrissy, in her harsh undertone, "he'll never disgrace you." Both parents heard these unkind words, and they cut painfully into already bleeding hearts; but the woman's peculiarities were too well known to them to elicit any comment. She stood there half smiling, grimly, as if in some sort taking pleasure in the calamities of others. It made her own misfortunes less dark by contrast.

"There, I've made the tea. It wont do any good to sit there mourning.   I told you how you'd feel, but you did n't believe me.   Come, Bernice, let's eat one more meal together before we all go to the poor-house — at least, before I do."

Mrs. Franklin looked up drearily.

"You did n't know I was going, I suppose, but it's the Lord's living truth.   Joseph is sick again, and the landlord threatens to turn us out to-morrow, unless I give him ten dollars.   I can't give him ten, no, nor one ; can't even get anything for Joe's sickness.   Sha' n't I be glad when I 've done with this world for good and all?"

CHAPTER IV.

"YOU DON'T ASK ANY QUESTIONS."

IT was late in the evening. Bernie slept sweetly as her mother ascertained by repeated visits to her little bed. Chrissy, the wife of an unfortunate brother of Mr. Franklin's, had gone home, consoled somewhat by the promise of her brother-in-law that he would see the landlord in the morning. The woman, though care-worn and crossed with trouble, had been a neat, good looking girl at her marriage. She was, besides, something of an heiress; had inherited a pretty cottage and piece of land, which, as misfortunes crowded her, she had foolishly sold, and repented ever since. Her husband had fallen down the hold of a vessel and injured himself for life. Her children grew up almost to the ages of man and womanhood, then sickened and died. From one condition to another of penury she had passed, till heart and face were hardened and misshapen by trouble.

As I said, she had gone, scarcely comforted, bearing with her some little delicacies for her husband, whom she loved almost idolatrously. Mrs.

Franklin had quietly cleared up the table, and put things in their accustomed places Then she sat down, taking her knitting sorrowfully. It was a stocking she was shaping for the absent boy, but she tried not to think of this, as she said softly and sorrowfully, " it will do for Bernie."

Mr. Franklin had not yet shown her that dreadful bill that weighed down his spirits like a nightmare. He gazed at her as she sat there — her once lovely face thinned and sharpened by affliction. The little store-boy, who, when Mr. Franklin was too ill to work, tended the counter for a trifle, was beating a tattoo with a wisp of tin on a tumbler.

" We did n't think of all these dark hours when we married, Bernice," he said.

" Trouble wont last forever, dear," was the quiet reply.

" No ; but I wish, for your sake, I had been more fortunate."

" Hush, dear, these are trials we could not avoid ; and for that other, that seemed worse than death, let us thank God that our dear boy is what he is. Do you know I long to have him home now, since · the news, more than ever?"

" I do n't then," replied Mr. Franklin, almost harshly. " Not but what I may forgive him," he added, touched by her imploring glance ; " but I do n't feel as if I ever wanted to see him agai ı.

He has bowed an honest man to the earth, with shame. Think of it; the son of George Franklin in State Prison. Great heaven! it almost drives me mad."

"George, he has been long repentant, and has conducted himself with so much propriety, that Colonel Willerton told me to-night he would probably be pardoned out this week. George, do n't hold that dreadful feeling against him, for my sake."

The man started and trembled from head to foot. Love for his first born struggled with the pride that was a heritage of his nature. Not once for the two years past had he seen or would he see his son.

" Let him go to Colonel Willerton then ; I cannot receive him."

"O, George!" and the woman threw herself on her knees, "I cannot bear this. Indeed, indeed you must be merciful, as God has been merciful to us. O! if you had seen the dear child go down—the black water closing like iron over her pretty, golden head! If you had given her to such a death as I had; if you had seen the white face coming up, drenched, dead, it seemed—our Bernie, George, the comfort and beauty of our sad life—" she bent her head and sobbed unrestrainedly. The tears began to roll out of his eyes also—great tears leaping from the troubled fountain of his heart, which the angel of memory was stirring. Involuntarily he let his shaking hand rest upon the head bowed there before him. He gave one gasping sob, battled down the strong power that had caused him to look upon his erring son with a feeling that was nearer kin to hate than he thought.

"Do n't cry so, dear," he said gently, his own voice almost drowned in tears; "I 'll—try—I 'll —I 'll forgive him; yes, yes, my poor boy—I *will* forgive him, freely, heartily, from this moment. There, dear, look up; you have conquered."

"God knows, I thank you," she said, lifting her drenched face. "O, George! if the angels do look down, our dear boy, our pretty Steevie smiles upon our joy. Many and many a time did I find him crying about poor Harry. And, just now, when you spoke—it might all be fancy—but oh! I saw him, our angel boy, and he smiled as if he saw and knew the triumph. I do feel now almost as if I had never known a trouble. And who can tell, dear, but brighter days are in store for us? I mean still to trust God, and hope."

Meantime, for some moments, a little old man, with a white bell-crowned hat, had been disturbing sundry people along the street by using his knuckles vigorously, where there was neither knocker nor other means of communication, and bringing various faces to the keen outer air, each of which displayed different phases of vexation as they answered his question with a curt "no," in all sorts of octaves.

The question was —

"Does Mr. George Franklin live here?"

Presently he queried, when a white-headed child volunteered the exclamation, "It's the corner grocery."

To the corner grocery he went accordingly, but not the right one. The mingled odors of garlic and bad gin saluted him unpleasantly, if one might judge by the way he lifted his immense handkerchief to his nose.

"If he's in this rascally trade," he muttered, "I'll know the reason why."

"Good evening, sir, what'll you have?" asked the burly-looking store-keeper from the midst of his canteens and gin casks.

"I'll have you, sir, if you can spare me a minute of your time, that is."

"Me, have *me!* what in the dickens does the gentleman mean?"

"I mean, Mr. Franklin, that I've got something to say to you."

"O, ho! you're dealing with the wrong man, after all. It's the *other* corner grocery — that small affair, yonder. That's kept by a Mr. Franklin. I s'pose you mean the one that's got a son in State Prison," he added, with a leer, that said, as

plainly as signs could speak, "strike him again,
he's down."

"I do n't know, and do n't care about his son,"
said the little man, sturdily bringing the point of
his green cotton umbrella against the floor. "I
want to see him, and I shall be disappointed if I
do n't find him more of a man than you are." So
saying, the old gentleman turned about and left the
store, while the laugh of the motley crew was
turned against the grocer. On he plodded to
where the one feeble light glimmered in the opposite corner grocery.

"Can't be doing a thriving business here, at any
rate," he said; "ah, I see! it's his reward for virtue. He do n't make drunkards, consequently he
can't make money, ha, ha!" Presenting himself
to the eyes of the wondering boy, he was ushered
into the little sitting room, just as Mrs. Franklin
had risen from her humble attitude and was com-
mencing her knitting again. Her cheek was flushed,
her eye shone with a pure light, she looked almost
young, and quite handsome.

"Right this time; I see the family likeness," he
said to himself; "everything neat and tight, too;
could n't be better. Like the looks of things."

"Good evening, friends," he said, laying his big
umbrella down quite composedly, and unbuttoning
his surtout coat, disclosing a gay colored vest, and
the very thin proportions upon which he stood.

"You are Mr. Franklin, sir, Mr. George Franklin, son of Thomas Franklin, of Deercut."

" I am, sir; wont you be seated?"

"Thank you, yes; believe I will, as I shall have
to go somewhat into preliminaries. If you wont
be offended, I should say you were in rather reduced
circumstances." George Franklin lifted his head.
The old latent pride flushed his brow, and his eye
was keener in its glitter. But, remembering the
bill, and suddenly foreseeing that this was some
form in which his relentless creditor was showing
himself, he suppressed the quick retort and merely
said,

" I am not as well off as I have been, sir."

" Thought so. From what I heard some twenty-
five years ago, you were in good business and bade
fair to go up hill instead of down."

All this time he had been quietly taking from his
capacious red pocket-book several papers, as if in
search of some particular one, which at last came
to light.

" How many of you were there, eh?" he asked,
looking up comically from under the blue goggles
which he had just placed over his eyes.

"There were seven of us, sir."

" Seven — hum — not all living, I suppose?"

"No, only one; Bernice, dear, get the family
Bible. There it is, sir, the record," said Mr.

Franklin, wondering what could be the occasion for this extraordinary proceeding.

" Yes, yes, I see — Jabez, mum, mum ; Charles, mum, mum ; Enoch, James — yes, all right, all perfectly clear. Now, sir, if you please, what relations have you besides this Joseph Franklin ? "

" None, that I know of. My father had an only brother; he went from home nearly forty years ago, or more. I presume that he has been dead for some time, though I never knew."

" Be kind enough to read this," said the little old man, handing him a slip of paper cut from an old newspaper. While his auditor read, he twirled his white hat, put it down, frowned, looked about the room narrowly, smiled, and at last crossed one knee over the other, sticking both thumbs in his vest pockets.

It was a short paragraph, dated a year back.

" Died, in Australia, of fever, Zacheus Franklin, aged sixty-seven."

" Then I am alone in the world," said Mr. Franklin, quietly. I have neither uncle, aunt, nor cousin. Did you know the old gentleman? "

" I knew him very well, sir."

" I'm almost sorry you told me ; it 's not pleasant to feel yourself, as it were, the last of your family. I wonder if he grew to look like my father? He was much younger, and father was always longing to see him the year he died. Death makes great inroads in some families, sir."

"Exactly so," said the little old man, nodding. "But do you know that you have done, or rather you have *not* done one thing, that surprises me rather?"

"And what is that?" asked Mr. Franklin, half smiling himself, at the quizzical look in the stranger's face.

"You have not once asked if this uncle of yours left any money. Now, that seems a defect in the moral constitution of man, for which I find it impossible to account.

"Perhaps if I had been more fortunate myself in money matters," replied Mr. Franklin, "I should have shown more anxiety. But my present perplexity, and the sad news we have received by the 'Laura,' quite changes the aspect of things. Besides, my uncle had no particular regard for me that I ever knew. Indeed, I was too young to know much of him when he went away."

"I should judge so. According to his account, you had then seen the light but a few days. But it seems," added the old man with a solemn assumption of dignity, "that he did not forget you." His eyes twinkled with some pleasant emotion. Mr. Franklin started — his wife grew pale.

"I was your uncle's chief man of business," said

the little old man, still with that air of importance, as he sorted out papers, and flashed blue light from his spectacles, here, there and everywhere — "his chief man of business," he added, peering over at the fire; "ain't you rather chilly here?"

Mr. Franklin piled on the wood till his wife was obliged to stay his hand.

"Do n't dear, it will smoke," she whispered; and he desisted, looking about him in a distraught way.

"Your uncle never had any family, poor man. He did n't care much for home comforts, fortunately for *you*. Let me see — oh! here it is — 'Mr. George Franklin, if he be living, otherwise his heirs in the male line, etc., etc.;' that's the very paper," he. cried exultantly. "Now, my dear madam, and you, my dear sir, it's a very great pleasure for me to inform you, that by your uncle's will, you are left — well, now — quite tidily provided for; indeed, I may say, respectably rich."

The burden of poverty began rolling off the tired shoulders of the man who had fought so steadily for a mere pittance — the four narrow walls to widen; up lifted the shining curtain of the future, revealing a dawn softened and shadowed yet by the fading mists of darkness, but, nevertheless, the capacities of boundless beauty were there. Sunlight and glory, ease and a competence; he thought of nothing else. Moving back hastily against the low mantelpiece, he brushed aside something that fluttered down to the hearth. His wife lifted and handed it to him. Her eyes were moist with happy tears. He glanced at it, it was the threatening account of his relentless creditor.

"Well, sir," said the little old man, drawing a long breath, "you do n't ask any questions. Why do n't you go into tantrums, you and your wife, there, and knock things down, generally?"

"It is n't our way," said Mr. Franklin, with a quiet smile.

"No, I see it is n't; and I can't say but I like you the better for it. It rather argues in favor of your poor relations. People who take matters calmly, do things reasonably. I've seen a man who raved on his wife's tombstone, married in six months. I decidedly like the quiet aspect, though I'm something of a blusterer myself, I expect. But you do n't seem in the least interested to know how much it is. However, we 'll put that to the account of temperament. I've a copy of the will, by the by, and this is it. Your considerate uncle has left you — I wont trouble myself to read the whole — a hundred thousand pounds; *now* what do you say?"

This astounding intelligence produced strangely different effects upon George Franklin and his wife. The former turned pale, and staggered to the table

like a drunken man. The latter moved towards
her husband, and with the exclamation, "Oh!
George, at last!" threw her arms around his neck
and burst into tears.

CHAPTER V.

HOW IT AFFECTED THEM.

THE little old man, umbrella, bell-crowned hat and all, had disappeared. There was the wooden chair in which he had sat, still drawn up to the table, wearing an aspect it never had before. There were the four dingy, dull papered walls; the fire blazing over the iron-dogs, the red coals winking and blinking at them, as if to assure them that however indifferent coals generally were to happiness of their possessors, these coals in particular were rejoicing over the good news, in their most cheerful manner. As yet there was only one candle burning. As yet the little store-boy drummed monotonously, wondering if it was not past the time to go to bed. The proprietor of the corner grocery walked into the little shop, still in a maze. Pete looked up and tried not to blink with his sharp little eyes, sleepy as they were.

"Please, sir, ain't it most time to shut up, sir?" he asked anxiously.

"Quite, Pete; but here, before you go, weigh out a pound of tea, and four pounds of sugar."

"Yes, sir," and the busy fingers hurried to the task.

"Now, can you lift a bag of flour?"

"Yes, sir," replied Pete, dubiously, wondering where he was to carry it at this late hour.

"Very well; take the tea and sugar and flour home to your mother, then; tell her I make them a present, and will send her something more, to-morrow."

"Yes, sir," said the boy, blankly, his mouth agape, and his eyes opened to their widest extent. He shouldered the flour, and took the tea, but turned on the threshold to give one more stare, still with his jaw hanging. Poor child! he never could remember seeing a bag of flour in his miserable home at one time.

Mr. Franklin closed the shutters like one in a dream; indeed he pinched himself now and then, to be sure that he was awake. Wherever he looked, there blazed the magic words,

"One hundred thousand pounds!"

Heaven help those who are suddenly lifted into prosperity.

> "*Wealth heaped on wealth, nor truth nor safety buys,*
> *The dangers gather as the treasures rise.*"

When he went into the little sitting-room, Mrs. Franklin stood there, candle in hand. She beckoned to him; her eyes were not quite dry, though smiles trembled on her lips. He followed instinctively, knowing why she wished it.

Upon pillows, white as snow, laid the angelface of little Bernie. More etherial and spiritual she looked in that innocent slumber than ever, the red and fragrant lips parted and smiling.

"Does it not seem as if the light of her forehead was something more than mortal, George; do you think that would change her?" she asked, after a pause, referring to their great and sudden wealth, with quivering lips.

"Nothing would change her, wife. She will always be our pure little daughter; and God grant that for her sake we may keep ourselves pure. But what of Irene?"

"I have been thinking of that, George. Irene is not at all like her. If she is so proud and unsubdued, now, it will turn her head, I fear."

"And Harry," murmured the father, struggling even yet to forget the shame to which the boy had brought them. "It will be a strange ordeal for him. He was prepared to battle with every thing but that."

"God will help us all, husband, if we ask Him," said the wife. "It is pleasant to know that we can aid others. That is what I cling to, though when I think of the hardening nature of riches, I tremble for all of us. Poor Joseph!"

"Poor Joseph no longer," said her husband. What will Chrissy say, when she hears the good news? Wife, I must buy her cottage back again. I heard it was for sale a day or two ago."

" That will be beautiful !" exclaimed Mrs. Franklin, her eyes lighting up. "It may prolong your brother's life. But see, what is this?"

"A folded paper. The husband took it from her hand. He opened it. It was a check on one of the banks for five hundred dollars, payable to George Franklin. It is from the old gentleman; he writes 'that we shall need some ready cash before the business is settled,' read Mr. Franklin, 'and has taken the liberty to leave this for our accommodation. What a strange, clever, eccentric old fellow !' Now, darling, I am a free man; I can't quite say a happy one, when I think of poor Harry, and little Steevie. But at least, I can look my creditors in the face again, thank God !"

It was a point gained, that he spoke freely and willingly of his erring son. Since his incarceration he had never uttered his name before that night; had neither seen him, nor expressed a wish to do so.

"You cannot tell what a dreary blank my life appeared at the moment you came in with little Bernie," he said a moment after. "Poor Tim was here with his sorrows and losses; Chrissy with her troubles; and to crown the whole, that frightful debt that seemed to add the last drop to my full cup. I think I was never so thoroughly miserable in my life before."

Into midnight they sat up talking of the wonderful fortune. And even after they had retired, the wife could not sleep for anxious thought.

She saw her bright haired boy in his wearisome prison-duties, pale, but resigned; suffering in body from irksome restraint and the long privation of exercise, yet gentle and Christian in all his ways, never murmuring, singing pleasant hymns in an undertone, what would he say when the news met him? And then her heart brimmed to the full with gratitude. Whatever trials were in reserve for him, the humiliation of pleading for work where he might be spurned and despised, would not be one. Some business he must have, but that she trusted to the kindness and discretion of friends.

And Irene, with her haughty head and proud spirit. She toiling day after day, for the wealthy, envying — for the mother knew her heart — the rich materials upon which she put the finishing touches of her swift needle; longing for the splendors and vanities of the world, beautiful, intellectual, even imperious, in her lowly circumstances, what would she be when the full fruition of all she wished, was thus showered upon her! The mother trembled and dreaded; but this, as every other expected trial, she carried to that Power who had sustained her through all her eventful life.

Meantime, the little old man was cosily seated in his room at the hotel. In one of the easiest of rocking-chairs he lounged, beside him a tumbler of steaming lemonade.

"Queer old gent that," the waiter had said when he made it; "it would have been such a comfortable punch!" But the little old man has not tasted his drink yet; he sits there rubbing his hands and chuckling to himself, as he mutters, "after all it's a nice thing to make people happy; a very nice thing. I must go there to-morrow and offer my services; they'll need 'em; he's not fit to work just yet; and she's not fit either, after *that* shock. Now we'll see what'll happen next; and then for my own pet plan. Upon my word, I never felt so good in my life. Pity a body could n't live forever, with the means and appliances to help the needy. Ah! yes, pity there's an end of it, sometime.

CHAPTER VI.

IRENE IN NEW CIRCUMSTANCES.

THE little room was very brilliant. It was called the "Colonel's room," the "Colonel's corner," "head-quarters," and sundry pet names through the household. A splendid copy from Teniers made the atmosphere ruby-colored, particularly when the glowing dyes of an anthracite fire incarnadined it. Red-gold paper on the walls, crimson and brown covering on the floor. Lilies of flame above, casting a rich light over all. Snug lounges brightened up with ovals of white, knit by the untiring fingers of the Colonel's wife; heavy fall of thick red curtains, softened by exquisite lace.

The Colonel loved luxury as thoroughly as any Sybarite of old. He encouraged the fine arts liberally, as his garden walks and the walls and niches of his home testified. He had fought in Mexico, had left a buried leg there, and brought home a deep white welt on his bronzed cheek. It was rather curious he said, but his wife always kissed him in that spot.

He had been a noble fighter — this man with the Leonine head and nostrils.   Many a Mexican vete- ran painted him as the Yankee devil, with red eyes and a flaming visage, for he led more than one charge that crushed the legions of the fiery astec. He had long been a friend of the Franklins, and had in various ways tried to better their for- tunes; but the sturdy and perhaps sullen pride of Mr. Franklin would.never accept that as a boon which he had not fairly earned, and half resented even the friendship of richer men, since his bitter shame in his boy.   So the Colonel turned his tac- tics in that direction, working hard for the poor victim of his one. mad act of folly, concerning which there were many extenuating circumstances.

Captain Gurney was this man's nephew, and hither Laura always came after a voyage, for the old man was as fondly attached to her as if she had been his child.

A few nights after Bernie's accident, Laura re- clined in a great easy-chair, drawn up before the fire, in the Colonel's snuggery.   A dress of some foreign material hung in soft folds around her; a dainty chain to which was attached a miracle, of exquisite workmanship, in the shape of a Venetian watch, fell from her girdle.   It pleased her hus- band, whose tastes were like his uncle's, to see her richly attired.   The Colonel came in just in time to catch the smile on her lips.

"Well, pet," he cried, throwing his shaggy white locks with a toss, and drawing the companion chair towards her, "so they 've left you by yourself. What do you do when you 're alone?"

"I wonder if any body else beside me has an aunt Madge," said Laura, laughing.

"What a thought, you chit! Pray what special mission is that uneasy little woman engaged in now?"

"Do n't you know?" queried Laura in surprise.

"Should you think so, when she observes that Christian injunction with the utmost possible strictness, never to let the left hand know what the right one does."

"Ah! but fortunately I 'm on intimate terms with that right hand, uncle; and to day I saw it do — what do you think? Take a poor sick painter out of a damp garret, and put him in a little snuggery, almost as comfortable as this."

"You did, did you? So my wife employs herself running after sick painters, does she? In confidence now, pet, was he handsome?" and the old man laughed till his shaggy locks shook silver gleams out of their whiteness.

"Ah, poor soul!" sighed Laura, suddenly grave; "he was only handsome with the hectic of the tomb. But he will have his easel drawn up, and now and then gives a tremulous line to the blank canvas."

"Ah, poor soul, indeed!" ejaculated the Colonel, all the glow of merriment fading out of his face. "Ah, poor fellow! poor fellow! is he so bad as that?"

"He will only live a month or two," sighed Laura.

"Pshaw!" ejaculated the Colonel, almost angrily; "the doctors say that, of course. Now suppose Madge cossets him a little, gives him her strengthening cordials, and we send nourishing food to the poor fellow, do n't you think we could coax life into him?"

"Aunt Madge says she do n't believe he 'll live a month," murmured Laura, with pitying accents.

The Colonel pushed his chair back. This stranger had become to him in that short moment as a bosom friend, and though he had not seen him, his generous nature looked upon the inevitable doom as a calamity to himself.

"Then it 's all up," he said shortly. "Madge knows. She can always tell. Jove! once when three doctors gave me up, she just put her lips on that scar, and says she, 'Percie, you 'll get well, dear,' and I did in spite of three doctors," he thundered with energetic gestures, the tears moistening his honest eyes.

"I'm so glad he was n't left to die in that horrid ga ret," quivered Laura.

"Yes, thank God! thank God!" murmured the old soldier, fervently. "If I had my way, I'd hang every landlord that rents a garret, and forbid cellar kitchens on penalty of banishment or death," he cried; "the scoundrels! with souls no bigger than a grain of gunpowder and twice as black! Laura, child, this is a heathenish world, after all."

"Perhaps it's the landlords — the wicked, griping, grinding landlords," said Laura, softly.

"Yes, child, the world's well enough, I suppose; but it is a relief even when it looks its best, to get in some high place and throw a glance as it were, across to the better land. Did Madge tell him that he — how it was?" he asked, abruptly.

"She led him to talk of his feelings and managed to give him some sweet thoughts of heaven. I think it did him good, for his face brightened, and his thin fingers worked as if he were planning out some beautiful creation."

"Poor soul!" cried the Colonel, again, yet with a tremulous smile on his lips.

"I never heard any one talk of heaven like aunt Madge" — Laura went on earnestly — "it refreshes one; I seem to have come from some consecrated place; to have been looking at some noble picture that has elevated and purified my nature. And it strikes me as rather strange, uncle, that people seem to hold heaven in such niggardly estimation. It is as if I, owning a beautiful jewel which would delight so many eyes, steal away once in awhile to where it is locked up, and take selfish glances. And yet if we intend investing money in a house, how we study plans for months, talk of scarcely any subject else, put ourselves out immensely to inspect the work as it is carried on, think of it, dream of it; but how seldom do we talk of the eternal mansions. Indeed, uncle, I never heard any one but aunt Madge talk freely of heaven."

"That's because she lives next door to it," my little philosopher," said the Colonel; I expect she has a key that none of us can duplicate, and so opens the gates of her soul, and catches glimpses now and then of the country she loves."

"It is something to share in the beautiful memories she retains, if indeed she sees more than we do. How she would enjoy life in the tropics! It is easy to dream of paradise there; particularly in those clear, white moonlights, when the palm trees seem almost to rain silver."

"Do n't talk to me of heaven where those deadly malaria breezes blow one's joints supple. I've had the yellow fever, thank you."

Laura laughed, then sighed.

"It was a terrible time in Barbadoes," she said. "When we went into harbor the English flag was half mast. We thought surely the Governor was dead. So when the health officer came on board, Philip asked what had happened."

"Happened, sir! enough I should think," he replied; "plague, sir, been raging for a fortnight; very terrible, sir, very terrible, indeed."

"The plague!" exclaimed Philip, aghast.

"Yes; one of the worst that has ever visited our island. Unfortunately, you are here, sir, and here you must stay; no vesssel goes out of port. English residents all left that could; your consul gone too at the first outbreak, but none allowed to leave the limits now, sir."

"So you see, uncle, we had to make the best of it; and there we lost our dear little cabin boy."

At that moment Mrs. Willerton entered, followed by a black servant; who carried a waiter filled with fruit. The Colonel sprang up and wheeled the easy chair he had just occupied on the other side of Laura, removing from a tripod that stood between them a willow basket shining with flosses and cambrics, for the accommodation of the waiter. Then the fruit was passed, eliciting comment as well as commendation.

"My dear, I have the happiness to inform you that young Franklin leaves prison the day after to-morrow," said the Colonel to his wife.

"On New Year's day!" exclaimed Laura.

"Yes, it will be a present worth having, poor fellow. And then we must set our wits to work in finding him something to do. I've a great aversion to giving a man his liberty if I can't secure his independence."

"What a beautiful boy he used to be," said Laura. "I suppose he is very much changed since I saw him three years ago."

"Dear, yes," replied Mrs. Willerton; "he is twenty-one, now; a fine, broad shouldered young man; and I hear that the warden gives him the very highest character. It is unfortunate that his father feels as he does towards him."

"O, Franklin will get over that in time," responded the Colonel.

"My dear," said Mrs. Willerton — whom her enemies denominated an ultraist, and her friends an angel — "Why is not Irene here?"

"That I can't tell you," replied the Colonel; "has n't she gone home?"

"Of course not; I engaged her yesterday to sew a week for me, as Mrs. Archer could spare her. I wonder she has n't come down."

She rang the bell. A red faced, intelligent looking girl answered the summons.

"Maria, tell Miss Irene to come down stairs," she said.

"I 'll tell her, mum," said the girl, with a shy look; ' but she is very queer to-night, mum."

" Queer ! what do you mean, Maria ? "

" Why, mum, you see she got a letter jest a little ago that sort o' upset her.   I expecs her intellecks is wandering, mum."

Mrs. Willerton turned aside to suppress a smile.

"A blue stocking in embryo, as well as a blue nose," whispered the old Colonel, laughing.

" Yes, mum, she flewed round and flewed round, and laughed asterically, and then she cried mum, and then she stood like a queen, mum, and then she looks at me black, mum, and orders me to leave the room, and then bursts into asterics like agin.   I 'm quite afeared of her intellecs, mum."

" What can the girl mean ? " queried Mrs. Willerton, the Colonel, meantime, rubbing his hands and enjoying the scene highly.   " Maria, I really cannot allow you to speak so freely of any lady in my house."

"I begs your pardon," said the girl, who was fresh from the provinces ; " I thought like that she was n't a lady, particular, but a seamstrus—which a seamstrus is n't a lady in our country, mum ; " and the girl gave another short curtsy and folded her hands demurely over her blue apron.

" We 'll go up and see what it means, Laura," said her aunt ; "perhaps she is in grief about her brother and wants comforting."

The Colonel made a wry face at this proposal, which would leave him alone. He solaced himself, however, with an orange, and settled down in his chair, the thick white locks clinging to the shaggy velvet.

Irene Franklin had been sewing all day in a room just over the Colonel's famous parlor. Neatness and a certain style made her plain gown of cheapest fabric fall round her like the folds upon a perfect statue. Grace was not wanting in any of her appointments. She turned a colorless face, over which the crimson tide poured as they entered — Laura and her aunt Madge.

She was a handsome girl, with gleaming dark hair and full red lips, on which, notwithstanding, the smile appeared wintry, and the light of whose large eyes, brilliant though they were, seemed like the sun-glare on ice. Rising slowly from her seat, she came forward to meet them, with something imperious in her manner — rather like one who is served instead of serving.

For a long time, Irene had struggled with the, to her, bitter fate of poverty. To see others feasting when she fasted, to see others in possession of what she never hoped to attain, made her rebellious. Perpetual struggles between the inclinations and the realities of her life had given her, though so young, a heart that was prematurely old and hard.

"Why did n't you come down, dear? Why sit here in the dark?" asked Mrs. Willerton, quietly, as she took her by the hand, remarking its coldness.

"O, Mrs. Willerton, I have heard such strange, strange, exciting news! I thought at first it would set me wild; but I feel calmer now."

"Why, what is the news, my dear?" asked Mrs. Willerton.

"Will you read this note? It came from my mother. It was sent yesterday, to Mrs. Archer's, and some way she neglected to forward it to me, till quite late this evening. Mrs. Willerton heightened the gas, and standing near it, read the following:

"MY DEAR IRENE:

"I do not know how you will receive the intelligence which I am about to communicate, and of which we have been in possession but a few hours. You will be obliged to work for your living no longer, my child, for your father inherits a large fortune, from an uncle recently deceased, in Australia. I write in haste, merely to inform you of the fact, and intimate that you had better remain as you are a day or two — or at most a week. Your uncle's man of business has taken our affairs into his own hands. His name is Lyons, and he came over from Barbadoes with Capt. Gurney. In that time, we shall probably be removed to better quarters, and then you must come to us. Your father is now occupied in arranging his affairs, and the place is in confusion.   *"Most affectionately, your mother,*

"BERNICE FRANKLIN."

"P. S.   I might as well say that the fortune which your father heirs is a hundred thousand pounds."

Mrs. Willerton looked half in delight, half in dismay, at the young girl who was yet trembling with excitement.

"I do n't wonder it unsettled you a little, my dear. Why, it's like the fairy tales we used to read. It is the purse of Fortunatus, inexhaustible. You have not got used to the thought of it yet, I see."

"No, indeed. I fear all the time that it is a beautiful dream; that presently I shall wake up and these illusions will all vanish. It is so hard to realize that I am rich; that no one can control me. I thought the gates of fortune were shut on me forever. O! it is such joy — such joy — if even it is only a dream!"

"My child, do you indeed attach so much importance to riches?" asked Mrs. Willerton, a momentary sadness clouding her face. "There are some circumstances, remember, that make even wealth a burden."

"O! I know, I know," cried Irene, passionately, clasping her hands and bursting into tears. "My brother's bitter disgrace ruins everything. How *can* I ever be happy with that knowledge?"

"I beg you to believe that I never meant to allude to him," said Mrs. Willerton, in great distress; "if I have hurt your feelings unintentionally, I am very sorry. And let me implore you to look

upon his situation in a different spirit. Your brother will come forth a noble young man, like gold
purified in the fire. He will be worthy your esteem, your love, much more than if he had never
passed through this terrible ordeal."

"I cannot view it in that light," said the young
girl, bitterly. "It has cast an awful shadow over
my life. From the first day he was carried where
he is, I have been wretched. Sometimes I have
wanted to die. I think when I pass through the
streets with my veil down, that the finger of scorn
is pointed at me wherever I go. And I am sure
it has ruined my father; he used to be so strong
and handsome, and now he is but a wreck of his
former self. It is a most fearful humiliation."

"Then you don't mean to be happy in any
state," said Laura, gently.

It is conceded, I suppose, that there are chronic
cases of mental malaria as well as physical. The
mind that is wholly wretched in the midst of ad-
verse surroundings, need not calculate to be happier in the possession of everything that heart can
wish. If a room with one window in it makes me
miserable, I am not curable by any quantity of light.
If my one good picture, placed on dingy walls,
does not thrill me with a sense of the beautiful, a
gallery of the choicest masterpieces would satisfy
me only with the first superficial glance. If my

mind is not susceptible of the keenest emotions in reading a line of choice poetry, a hundred volumes would be as chambers furnished richly, but locked against me forever.

As some believers cling to a creed they cannot understand, so Irene clung to a sense of her own wretchedness in thus being cursed with a brother who had dishonored her.   She had not magnanimity enough to forgive, or grace to forget.   The evil was ever present with her, like some coiled serpent, ready to sting.   Alas, for poor Harry, when he should come to a knowledge of this fact. A few moments before, Irene had been deliriously happy ; now she was plunged into the deepest mental darkness.   So much depends upon the make of one's mind.   Surely a cloud not the bigness of the hand will cover some skies.

"Of course I shall try to endure it.   I suppose my father will send Harry away, since he is to be pardoned soon, I hear, or else, we may all leave this hateful city.   At least " — she poised her head haughtily — " no one will dare to fling it in our teeth now that we are rich."

" Your father will need Harry's assistance I should think, more than ever.   In his sad state of health, care will be burdensome ; he requires a strong brain to think for him, and a strong will to execute," said Mrs. Willerton.

" If my brother remains at home, *I* do not wish to," Irene responded, half angrily.

" A sad want of submission here," thought Mrs. Willerton.

A slender figure crept in and came gliding towards them. A rich, low laugh, and Bernie hung on her sister's neck.

" O, Mrs. Willerton! and you, dear, dear Laura, how glad I am to see you! "

Irene loved her sister as thoroughly as, I am sorry to say, she hated Harry. Her face brightened in a moment at sight of those heavenly eyes.

" Irene, darling, mamma was frightened a little because you did n't answer her note, so she sent me in a carriage to Mrs. Archer's. When I found you were n't there, I drove here. O, Irene! what *do* you think of the great, good news? Is n't it perfectly splendid? We 've had such a time at home; for papa has been giving everything away out of his store to the poor people, and they 've all been crowding in and thanking him, and laughing and crying. It was a rare sight to see. Poor mamma! I never was so amused. It would have done you good. The funny little man was there, who brought papa the news, you know, and he is seeing about a fine, large house, all thoroughly furnished, so we can move in to-morrow or next day You can go home with me, if you wish."

" I 'll go, I think," said Irene, and she arose to make preparations.

" And how do *you* look at this new fortune?" asked Mrs. Willerton of Bernie, who followed her sister's motions with a dreamy smile on her lips.

" Why, I think it has almost turned my head, I 'm building such castles, you see. In the first place, I shall try to find out that noble fellow who saved me from drowning. For don't you think he must be noble to risk his life, even if he was a poor, miserable fellow, as some say he was. I 'm so afraid he 'll go away before I can find him that I do n't know what to do. I shall present him with a suit of clothes — the very best, you know; and if he 'll only be good, I' ll take care of him all his life, or at least, help him to take care of himself. O, Mrs. Willerton, it kept me awake last night, I was so happy thinking what I should do. Papa says the shoes I 've spoken for for my poor children will come to a hundred dollars ; just think of it ! "

" And Harry, what do you think he will say about it?" asked Laura, tears of pleasure standing in her eyes.

Bernie drew a long breath, and her beautiful face for one moment reflected the pang that shot clear through her heart.

"I'm sure he'll be very thankful, Mrs. Gurney,"
she said in a low, earnest voice. "And my father
has spoken of him once or twice to my certain
knowledge, and mamma thinks he feels differently
towards him. Ah! but don't I *long* to see him?
I never loved anything better than I loved Harry,
he was so kind to me. As for the disgrace, I'm
determined not to think of it. I shall just open
my arms and say, come here Harry, you're just
as dear to me as ever. And why should'nt he be?
Does not our holy Christ love those who have repented just as well as though they had n't sinned?
But Oh! Mrs. Willerton, I'm afraid everybody
wont think so, and the little that we can do for
him will hardly compensate for the slights and in-
sults he may receive in other quarters. It troubles
me to think of it."

Here was the golden heart, sunny amidst poverty and privation; sunny still, but not over elated
when prosperity came; the key of her treasures
was still that undoubting, gentle, innocent faith.
The veriest fiend might have hesitated to assert
that there was no goodness in the world, looking
into that harmonious face, soul shining through
azure eyes, simple goodness permeating every
feature.

Mrs. Willerton, in her own gentle way, tried to
reassure her, and as Irene glided in, now self-pos-

sessed and quiet in her cold beauty, Bernie gave her farewell kiss, and the two drove home.

"I wonder whenever a carriage waited for us before?" queried Irene, sinking back on the soft cushions.

"It does seem odd, does n't it? But I suppose we shall get so accustomed to it that we shall think nothing of it."

Irene did not answer; she was so absorbed in visions of splendor as she reclined there, her brilliant eyes closed, her lips tightly locked. The carriage stopped at the little corner grocery, now quite dark. There were brilliant lights however in the sitting room. Shrunk, and mean, and almost contemptible as this place had always seemed in Irene's eyes, it was scarcely endurable now. She bowed her haughty head under the low doorway. Her mother sprang forward with a quiet pleasure subdued on lip and brow, her father took both hands in his and imprinted a kiss on her forehead. She was introduced to the little old man, upon whom, in his outlandish habiliments, she looked in her inmost soul with something like contempt.

"So this is the elder daughter," he said, rising, as he took her hand after a courtly, old-time fashion. "I wish you much joy, Miss Franklin, and I 've no doubt you 'll grace your new circumstances, royally. Yet remember an old man tells you,

"Much wealth brings want, that hunger of the heart,
  Which comes when nature man deserts for art."

He scanned her thoroughly as he spoke, and his
eyes turned with a strange smile from her to the
starry eyes of Bernie, that were fastened with a
look of pride upon her queenly sister.

"A woman that either loves or hates," he said to
himself, then added aloud, turning several plans
and papers; "we'll submit this matter to your
daughter, Mr. Franklin. She is old enough to
give her judgment an airing, I should think," and
he handed her the plans, adding here and there a
hint or an explanation.

"Here is one, he said, which is rather comfortable than splendid. I think Mr. Franklin prefers
it."

"O! papa, that will never do," she said hastily.

"Ah! I see; I thought so," replied the little
old man, with a shrewd smile. "Youth at the
prow, pleasure at the helm. Not a mere barge,
with a pennon and a flag, but a royal yacht streaming at every point; room for us to move in, eh? so
we sha'n't capsize the thing by a heedless misstep.
Well, well, I can't say I blame you, especially
with such lee way, and the sun shining on it, just
now. But you know the smoothness of the brightest sea is treacherous. There; this is the house
that will suit your daughter, Mr. Franklin."

Irene smiled, and half pouted too. There was something in this queer little man whom Bernie gazed upon almost in rapture, as the deliverer of her father from a majority of earthly ills, that she did not quite like. She expressed her approbation of the place, however, and its neighborhood, clenching her arguments by the remark that the location was in the vicinity of churches and schools.

"Yes, of the most fashionable kind," added the little old man, with a spice of sarcasm. So the house was chosen, and the premises made ready or the following day.

CHAPTER VII.

I TOLD YOU SO.

IT'S turned out just as I said it would, Stebbins.
You always *was* that obstinate, — and I *knew*
how it would be. Why could n't you let the chist
alone?"

"It was so bad to keep running home for
tools," said Tim, meekly, tilting back and forth in
a wooden chair, his hands in his pockets.

"I'm glad of it — I'm glad of it," cried the old
lady, with a spiteful grimace. "So much comes
for not taking my advice. Stebbins, did n't I *tell*
you harm would come of your taking that chist
off, not to say nothing of seventy-five cents all in
silver, that was paid for the carting? Did n't I
tell ye?"

"Yes," replied Tim, meekly, cowering under the
severe glance of her spectacles. Poor Tim; the
very chairs and tables, in their prim way, seemed
all gifted with speech. Everything that he looked
at, said as plainly as word and paint could say,
"did n't I tell ye?" How could they help echoing
what they had been hearing all the morning.

Dame Stebbins was a good woman in the main.
She read her Bible night and morning; would n't
have missed church on Sunday for twenty rheuma-
tisms; enjoyed the delightful privilege of meeting
with the children of God at all times, and tried her
best to live for heaven; but she did n't quite comprehend the beauty of that exceedingly beautiful
line — that pearl that dropped from lips touched
with the fire of holiness —

"Little children, love one another."

Not but what she would have been rightly and
righteously indignant if any one had hinted that
she did not love Tim. Years of constant assiduity to his interest, days and nights of ceaseless
watching by his fevered pillow, careful attention
to his comforts bodily, all attested to that; but if
Tim failed in anything, he always came home with
a dejected air, sure of a good scolding, and the inevitable "I told you so!" The last thing that a
man likes to confess, under any circumstances, is
the mishap that has occurred through his own folly.
But when he does confess, do n't suck your thumb
mentally and look sullen at him, if you have any
respect for the manhood he wears; that is, supposing I am talking to some wife, married to a mortal
who *will* at times make mistakes. A few such
still exist, even at this enlightened period. For
sins of carelessness committed in defiance of your

better judgment, soothe while you sorrow. Tim
felt worse than his wife about the tool-chest.

His very means of support were taken away.
He sat down to the tidy little breakfast-table dejected, and minus an appetite.

"I do n't wonder you can't eat," said Mrs. Tim,
harshly. The wiser way would have been —"Tim,
dear, you'll feel better for a cup of tea." But, no;
her gentle heart that ached at sight of a famished
cat, felt no sympathy for the dejected man. He
was a broken reed, not a handsome one by any
means; fuzzy, ill-shapen, homely at his best; but,
oh! dear, how his honest heart ached for one word
of consolation! No, he could n't eat; the bread
choked him, and though Mrs. Tim toasted him a
fair slice on her own fork, turning away from the
table to do it, her face was so clouded, so right
down and viciously cross, that he put it on his
plate instead of into his mouth.

"And now what are we going to do, I should
like to know? How are you to work without
tools? I can't help you with my swelled hands,
and patience knows we haven't anything to spare.
Why *could n't* you leave that tool-chist at home?"

O! Mrs. Tim, what is the use?

"I wish to mercy I had," said Tim — never de
fended himself, you see — which forbearance should
have called out Mrs. Tim's charity in an unusual
degree.

"Wish, yes, but what's the good of wishing? It was bad enough in you not to let me know of it for two whole days. But there! oh! dear, what *is* the use?"

That is exactly the question we asked above, my good woman; the shop is gone, the tools are gone, and the fire is gone that destroyed them; now suppose you let by-gones be by-gones.

Tim walked drearily to the window. I had forgotten to say that it was Christmas day, by-the-by. The fact made the poor carpenter all the more melancholy. For years he had not missed having a Christmas turkey; and as Mrs. Tim had sharply informed him, there was only a little cold meat in the house. The carpenter's wife still sat at table, thinking up, doubtless, some other tormenting consolation, when the door burst open, and there like a sunbeam stood Bernie Franklin, her warm heart shining through the transparency of her beautiful face.

"Here I am! a merry Christmas," she said cheerily.

"Bless me; why Bernie, how bright you look, child!" cried Mrs. Tim, bustling up. "And seems to me, you're altered," she added, scanning the soft, warm materials of the girl's cloak. "Why Bernie, you never was so pretty in your life."

"Thank you, Mrs. Stebbins; but oh! Tim, I

was *so* sorry to hear of your misfortune," she said
softly, her angel eyes beaming a gentle pity.

Tim had steeled his heart a little, as much as
his soft nature would allow, at his wife's fretful-
ness; but this kind little voice was a trifle more
than he could bear. He winked a little, and gulped
a little, all the time trying to draw forth his handkerchief that would n't come, until he turned away
fairly crying.

" It was his own fault, Bernie. I *begged* him to
let that chist stay at home," said Mrs. Tim, though
her voice had lost its acid, for she was taken aback
a little herself at this unusual sign of feeling.

" Papa has been so busy, so very busy, that he
did n't think till last night about it; so this morning he sent me over here to — to — well, to say
how bad he felt, and — to — "

" I 'm sure I 'm much obliged," said Tim, giving
his handkerchief one final flourish against his moist
eyes. "Your father felt sorry for me, I know;
for when I told him the day it happened, he expressed the kindest wishes. It goes to my heart
to have any one speak so."

" It was a great loss to us, Bernie," said Mrs.
Tim, dolefully, twisting the corners of her mouth.

" It must have been ; and here," said Bernie, her
sweet face flushing up to her temples, speaking as
rapidly as she could, "here is a little Christmas

present papa begs you'll accept," and she laid it on the table. "And if you please, Tim, just come down stairs with me; I've got something there for Mrs. Stebbins — come."

Someway Tim felt as if an angel had hold of his hand, and that the door opened into heaven, the fingers seemed so etherial — the little white fingers that were destined to be so busy in the Father's work. He went in his usual subdued manner, and in a few moments came up-stairs loaded with a large turkey and a ditto bundle. There he stood in the open door-way, sending towards his wife an incredulous, comical stare; there she stood, looking at him, a small roll in her fingers, her glance as incredulous, her expression as comical as his.

"Tim," she cried, in a hollow, measured voice, expressive of mingled awe and gratitude, "I've counted it and counted it, and it's a hundred."

"A hundred what, wife?" gasped Tim.

"A hundred dollars."

"Two tool-chests," said Tim, sententiously, and solemnly walking forward deposited his burden upon the table, wondering whether he wasn't going to laugh presently.

"Wife," he said not long afterwards, as he stood surveying a glorious woolen shawl that had opened out of the bundle, "for once you can't say, 'I told you so.'"

CHAPTER VIII.

THE SUDDEN DEATH.

BERNIE rolled off in the carriage, her little heart full to the brim with the pure, sanctified love of doing good. It was a sumptuous, not to say luxurious carriage, and the coachman, whose stable and stand were not far from the little corner grocery, was a most ardent admirer of Bernie Franklin. He never forgot that when once he went into the corner shop, the tears in his eyes, forced there and almost freezing on his lashes by reason of the terrible cold, slapping his poor benumbed hands to bring a little warmth into them, how an angel-face had appeared at the door, and the pitying eyes watched with quivering interest. He never forgot the look that accompanied her question —

"Wouldn't you like some thick, warm mittens, sir? I've got a pair I knit myself, and you can bring them back to-morrow, unless it's another cold day."

Jehu was not used to kind words. It was something entirely out of his line, as he would have said. Who ever took one thought of *his* comfort? It quite broke him down, and although he intended to refuse, yet when the soft, warm mittens were held up to him, something impelled him to take them; and the spiritual beauty of that child's face haunted him forever. It was as if he felt that nothing common nor unclean must come between his heart and that image. When he heard, therefore, that the proprietor of that corner grocery had by some unaccountable means grown rich all at once, he was the first one to ask for employment. Bernie remembered him, and said yes; and Bernie usually had it all her own way.

They stopped, Jehu and Bernice, once more at the door of a dilapidated house, much worse than that which held the corner grocery. Bernie sprang out and hurried into the dark door-way. Poverty lived there, armed to the teeth with pride; it was not yet the abode of crime. Poor widows, scantily paid; poor girls, fighting off evil with a few coals, set teeth and numb fingers, as they sewed that for which many a rich and lordly man grudged them the meanest pittance.

On the second story Bernie stopped, quite out of breath, her heart beating against the frail body so fast and so loud, that it made her tremble from head to foot.

The door opened.

"You dear, blessed child!" cried aunt Chrissy, whose personal peculiarity was an indifference to her outward appearance. On the present occasion she had perched an old military cap over her somewhat neglected visage, and had thrown her husband's well-worn dressing-gown over her own ill-worn one.

"I'm just as happy as I can be, only I think that old uncle of ours might have divided his property more fairly. However, it's all for the best, I suppose, for George is the oldest, and Joseph has n't any business turn whatever, and I'm sure I have n't. Just look at that chair, you darling; your father sent it up last night. My poor sick one is so comfortable in it! And the jellies! Why he'll get well, now — he can't help it. There, take care how you rock, or you'll break the window; and there goes a quarter, cash.

"I'll be careful," said Bernie, with her grave, gentle smile. "Can I see uncle Joseph?"

"No, you can't; I wouldn't let the king see him, for he's in the blessedest sleep! Look at what your father sent me from the store;" and opening a closet, she displayed rows of packages and bundles. "They're all very nice," she added, with a short, dissatisfied nod," but I do wish he'd thought of molasses."

Bernie turned away to smile.

" Did you know that your old cottage was for sale? " she asked.

" What if it is? " queried Chrissy, coldly ; " I 've got no money to buy it."

" But papa has, and I suppose I ought not to tell you, but I must ; he 's going to buy it for you, aunt Chrissy."

The woman looked up, incredulous.

" Bernie Franklin, you know better," she said sternly.

" Well, you 'll see. I am sure that he has seen the man who owns it, and made almost all the arrangements."

" O, the good Lord of heaven ! " exclaimed Chrissy, in a burst of irrepressible gratitude ; " your father 's a prince, Bernie Franklin. Well, well, the house that my mother left me ; " and she burst into a passion of tears. The shower subsided in a minute, however. She looked up brightening.

" I sha n't believe it till I see it," she said, in her old odd way.

" We shall go to *our* new house this afternoon," said Bernie, " and Harry will be with us."

" That prison-bird? " muttered Chrissy.

Bernie burst from her calm, sprang to the floor. Her lucid eyes flamed ; her face flushed scarlet from her throat to the roots of her hair. Small as she was, she looked regal, as she confronted her coarse-tongued relative.

"Aunt Chrissy, how *dare* you?" she cried; then choked then turned away and dropped her head upon her palms, shaking to her very heart with agony and constrained passion. By-and-by she dashed away the tears, and stood up, white, weak and quivering.

"Aunt Chrissy, you say such things to papa, and he do n't answer you," she cried again," but I *will*. I will tell you how cruel and beneath any woman it is to taunt us in our affliction. O, Harry, Harry! what shall I do if they say these things to you — what shall I do?"

The woman was first frightened, then angry, then touched even to tears."

"Bernie, child, do n't looks o," she cried, with a scared face, as the girl sank down feebly into the chair. "Bernie, do forgive me, child."

"What he will have to suffer," sobbed Bernie, though she did not shed a tear. "It is so cruel, so unchristian! Even my own dear sister, *his* own sister refuses to love him. But he shall find one heart, at least, that will not turn away from him. He is my dear brother, he always shall be my dear brother. I am going," she added, rising up weakly.

"You 're dreadful put out with me, child."

" No, aunty, I'm not put out; at least, I'm not quite sure I ought to say that, but I'll try not to think of it. You do n't know how you've hurt my feelings, aunt Chrissy," she added, in a voice so plaintive that it went straight to the heart of her aunt.

" There, child, I promise you I'll never speak so of him again; and more than that, I'll tear this ugly feeling out of my heart, so there's welcome number two for master Harry. He was a dear, kind lad, I remember, and I've been a heathen to feel so set against him. He shall never know that I think there's such a word as prison in the dictionary, I give my honor."

" O, I'm glad to hear that, aunty; perhaps it is better everything has happened as it has."

Very likely it was, for the woman possessed one of those unforgiving natures that made her blunt tongue as keen and cruel as a razor, sometimes. But she also possessed the virtue of standing to her word.

Bernie had risen to go. Chrissy thought the sleeper stirred in the next room. She went in, came out again, with blank, scared face, fallen jaw, and eyes that saw nothing.

" What is it aunt Chrissy?" cried Bernie, in affright.

" Go home," cried the woman, hollowly, like an

automaton, her teeth chattering as she spoke; "go home and tell your father to come up here; Joseph's dead."

"O, aunt Chrissy!" cried Bernie, breathless, as she tried to take her hand.

"Go home, I say, exclaimed the other; "do n't stand there like a fool. What do you know of trouble? O, good Lord! what shall I do without Joseph?" she shrieked, her arms uplifted, her eyes dry and glazed.

Bernie sprang from the door, down the stairs, and hurried home with the sad news.

CHAPTER IX.

THE NEW YEAR'S GIFT.

ROWS upon rows of dead blank faces stared at the old minister as he said these words:

"One of you will receive a new year's gift to-day of worth beyond computation. Of all offerings that change hands in the stately homes, in the humble cottages of our country, none will be so valuable as that which you are to take with thankfulness, I trust with Christian humility."

"That gift is liberty."

How strange the word sounded in that dismal place. Every man turned to his neighbor, some glances mournful, others defiant.

The preacher gazed about him. He was a good man, and loved to speak comforting words. All his life he had been an angel of mercy; around the brows of such, one seems to see a halo — a faint reflection of that which glorified the head of Christ.

"*In prison and ye visited me.*"

The chapel of the prison was a semi-circular room, which, with every contrivance of art, could

not be made to look cheerful. God only knew the
hearts of the men assembled there. Some of them
might have been easily touched by kindness, but
the many, though they listened with an assiduity
that was almost painful, ground their teeth with a
bitter hatred of everything good. Here and there
such faces looked out as might have startled
angels. The senate chamber, the sacred desk, the
bar, seemed fitter places for them than this dreadful prison. And yet murder, arson, theft, adul-
tery, every crime under heaven, had here its un-
hallowed exponent.

I dare not think of the pangs hidden by such
walls. My heart sickens when I remember the
words, the eyes that greeted me on one weary
round. My very breath was an agonizing prayer
to the Eternal —"Oh! pitying Christ, save these
lost souls!"

I fancy how the moonlight must look to such as
are not wholly bad; whose inclinations lead to
graceful, pleasant avocations, and who would not
touch the hands of crime if they were soiled. See
that patch of white against the dull, black blot
yonder; it is a man's forehead. Does the cool
air bring an odor of new mown hay, or the breath
of his mother's lips as she kissed him once, when a
kiss was worth so much? Ah! to him the chances
of life and death are too evenly poised for the out-

side world to have much attraction; still, he cannot resist that one yearning look at the moonlight, nor the soothing influence it brings.

But I forget my souls in the prison chapel. Right forward of the preacher, on the second seat, sat a handsome young man, his face returned to the fairness of infancy, through the confinement of years. His bearded lip had quivered more than once as the quiet-voiced chaplain pictured many a fair scene. Heavy bolt, dungeon bar, midnight blackness were all forgotten, for was there not the transcendant brightness of another and a heavenly home awaiting him?

Upon him the announcement just made fell like a thunder clap. Not because he imagined, or even fancied that it might be himself. His term had been shortened from the first to three years. But for whom was this priceless boon? Over his mind swept all the sweet remembrances of liberty. A wild, almost irrepressible yearning came over him to rush into the outer world, and quaff the vital atmosphere of freedom. Even if it lasted but a moment; oh! for that moment he would have given a year of life.

But see — the warden was rising. Now the announcement would be made. He wondered whose heart beat the loudest; he could hear his, like the strokes of a hammer. The silence was almost

frightful.   Of the hundreds there, not one moved
hand or foot.

"I am empowered," said the warden, a pale, tall
cadaverous man, "to give to one of our prisoners
the restoration of his liberty, and to say that by
uniform good conduct he has merited the same.
Harry Franklin, you will step forward."

No language can describe the light that flashed
all over that pale face, fired the patient eyes with
a luminous splendor.   He sprang up wildly, threw
one triumphant glance around, stepped to the
front, lifted his arms, staggered blindly a few
steps, and fell prone his whole length.   He had
fainted from excess of joy.

The surgeon of the prison happened to be present.   The men stood up, but a look of authority
seated them again.   Not one there, hardened or
otherwise, but felt some spark of gladness thrill
along his frame, when Harry came to consciousness.

"Are you able to go out, now?" asked the
surgeon, kindly.

"I am much better, thank you.   It was very
weak of me, certainly.   But — are you *sure* — it's
true?" he put his hand to his head in a bewildered manner.

"Be careful, or we must detain you here; if
any serious injury should result from this excess of

feeling, your liberty would not be worth much."
Harry smiled sadly, as he replied, "Ah, sir, you
do n't know what it is to lose it."

"True, said the surgeon, smiling, "but are you
able now to go in the warden's room?"

"O, yes;" and rising, with the aid of the surgeon he walked quickly to the place designated,
never once looking behind him. Seated there,
left to himself, he felt oppressed, uneasy. Over
and over again he gazed at the little shelf of books,
the round table in the centre covered with a red
and black cloth, the dull carpet, here and there
plashed with faded blotches of ink, the great, dusky
inkstand with quill pens scattered round, the worn
chairs, their hair-cloth seats grey and white with
time, the rusty frame around the grate, the fire
smouldering within. Strange he did not take
the first step towards the window that looked
upon the busy street. A dull apathy, or perhaps
a dread prevailed whenever he thought of it. In
vain he tried to persuade himself that the faces
would be all unfamiliar there and everywhere in
the crowded city. A shuddering impression that
"convict" would be branded on his forehead, possessed him. In the first gladness he had not
thought of that; now it overwhelmed him.

"Have I lost my faith?" he gasped, with white
lips. "Oh! Christ, forsake me not."

No, Christ had not forsaken him. Came that sweet sentence breathed by some spirit voice, " Lo ! I am with you *alway*." It lulled all apprehensions. It gave him a perfect calmness, such as visits only those who can claim loving nearness to the Father.

Some one entered the room. Through misty eyes he saw the warden — then the surgeon. The former brought in a large package.

" If you will step into one of the side apartments," he said, " you will find everything you want in this bundle."

The poor fellow had almost forgotten that he wore his convict clothes ; seeing them so constantly had dulled his perceptions. When he came out, some forty minutes afterward, in a suit of the finest, black broadcloth, there was a perceptible change in his demeanor. He looked the finished gentleman ; he had always been a handsome youth. The surgeon was there ; he smiled approval. He from the first had taken a lively interest in this superior young man. In fact, he knew then, more than he chose to tell, about the altered circumstances of the family. He went out, smiling to himself. Harry stood, thoughtful, in the centre of the room. Now that the ordeal was really to come, he began to tremble. How should he meet his father ? Had he ever forgiven him ? would he ever forgive him ? His mother, he was sure of ;

that dear heart had not been closed against him. Little Bernie, whose angel-hood he had never doubted, he felt no fear on that score; but Irene, proud and imperious in her very childhood, a born aristocrat, her sympathies he feared would be closed against him. These varied emotions whirled and seethed in his brain. His intellect was intensely acute to all fatal contingencies. It was well for him that his attention was distracted by a low cry, a cry that was very music to his ears, though it smote every nerve with pain. He turned; his mother stood there — her arms opened, even as when a babe he learned to toddle into them.

"O, Harry, my son!" she cried — some pride in her sad face as she marked how nobly he stood.

"Mother! mother!" he half sobbed, and sank on his knee as she came towards him. She drew the bright, young head closer to her bosom. She patted the brown curls, childishly, scarcely knowing that her tears brightened them. Over his memory rushed every sacred heroism of her patient life, and the blessing she had been to him, deserted by all else. O! what deeps of anguish, what heights of love seemed to open to his desolate heart, folded there in the arms of his mother!

"Look up, dear, somebody else wants to see you."

Harry lifted his head. He flushed to the roots

of his hair, meeting that face, aged by ten years it seemed, rather than two.

"O, father, is it possible? Father, dear father, have you at last forgiven me?"

"Harry," said his father, and stopped, for self-command was fast deserting him — "I — have forgiven you. After this stern encounter with suffering, I" — there he broke down, threw his arms about the neck of his boy — his first born — now his only one. Steevie's bright young image came freshly before him. Was it for this reconciliation that God had taken him? The father wept on the neck of his son.

"This is too kind of you," said Harry, in broken tones. "But I will try to repay you, believe me — I can't say much — but I will prove how sincere my repentance has been."

Bernie could be denied no longer. She went round on the other side. She touched him with her little, helpless hands.

"O, Bernie! angel sister!" cried the young man, catching her in his arms, and pouring out the long-hoarded love of his heart in lavish, rapturous kisses.

"If you knew how that sinless face has smiled upon me in my dreams. Ah, if I were only worthy of all these blessings! Heaven helping me, though you may blush for my past, you shall have

no cause to dread my future. Irene did not
come?"

Bernie's tear-dimmed eyes fell, her cheek crim-·
soned.

" Irene was too busy, dear," she said.

" Come, the carriage is waiting;" and Mr.
Franklin touched his son upon the shoulder.

Not until this moment did Harry notice the al-
teration in the garments of his mother and sister.
The richly furred coat his father wore, the fineness
and glossiness of his own suit; now following
them he gazed on these evidences of better fortune
with growing surprise.

" It must be that Irene has made a great match,"
he said to himself.

In the large circular hall, which for months he
had only seen at a distance, going down the neat
staircase that led to the warden's private parlors,
how his pulses bounded ! The sweet air of liberty,
like some rare gift fresh from God's hand, breathed
over his brow, quickened his pulses, swept every
vibrant string of his nature, till his whole being
seemed glorified. For the moment he felt that this
was his first draught of pure, unalloyed happiness.
At the door of the parlor, the warden's wife stood
smiling and wishing him joy. In a group stood
the warden, the jailor and little black-eyed Benny,
the jailor's son, who held a package mysteriously,
well wrapped up.

"It's the paint box," he whispered — "the old box you liked so well. Papa said I might give it to you if I liked."

Harry kissed the boy, and accepted the little gift with tearful eyes. Then, after he had shaken hands all round, and said good bye, he walked quickly forward and stood upon the stone step, out under the open sky, exulting in freedom.

"We have changed our quarters, Harry," said Mr. Franklin, as the carriage stopped.

"But *this* house!" cried he, breathlessly.

A noble edifice, the portico fitly finished with pillars of marble — the lustre of plate glass shining everywhere. What his sensations were, it is not possible for pen to define. Had any one asked him, he would as likely have answered with reference to the sun or moon as anything else.

"Where are you going?" he queried, confusedly.

"Home, dear," his mother answered, with her soft, sad smile.

"Home! this?"

"I will tell you all about it; wait."

And not long after he was put in possession of the facts. Quietly he listened; only a little pale, a little bewildered. The transition from a dreary prison, and the discipline of weary months, and almost years, to these luxurious surroundings, was almost too much for his self-possession. Irene, at first steadily refused to see him. It was not till her father commanded that she met him coldly, coldly offered her hand.

" She has ceased to love me," said Harry, mournfully. He might have been comforted; Irene loved few beside herself.

At the sound of a silver bell the folding doors were opened. There stood beside a little arch which Laura had erected, Colonel and Mrs. Willerton, Captain Gurney and his wife. Wrought in evergreen and bright flowers on the arch were the words, " Welcome home ;" a beautiful tribute to forgiveness and redemption.

Harry, if he had been allowed his own way, would have thrown himself in some curtained recess, away from every eye, even those that loved him best. As it was, he bore himself with a quiet dignity, though blanched cheek, and a certain pallor of lip and brow told how keenly he felt this unlooked for kindness. The strangeness of the circumstances wore off as dinner was announced, but Harry experienced no new humility. Everybody treated him with kindness and delicate consideration.

Bewildered and happy, in spite of all his remembered shame, he sank to a dreamless slumber that night—not on the narrow pallet, hemmed in by pitiless stone, but the soft, luxurious width of a bed in his father's house. Was it strange that he could not yet realize the extent of this day's blessings?

Irene stood combing out her long curls in the chamber of her selection. A very fine affair it was; the predominating colors, crimson and green. The cheval mirror gave back the outlines of a face, more fascinating in its perfect contour, than attractive by its feminine graces. Her features were almost faultless, her figure wholly so. Regnant, triumphant, there was but one shadow in her brilliant sky — her brother.

Bernie, in her snug little bed in the alcove, separated by heavy red curtains, lay with great palpitating eyes alive to everything.

" Do n't it seem so strange to be in this beautiful house? " she asked, childishly. " And only think, it was furnished for a sweet young bride, they say, who never came back from her wedding tour. She died in Venice."

" Who told you that? " asked Irene, hastily turning round with a startled look.

" Mrs. Kippet, the housekeeper. She staid here to be let with the other furniture, I suppose," replied Bernie, with a merry little laugh. " She 's nice, though, but the whole thing seems so queer to me, I can 't make it out."

" The whole thing seems just *the* thing," said

Irene, proudly. "It comes natural to me to wear purple and fine linen, I suppose."

"If we could only give everybody else purple and fine linen; or at least, make everybody comfortable, if not as rich, as we are."

"I expect you'll go poking about in dark alleys all your life," said Irene.

"There's nothing I should like better, if I could do some good," replied the gentle Bernie. "I thought of it after I was half drowned the other day. I was so glad God had spared me to do something."

"Of course you'll be somebody's good angel all your life — I shall have to subsist on charity. People *love* you, but they will only admire me, I suppose. There's nothing lovable about me."

"O, Renie, don't say that. You'll be a princess — a queen, and I only your poor little admirer and shadow. I never can shine, you know; even if I live to your age, I shall not be a beautiful or fashionable woman."

"*Even* if you live to my age — why, Bernie!"

"To be sure, dear. When I have these dreadful turns of heart-beat, I commend myself to God. I say, now perhaps I am going to die; Lord Jesus, may I be ready. If He spares me, why, it is all right; but if at any time He should take me"—the light in her eyes grew solemn—"do you know I should be *glad?*"

"O! Bernie, do n't, do n't talk so." Her voice was petulant, but it was the petulance of sadness. Did ever any created thing live near Bernie and not love her?

"I can almost see heaven, sometimes," whispered Bernie, her dreamy glance now upturned. "O, you can't think what strange joy comes over me when I think of it. It's like pouring a liquid, bright as gold, into some clear, slender vial. Do you suppose angels do come near us?"

"I never think of it," was the light reply.

"Did I ever tell you that the strange, heavenly music waked me up, now and then?"

"Why, Bernie, child, how you run on."

"Let me; I feel like talking. Well, sometimes, (it must be in my sleep, of course,) I hear thousands upon thousands of angel voices. It's like a great, solemn choir in circles, each circle nearer heaven; and oh, the music! O, if you could listen to it one little moment, you would never think what you hear on earth was music, never. And it grows louder, and richer, and clearer, till it comes close to my pillow; and then, as I am waking up, the sweet sounds grow so soft — oh! so soft — floating up, up, till they are like little infant's voices, and so they die out."

"What a strange child you are, Bernie," said Irene, conscious of a choking sensation in her throat, akin to tears.

"Why, I think I'm just the happiest creature alive," said Bernie, her little musical laugh rippling out—"so happy, that sometimes I hold my hands to my heart. It almost hurts me. I want to be outside, somewhere, floating up in this great universe of God. Just stop till my wings grow"—and she laughed again, at her own conceit—"for," she added, "such a queer little body as I have, never was meant for such beautiful things as the world loves. I must keep it out of sight all I can, now we have come to this great house."

Irene looked over. It frightened her to see the luminous beauty that seemed playing over the heavenly face. "Is she already half angel?" she murmured to herself.

"Come here, and kiss me," called Bernie. "May I whisper something?" she asked, her thin arms folded round her sister's neck.

"Certainly, dear."

"Pray that you may be able to forgive poor, dear Harry."

Irene arose with face and neck crimsoned. She had forgotten how to pray. Bernie's gentle eyes watched her till the light was put out, then she whispered grievingly,

"I did not see her kneel, but God will hear her if she will *only* pray."

CHAPTER X.

WILL YOU HELP HIM?

THE little old man was down on his knees rubbing the large, uneven hearth. By his side a cracked bowl sat, filled with a dingy, red liquid. The room was large and faded; the carpet was faded too, and every item of furniture seemed to possess a decayed constitution.

"Poh! this will never do. With my notions of neatness I shall be obliged to have a servant;" and he stood upright, wheezing with exertion, the bald spot on his head shining in the candle light. "Work conduces to one's happiness, no doubt," he continued; "is a sovereign balm for dyspepsia, and its manifold woes, but it's rather fatiguing to red up one's own hearth. Would n't it be charitable now"—he darted to the door, leaving his sentence unfinished. "Yes, there the young rascal sits, still," he muttered, *sotto voce;* "has n't moved, I'll be bound. Here, boy, I want you."

The ragged lump of humanity listened at first with an incredulous stare. Then, after another, raised himself slowly and came over.

"Monstrous dirty!" muttered the old man. Come in here and earn a quarter honestly," he added, in a louder tone, as the nondescript looked in his face with a stupid leer. At this offer, however, the sluggish light of his eyes quickened perceptibly. He went in, listened to instructions, and was soon at work.

"Tolerably well done; here's a quarter to carry home to your mother."

"A'n't got none," said the boy, doggedly.

"Well, your father, then."

"Nary father, nither."

"Both dead, eh?" and the old gentleman surveyed the boy with a glance of benevolent dejection.

"No, they a'n't dead, either. They're to State Prison, both on 'em."

"And where's *your* home?"

"I a'n't got what you might call a reg'lar home. There's a shed or two and some door-steps where I do n't pay much for board:" and a latent love of fun twinkled in the boy's steel blue eyes.

"But how do you get your food?"

"I begs, and sometimes I steals."

"Then you are not honest."

"No, sir; not when I'm so hungry I could eat my shoes, if I'd got any."

"If you had n't confessed yourself a thief, I

might have helped you," said the little old man, mildly. The boy looked down, and bit his lip. "That's the way your parents got into State Prison."

"Yes, sir, they lifted, both on 'em," was the reply; "but I do n't think I'd ever lift if I was decent and got enough to eat."

"Go buy yourself a supper, and come here tomorrow," said the old man, touched, he hardly knew why, by this specimen of forlorn humanity; and the boy, with a duck of his head and a scrape of his bare feet, vanished.

Mr. Lyons now commenced walking the floor, his hands folded under the long, blue coat-tails, his head bent.

"Poor young fellow!" he murmured, after a long silence. "I pity him. To carry with him the knowledge of this matter wherever he goes; to have that forced upon him that will fire his blood, and possibly nerve his hand to retaliation. It's a hard case, very hard. No doubt he did the thing in a moment of excitement — in the delirium of passion — half drunk, perhaps. But we must help him; if all things are true, he is a Christian, they say. Let us see what this religion will do for him. I wonder why Mr. Romaine do n't come? It's almost time for a game of whist with my old friends. Ah, here he is!"

A handsome, middle aged gentleman entered — the one who had been so much struck with little Bernie's beauty on the day of the accident. A mild and dignified urbanity marked all his movements. He was reputed to be the richest man in the city, and his only daughter was heiress to his immense wealth. Mr. Lyons received him cordially, drew a chair out, a small table, and the two men sat opposite each other.

Mr. Romaine had some papers drawn up, which he placed upon the table.

"I cannot conceal from you," he said, "that it appears to me a very singular notion;" and he smiled.

"Because I wish to rent the whole of this house?" returned the other, smiling, too. "O! that is a whim of mine, over which I have spent a good deal of thought. You know we all have various ideas of happiness. You, for instance, enjoy the comfort of your splendid house, and the society of your charming daughter. I do not quarrel with your taste, though mine is essentially different. There, sir, the papers are signed, and I may do what I please with the house for a twelvemonth, at least."

"The house is nominally yours, for that time, sir," replied Mr. Romaine, "and I wish you joy of your bargain. It certainly is not in the most *fashionable* location in the city."

" I am not a fashionable man, sir," was the grave reply.

" As to that, neither am I, in the strict sense of the word," said the banker. " Before I go, however, let me congratulate you on being the means of bringing great happiness to a very interesting family."

" You mean the Franklins; ah! I thank you. Yes, it was really a desirable piece of business; something especially agreeable to my feelings. How do you think they will stand prosperity, sir?"

" I have no fears whatever, except in the case of that son of theirs. Ah! a great misfortune that!"

His listener pursed up his lips and looked meditatively forward. " Well, sir," he said at length, " if you and I do our duty, he will go straight, I've no doubt."

" I!" exclaimed Mr. Romaine, "what have I to do with him?"

" A great deal; you have a great deal to do with him, sir," said the old man, almost sternly.

" Indeed, I was not aware of that," was the cold reply.

" Mr. Romaine, that young man might have been your own son," said Mr. Lyons.

The merchant shrugged his shoulders — moved uneasily.

" I am very glad that he was not, however," he said, in an undertone.

"That may be. We are all sensitive to disgrace, when it comes in any shape. But, sir, supposing him to have been a son of yours; an impulsive boy easily led astray, and who in a moment of temptation, after having his morals undermined by vicious companions, had at one step precipitated himself to the lowest moral standard. Then suppose him to submit to his punishment, as they say this young Franklin has, with a Christian resignation, behaving with such circumspection that the vilest inmate of that terrible place respects and honors him, and the Government even pardons and commends him; how would you wish to see that boy treated when he enters society again?"

"I should wish to see him taken by the hand, of course. I should wish to see him respected; but, I could not reasonably look for it, as society is constituted."

"A fig for society!" exclaimed the little old man; "society, as it is constituted, is a sham!"

"To you, perhaps," replied the banker, suppressing a smile.

"Ah! I see you are doing as all the world does, judging me by outside appearances; my merits from the cut of my coat, my position from the odd fashion of my trousers; but let me tell you, sir, I am no novice, even in that fashionable circle in which your high standing has enabled you to move."

"I beg your pardon," said Mr. Romaine, coloring, "and give you credit for your shrewdness. I certainly should never suspect that you had been a man of fashion. But I am always willing to rectify mistakes."

"You have not hurt my feelings at all, sir," replied Mr. Lyons, with vivacity. "I do not place any value whatever on that position which makes of man a mere automaton, and does not finish him till it has deadened almost every beautiful impulse of his nature. But what I was coming at, is this. Very likely this young man will need a helping hand. His father, to be sure, is a rich man, but the son scorns to live a mere gentleman — or rather, as any right-minded man would call it — a beggar on the bounty of his connections. He needs a friend who will not only counsel him, but protect him valiantly against the slurs and animadversions of his fellow-clerks. You see, of course, what I am driving at. Will you take him into your banking house?"

Mr. Romaine flushed again. He considered, twisting and tearing small bits of paper that he had taken from his pocket-book. Uppermost in his mind was the query of who this man could be, so insignificant in appearance, and yet by the interest and confidence he inspired, so much beyond any other mere stranger he had ever met with, as

well as in native nobleness of character.   He was
not a poor man, certainly, or he could not afford
to rent a house which divided among tenants yield-
ed an immense profit.   He did not appeal to his
religious feelings or to his passions — simply to
the justice of his nature as illustrated by the gold-
en rule.

" I do n't know that I have a vacancy," he said,
thoughtfully.

" You are a man of great resources, Mr. Romaine ;
surely you would create one for a favorite.   This
is a louder call of duty than that would be."

" The fact is," so spoke the man of the world,
" the young men in my employ are well connected ;
many of them are my personal friends.   I do n't
know how it would do to place this Mr. Franklin
among them.   The institution from which he has
just graduated does not find much favor in the
eyes of honest men."

" I am glad to hear that virtue is in such high
repute," said Mr. Lyons, dryly, " particularly
among young men.   What a school of morality
your banking-house must be, Mr. Romaine, since
even a reformed man cannot be tolerated because
of what he has been ! "

" You are rather hard upon me," returned the
banker, smiling in spite of himself.   " I do not
boast of the morality of my young men ; it is of

course a merely conventional feeling. I would not insure one of them that I know of, against crime, if temptation came through any particular channel that commanded their weakest points."

"Then pray do not fasten your heart against this man, whose struggle, at the best, will be hard enough. I want him to feel that, if he has earned a good character, even in State Prison, and through the severest discipline, he is thought worthy to be trusted by such an influential man as yourself."

"It seems to me you take an unusual interest in this young fellow," said the banker, with a steady look.

Mr. Lyons bit his lips; his eyes fell.

"Yes, I confess I do, sir," he said quietly, after a moment of suspense; "but, sir, if you had seen a little sister of his, a little helpless angel, bless her! whose eyes go to the very core of a man's heart; and more, if you had listened to her as she talked of her erring brother, you, too, Mr. Romaine, rich man that you are, would feel almost as deeply as I do."

"You mistake me, Mr. Lyons, if you think I do not feel for this young man. I am not hard in my nature, as perhaps you take it for granted most rich men are. You touched me in the right spot, when you spoke of that little woman, Bernie, I think they call her. Her face is certainly an index of a heart as pure as angel-hood. I never was so affected in my life by mere human beauty. I cannot say how often I have reverted to the time when rescued from the dock where one of my vessels was coming in, she laid in my arms. My daughter and I talk of it oftener than of any chance incident I can recall, and Cecil longs to see her. She is, I have heard, a sweet almoner to the poor."

" I told you she was an angel," said the little old man, softly; "a creature, whom religious people would say, was sent by the express will of God to show humanity the perfection it will attain hereafter. Unfortunately, perhaps, you will think the only angels I believe in are such as she; and when the time comes in which science shall bring her conserving influences to bear upon the being of man, then the continued existence of such as she will tend to purify the whole race."

" That is a very singular remark," observed the banker.

" And very ill-timed, I acknowledge," was the reply. "However, let it die where it fell. I never talk much about my peculiar opinions. The question is, will you take this young man into your employ?"

" I will think of it," said the banker.

" Thought is a tyrant in such a case as this," returned the latter.

"I will go so far as to promise that if I find I can easily create another office, or if I have one already vacant in a minor department, I will willingly give it to Henry Franklin."

"Willingly; I like that word," cried Mr. Lyons, eagerly. "Thank you, sir, thank you in little Bernie's name. And I have only one more favor to ask. If any one speaks to you about it, don't say, "O! poor devil — I pitied him."

"It's the way of the world, you know," he added, as the banker laughed at his comical grimace; "and if you will not think me officious, I would suggest that you make the offer to Mr. Franklin, or rather," he added, noting the coming frown, "allow me to do so, in your name."

"I shall have no objection," replied the banker, "provided I find him a place."

CHAPTER XI.

THE BANKER'S LETTER.

THE old clock in the corner struck eight with such a wheeze and rattle that the banker nearly sprang from his chair.

"I beg your pardon, in the name of my clock," said Mr. Lyons, laughing. "I bought it for a mere song, because, in my mother's old kitchen, such an one stood in the corner. We children used to look with awe at the rising sun over the old eight-day time keeper. Broken as they are, those tones recall my mother's voice, and I see her moving softly round, busy with household avocations. I wonder if anywhere there are old kitchens and old mothers like those of lang syne?"

"Very few exist now," replied the banker, a shade of sadness in his voice. He, too, was thinking of a sprig of mignonette on a certain stand, and the sunshine streaming in over a sanded floor.

"And that leads me to ask another favor. I want something to brighten up my old clock and me—say, an honest, upright and venerable octogenarian; a mild sort of superannuated clergyman,

poor enough to make the offer of a shelter a pleasant contingency, and independent enough to hold
his own views at the risk of some personal incon-
venience.   Can you tell me where I can find such
an one?"

The earnest, eager look of inquiry, coupled with
the oddity of the request, struck Mr. Romaine as
something too irresistibly *outre* to emanate from
the lips of a sane man.   He looked all his perplexity, as how to treat and answer the question.

"I am in earnest, Mr. Romaine, as you will
understand when I tell you that I am by constitution and education a sceptic as to the truths of the
so called revealed religion.   I am what might be
styled a hard-shell nothingarian, and I am willing
to give myself every chance to be convinced that I
am as wrong-headed as I am obstinate.   Now, with
a man such as I have in my mind's eye, who has
enough of what he calls religion to keep his temper
in an argument, I stand a chance of being converted
from the error of my ways, *if* the thing is possible.
He shall have all the comforts of a home, and give
me in return, not exactly Peter's pence, but the
coin of his experience.   But he must be patient,
for I have studied the Bible, in Greek and Hebrew
both."

" Your proposition staggered me a little at first,"
said the banker, who began to get an insight into

the character of the man before him ; "but, strangely enough, I think I know just such a person, who
lives in a very unpleasant family ; a man of great
refinement, a widower, a scholar, and so accustomed to the chances and changes of an eventful
life that I presume a quiet home would be a sort
of heaven to him."

"The very one," cried the old gentleman, rising
in nervous ecstasy. "Where is he? How can I
find him? Refined, intellectual, and alone. I am
sure I shall like him."

"He lives a few miles from the city, in the family
of a son's widow ; a good woman enough, but entirely unable to manage a household with dignity.
She is left with several children, and takes
boarders to eke out her slender means. Mr. Callender is an invalid, and unable to follow any business consecutively, therefore he is sadly dependent.
I fancy that his superintendence in part over the
widow's affairs is not as agreeable as his room
would be. I have often wondered how I could
proffer him assistance, without offending his deli-
cacy ; but the offer you have made will suit him
exactly. You are alone, and so is he ; and as he
is a very devoted, good man, I have no doubt that
you will be pleased with his efforts."

"All right, Mr. Romaine, it's exactly the ticket,"
cried the enthusiastic Mr. Lyons, his benevolent

face shining. "I'll take the address, and see after it to-morrow."

"Then I have the honor of wishing you a pleasant good night, and success to all your plans of usefulness."

"How do you know I've any plans of usefulness afloat?" asked the other, chuckling.

"How do I know that the sun rises?" was the answer.

The little man carefully bolted the door after his visitor had gone. Then, returning to the fire, he replenished it, hung a kettle of water over the flames, placed an enormous red apple to splutter at the coals, and brought out sugar and lemons and a small glass pitcher. Having brewed his harmless beverage, he unfolded his little pack of well worn cards and commenced his curious game, talking, and nodding, and smiling, towards his three invisibles, and apparently enjoying it heartily.

A few days after, Mr. Franklin quietly handed a note to his son. The latter read it, crimsoned, drew a quick, deep breath, and seemed for a few moments plunged in thought.

"Well!" said his father, expectartly.

"Mr. Romaine offers me a place in the bank; a miner position at first, he says, but it will be my own fault if I do not work my way up."

Bernie sat by, knitting a pair of white mittens for

one of her " children," a little flock of whom came
to the back door every morning, to the manifest
annoyance of the genteel servants. She looked
up, her splendid eyes all a-glow, her dewy red lips
quivering and parted.

" O, Harry, that is capital," she cried ; " and Mr.
Romaine is such a dear, good gentleman. I shall
never forget the time he gave me ten dollars when
he found me crying over a little boy, who was
hurt in the street ; and such a good time as I had
with that ten dollars ! He was so kind, too, the
day I was drowned — no, I mean half drowned.
You know, papa, he brought me home in his arms,
and — oh ! I 'm so glad ! "

" Shall you accept, Harry ? " asked his father.

The flush had faded from his cheek now, and the
young man was deadly pale. None but heaven
knew the struggle that was going on in his heart
daily ; the fierce conflict with pride, which, though
" crushed to earth," would so often assert its su-
premacy. To go among young men of his own
age was like death ; to enter the ranks of the class
that comprised the sons of proud families, seemed
pushing matters almost to the verge of insult.
How would they look upon him ? How treat him ?
And then came the sweet and soothing thought —
" Why should I care ? These men are dust like
myself ; and though their garments be not soiled

and spotted by the stains of an ignominious career, yet are they any better in the eyes of heaven than one of Christ's redeemed little ones? Was He not judged as a malefactor, treated as a thief and murderer; and should the disciple be above his Lord?'

The young man might have fled the country, or gone with Captain Gurney as a seaman; but exile would not alter the facts, and an ocean life was distasteful to him. No, if men troubled themselves about him at all, they should learn to speak of him as one who had earned, in the face of all opposition, in the very teeth of prejudice, an honorable reputation. He would not ignore the past, come what might come. Bernie gazed at him still, with soul-full eyes. She marked his slight yet graceful form, the firm poise of his stately head; for, whatever fault might be found with his reputation, in looks he was faultless. Brow, lip, and throat were all cast in the mould of manly beauty; the eyes, save that they flashed oftener and wore a more earthly light, were like Bernie's own great dreamy orbs. In prison, he had allowed beard and moustache their free will, and Bernie had begged him not to touch them with the razor, he looked so like a picture that she had taken to her heart (what did she not take in that priceless heart of hers?) when she was a wee child; strangely enough, an incomparably beautiful face of the youthful Christ.

"You'll go, Harry, you *will* go?" she said, that irresistible touch of the small fingers nerving his soul; she was so under the dread of a vague fear that he would leave them and find a home in some distant land. "And if that happens," she thought, "with no one to care for and love him, what might become of him?"

"I'll think of it, darling," he said.

"Think of what, Harry?" asked a soft voice that floated in from the hall, followed by the figure of his mother. "What troubles you?" and the caressing arm enfolded his neck. Doubly tender was she toward this sorely tried one; what true mother-heart would not be? With such love at home, why should he care for the world? He braced himself up, and grew grander in stature and expression. The native vigor of his soul was fairly roused. The manhood was in him, let who would dare revile him. A new sense of tranquility, a trust in the better nature of his fellows, took possession of his mind.

"Bernie, mother," he said, "I believe I'll go." Then he put the note in his mother's hand. When he met her smile, he added, "God is greater than man; I'll take Him for my defender."

And there was rejoicing in two womanly hearts — two hearts that fully understood each other, that answered to each, and beat responsive

with love and tender compassion for all the world
besides.

Irene, on this particular day, had gone to make
some calls. She had not developed gradually into
a fine lady ; her proclivities had all tended to this
consummation, ever since she could remember.
At five years of age she had stuck feathers in her
hair, and languished, and taken on airs, that would
have thrown a Hogarth into ecstasies. Poor herself, she had always looked down upon the poor.
Not thoughtlessly had she adopted her fate. To
reign, was her chief ambition. She had beauty,
she had wealth — wealth that to her seemed
boundless. And in believing that the very choicest circles would open to her, she was right.
Young, fresh, charming, liberal when it suited her
purpose, with infinite tact and feminine finesse for
a dozen dowagers, she did not have to fight her
way. The velvet hinges opened softly to her,
and she entered, as Bernie said, like a princess.
Flowers sprang up in her path, and the vista
glowed bright to its utmost point, with stars and
style, and splendor. The fascinating Miss Franklin ! the superb Miss Franklin ! the wealthy Miss
Franklin ! was the theme of the world of fashion.
She commenced by quietly ignoring the existence of her brother Harry. Tacitly, she gave him
to understand that to her he was the merest cypher

in the world. She spoke to him cold y, and
bowed politely, but socially he was dead to her.
She never could have dreamed how deeply she injured him. Unfortunately, he had a heart as tender and gentle as a woman's; it was stabbed
repeatedly, yet concealed the wound. Irene was
not accessible by any member of her household
save, only at times, Bernie. Her father, being an
invalid, left many things to her. Her meek mother could not understand her; she herself seemed
like a sweet blossoming rose-bush, beside a tall,
acacia tree, with one gorgeous flower a-top.

She could not help looking up to this regal off-
shoot of the house of Franklin, but any advice or
motherly talk was out of the question. Little she
dreamed to what a depth her vaulting ambition
might yet descend, and descend willingly. For
when such regal natures bend of their own sweet
will, they are most humble.

Nothing could be more touching than Bernie's
gentle admonitions, when she saw her sister plunging body and soul into the vortex of fashionable
pleasures. Irene would listen with a dreary smile,
and only brighten when she thought of her con-
quests and her power. She had become already
acquainted with Cecil Romaine. Cecil, though to
the manor born, was neither as proud nor as
fashionable as Irene. She was a noble girl, en-

tirely unspoiled by society, and prizing a social evening with her father above the brightest scene of mirth and revelry. A calm, strong soul, gave to her countenance an unusual serenity. She loved quiet pursuits, admired goodness wherever she met it, and when she smiled, gave a fresh impulse to the hearts that loved her.

To her little Bernie speedily became attached.

"Your sister's eyes make me think of heaven," she said to Irene, one day. "Pray, is she as good as she looks?"

"It would take an angel to measure her goodness," was the simple answer; and Cecil saw that Irene felt all she said.

Irene came in soon after Harry had gone to his own room.

"Father, if you are willing, I am going to give a party," she said.

"We are hardly old enough, yet, my dear, are we?" asked Mr. Franklin, from the depths of his great green velvet arm-chair.

"You mean known enough; yes, for all present purposes. I do not intend giving a large party; I shall invite only a few. It must be select, but very elegant. What do you say, papa?"

Papa looked up at his eldest daughter as she came and stood beside him, not caressingly, that was not her way; but queenly, commandingly.

"You will have to undertake and carry it through yourself, my dear," he said.

"There's Harry," murmured a bird-like voice.

Irene's brow darkened.   The suggestion did not please her.

"I shall manage it and see to everything myself," she replied.   "I feel fully competent to the task, and only want your consent."

"Of course, in that case, I have no objection to offer," said her father.

"Then, in three weeks, at the farthest, we will give the party," responded Irene, jubilant over her plans.

"Mamma," whispered Bernie, as the young lady sailed out, and there was a plaintive sadness in her always sweet voice, "mamma, is n't Irene growing very, *very* worldly?"

Mrs. Franklin answered nothing, save by a sigh.

"And oh, mamma! is there nothing we can say that will soften her toward poor Harry?   Does n't he grow thin, mother, or is it my fancy?   Poor, dear Harry!   You and I will love him, mamma."

CHAPTER XII.

BERNIE IN THE BY-WAYS.

A STRANGE hour for little Bernie to be in the street, and a very dismal, strange street for any delicate lady to be in, now that the twilight had descended.

"O, I'm afraid he'll never stop, and I've lost my way! What shall I do?"

So panted the child (a child to my heart she is always), as she struggled on in the March breeze, holding her rich furs close against her breast, that the chill wind seemed to penetrate. At the distance of two squares off loomed up a colossal figure, walking lazily, yet with strides, that, slow as they were, left weaker and faster pedestrians far behind. The splendid proportions of the man developed themselves even under the slouching garments, whose original color and comeliness were quite obscured. There were rents and ridges in coat and pantaloons, whose fringed ends hung shapelessly over the inelegant boots, whatever might have been the proportions of the feet they

encased, for it was very evident that they had been
cast from some wealthier proprietor to disfigure,
not adorn the present possessor. From his
physique one would have demanded bodily powers
of surpassing vigor, and mental traits to corres-
pond ; but whatever and whoever he was, it was
evident that poor little Bernie was keeping up a
very unequal chase, that bade fair to end in disappointment, for she was actually in pursuit of the
begrimmed and battered giant in the distance ; and
with strength and heart sadly wearied, she still
plunged on, until she lost sight of him. Even then
she walked drearily, till the occasional lighting of
a lamp in baker's and butcher's shops began to
startle her.

Not so the haggard and elfish faces that from all
sides peered into her own. She had seen too many
such to be timid now, but the consciousness that
her rich furs and apparel were sadly out of place,
and that she was scarcely safe in that motley neighborhood, quickened her steps and her breath. She
moved on, wondering to whom she should appeal
until turning the corner and emerging into a wider
but not more respectable thoroughfare. Here she
felt more lost and more defenceless than ever.
The low shops were crowded, there was a jabbering
of all the languages spoken under heaven in the
door-ways of the shambles ; oaths and cries re-

sounded, children fought and dogs howled. Bernie's heart began to beat with the first real terror she had ever felt. She did not know it, but she was in the vicinity of two or three Portuguese boarding-houses, and several crews having landed that day, the place was more than usually noisy. Looking round her bewilderedly, in her haste to get out of the crowd, and her fear of fainting, her heart beating almost to suffocation, she sprang towards a low door-way, attracted by the kindly face of a woman who stood on the steps, holding one child in her arms, and supporting another by the hand.

"O, please let me come in and rest a moment; I'm faint and tired," she said, almost losing her breath as she spoke.

The woman needed but one glance of those pleading eyes, one tone of the soft, low, rich voice.

"Sure, ye shall, Miss; here, Billy, clear the way; walk right in, Miss. It's rather a poor place for such as you, but you're welcome."

The room into which Bernie was ushered, served as a reminder of the old colonial times. It was, fortunately, as neat as hands could make it, and, in spite of the discoloration and grimness of the walls, the general dislocation of the wood work, the bare floor and scanty furniture, looked, with its blazing fire, almost comfortable.

" There, Miss, please ye, sit there or lie there
if ye 're not overwell.   And won't I get ye a cup
:f strong tea?"

" No, indeed, thank you," said Bernie faintly.
" When I feel better, perhaps you will find some one
who will call a carriage; I will pay you, if you
will."

" I 'll go myself, Miss, and that without pay, if
ye 'll jest keep an eye on the children.   Mike is
that busy whin evening comes on, that he never
steps out of the house.   Will I go now?"

" Not just now; wait, please, till I feel a little
better.   My heart beats so."

" And it 's lavender will do you good, which I
take myself when any ailing 's on.   See, ye look
so pale and faint, like, that I think I 'll be gettin
you a little dropped on some white sugar.   It 's
the most consoling thing for a flurried state; or,
would ye prefer whiskey?"

" No, I thank you; the lavender will do; I take
it at home, sometimes.   What 's that?"

" Now, do n't be frightened, Miss; it 's only the
creatures amusing themselves.   Sure, it 's the re-
spictible gentleman that might be, if it was n't for
the bad luck that 's allays follered him, poor soul!
And a more illiganter man, to my way of thinking,
is n't often seen, when he keeps out of the whiskey,
and the whiskey keeps out of him.   He 's spouting
now, I 'll be bound   Hear you that?"

A roar of laughter, that was almost hideous, went up from a dozen sturdy throats.

" Why, how near it sounds!" said Bernie, half rising, her face still white, and her breath short and tremulous.

"Yes, but never you mind, dear, they wont hurt nobody, not at all; they 're harmless felleys, all of them; only when the Duke gits at his play-speaking, it tickles 'em mightily."

" O ! is that the one?" cried Bernie, now sitting upright, the pale cheeks flushing a deep crimson in the firelight.   " It is the man who saved my life; the very man I 'm looking after.   If I could only see him ! "

" See him, you shall, dear," said the woman, laying the passionless baby down in a lump; but Bernie shrank back.

" I could n't go in there, you know," she said.

" Av course not; but if you 'll just look through this curtain, here; it 's right through in the shop there, and nobody 'll be the wiser.   It 's Mike's store, that 's my husband, Miss."

Bernie, forgetting her weakness in the new excitement, sprang from the old lounge and followed the woman down the long room.

"Now, Miss, is n't it a beautiful sight? and a shame it is, he 's that far gone that he 's forgotten all his better days."

The man stood in the centre of the small store, like a gladiator. He had bared his muscular throat, and thrown aside his slouched hat. His bold, sharply cut features, bearded lip, steady dark eye and thick hair, that curled almost like a woman's, shaken from a brow where might sit throned the very monarch of reason — so massive, broad and bronzed it was — would have thrilled a less impulsive child-heart than Bernie's.

" Now, whist ! " shouted one of the men.

Another threw him a blanket of some dark color, which in a moment he had disposed of in classic style, over his broad shoulders.

" Here, Duke, here 's another glass," said a sturdy, thick set man, coming forward, with a wink aside at his companions, which intimated that he had diluted the liquor so that he might not feel its effects too soon.

" O, that is too, *too* bad ! " cried Bernie, in a grieved voice.

" And so it is ; and so I tell Mike. But what do men care for, if they would n't lose their custom? It 's a bad shame, entirely, and he such a handsome man. But see, he be go'ng to speak. And when it 's through it is, they 'll give him another, and then more and more, till it 's like dead on the floor he 'll be, and then, heaven knows what they 'll be doin."

"O, I cannot bear it!" cried Bern e, sobbingly.

"Then do n't ye be seeing it, dear; sure, and I would n't av' telled ye, if I thought ye 'd look and feel like that. Go back to the lounge, and rest ye."

"No, no; I must see — I must — ah! he might be so good! so good and great. I know he might."

"True, for ye, dear, that 's what Mike says; but he *will* have the drink. There, now, hear that! If it is n't grand!"

The man had commenced Macbeth's soliloquy,

"Go bid thy mistress when my drink is ready."

The tone, the manner, the thorough impersonation of the character were most marvellously true to nature. Bernie fell back softly.

"I can't see him drink again," she moaned, shuddering. "What makes him destroy himself? If I could only speak to him — only a little moment. What do you think, would it be wild in me to wish to have him come here? I *must* say something; I must thank him."

"Not a bit of it," said the woman, soothingly, seeing the excitement into which she had wrought her slight frame. "Do you go back to the sofy, and rest yourself, while I speak to Mike. One tap on the windy always brings him; and I 'm sure the Duke will come in here, for it's had the baby upon his knee, he has, more nor once."

Bernie sank back. She had taken her bonnet off, and the rich masses of her splendid hair fell about her like a glory. So unearthly white was she, that the good woman was frightened. "For sure," she thought, "the angels that came down in the sepulchre could n't av looked much more holy than she."

She went to the window, and gave a ringing blow. A short conference ensued, and not very long after, shuffling footsteps were heard in the long hall.

" O, Duke ! it's glad I am to see you," said Mrs. Mike, bustling up to the door. "Look, how ye 're honored now; a real young lady wants to speak till ye. This way, here he is, Miss."

The man stood before her, his long locks falling low on his throat, his hat in his hand. So majestic he seemed to the little frail body half reclining there, that for a moment she felt afraid of him. It was only for a moment. She held out that little snow-white hand, as she said, pressing the other tightly on her heart,

"I am so glad to see you, sir ! O, how often I have wanted to thank you for saving my life. Please let me do something for you, to show my gratitude; please, do, sir."

He half bent over, then drew a chair up, and sat down, one elbow on his knee, to steady his head, her little hand still clasped in his trembling fingers.

"Do n't mention it, my little lady," he said, in tones soft as music. "I think the gratitude ought to be on my side, for having been instrumental in saving such a life."

"A very poor little life," she murmured, smiling; "yours might be such a grand one! Oh, sir " — the pretty lips quivered, she lifted her beseeching eyes to his, eloquent with tears. The shop-keeper's wife stood by, listening, uneasily shifting the uneasy baby from one hip to the other. He turned aside, and gnawed his nether lip, whether from annoyance or deep feeling, could not yet be told.

"I *must* say it," she cried, at last; "how *can* you let this dreadful appetite be your master? Will you forgive me?" she pleaded in a lower voice, seeing that he did not speak.

"Forgive you! God knows, my soul echoed the question," he exclaimed, shaking from head to foot. "But I have lost — everything."

She laid the other hand with a soft, fluttering touch on his arm. Her large eyes were full of a mysterious light that compelled his vision; a flickering radiance — it might have been the fire-light — touched and retouched the sweet face with a

clear, vivid splendor, so that the man was fascinat-
ed.   A great start and a groan followed the low,
earnest question,

"You have not lost *God?*"

"Child, what *are* you?   You shake me to the
very centre of my being," he cried, sharply.   "I
did not mean to be so rude," he added, in a voice
that changed like magic, as her hand fell off.

"No, no, you are not rude.   You spoke in earnest; I am not frightened, but — I want to save
you."

"If anything could reclaim a being so lost as I
am, it would be you, sweet child," he said, with
something like a groan, as he gazed at her again.

"What can I do?" The question was uttered
almost in agony.   "Shall I claim a promise?
Will you keep a promise?"

"I — I dare not say, now," he replied in a voice
that was almost unnatural in its depth.

"It's a very *little* promise," she whispered,
softly; "that you will let me see you again."

"O, I *will* promise you that," he said, much re-
lieved, unloosing the clasp of his hand.

"And where shall I send, when I want you?"

"Send here," he answered, abruptly.

"You will *not* leave this terrible drink alone,
then?"

"I dare not answer."   He covered his face with
both hands.

" Will you speak a carriage for me ? " she whispered, more exhausted than she dared allow. "They think I am at a friend's, at home, and if I stay longer, I shall frighten them."

" I 'll send one round " — the man rose up — " and vagabond as I am, I shall remember this kind little angel who cared enough for the poor outcast to warn him of his slippery standing. Perhaps I am not *all* gone ; hope so, at least, kind little heart, if it will comfort you."

" I *will* hope and *pray*," said Bernie, fervently, solemnly.

Alas, for the poor victim of his own passions ! Though the beautiful child-face had not faded from his mind, he was, before midnight, lost to all intents ; a helpless human mass, reduced to idiocy and mental death. Poor little Bernie ! In her innocent dreams she saw him restored once more to the perfect manhood to which her prayers would have led him. He had saved her life. Though fallen, he still bore the impress of inherent grandeur both of mind and body. And Bernie had great faith. Is it not said unto such,

" *Be it unto thee, even as thou wilt?* "

CHAPTER XIII.

FIGHTING WITH SHADOWS.

ON the day, the evening of which she met the Duke, Bernie had been visiting at M.'s. Willerton's. It was a rare treat to share the sweet society of Laura and her pure-hearted friend. The old Colonel, too, was a study to Bernie. She never tired of gazing at his fine face, so beaming with benevolence, or of treasuring up his witty speeches. The Colonel was one who believed, with gentle Sir Thomas More, that it was wise to " be merrie in God." Laura and Mrs. Willerton had been on some errand of mercy, and many a pathetic little story, as she listened, sank deeply into Bernie's heart.

" If I were only strong and well ! " she said, sighing, " how I should like to do some good ! But ah ! poor, weak little me ! "

" Great-hearted, strong little me ! " cried Laura, hugging her and showering kisses upon the fair brow. " Let little me be satisfied that she is her brother's comforter, guide and counsellor, and that he thinks of her as one of his greatest earthly blessings."

"Here's a lily, a calla, quite blown," cried Mrs. Willerton, from the farthest part of the room.

"Go see it, my dear," said the Colonel, "it is one of her pets. I think she prizes her flowers almost as much as she does her husband. Never was there a house so bountifully supplied — roses all the year round."

"Poor Henderson shall have it," murmured his wife. "Poor boy, it looks like him — just as white and thin; and, I might add, pure, if the Colonel would n't laugh at me."

"O, no, my dear, do n't say that; am I not almost as much an enthusiast as yourself? Henderson is a very nice little fellow, though he is in prison. He was a law-breaker through ignorance, and he shall have all the lilies you can raise. He's not long for this world, anyway."

Irene was absorbed in the preparation for her great party. Dress-makers were busy within doors, caterers without. Pale silks richly lustred, beautiful laces, all the pretty odds and ends, that go to make up a fashionable outfit, were strewed from end to end of the light, attractive sewing-room. Bernie was busy everywhere. Occasionally she would exclaim at her sister's opulence, especially when she put into her hands a little box containing a set of pearls, pure and clear as white sea-foam.

" These are quite too nice for me, Irene," she said, her eyes lighted up with pleasure at their beauty.

" Nothing is too nice for you, Bernie," was the tender reply; and then there was a clasping of the neck, and a warm kiss.

Harry had taken his place in the bank, and met, as he expected, but a half-way reception from the young clerks in Mr. Romaine's employ. His check paled more than once at some real or imaginary slight, but God was with him, and God and good angels are better company than even the better class of bankers' clerks; and so the young man was not alone.

" Is n't Harry growing pale and low spirited?" asked Bernie, one morning.

" I 'm sure I have n't noticed," replied Irene, indifferently.

" I 'm glad we 're going to have some company for *his* sake," Bernie continued, in her cheerful voice.

" For *his* sake ! Indeed," said Irene, hotly and bitterly. " I shall not expect him to come into the rooms at all.

" Irene ! "

The voice thrilled the haughty girl, as it would

sometimes. She did not turn, for she saw Bernie, who had stooped to tie the lacing of her shoe, now kneeling, leaning against the chair, her piteous glance appealing, the sunlight throwing a strange white glory over her brow as if loving to shine on her; all this she saw in the great oval mirror before which she stood. The anguish of that tone, while it touched, still annoyed her.

"I do n't know why he should wish to intrude on my company. For very shame's sake, I should think he would want to be seen as little as possible in society."

"And so you are not going to include him among your guests — your own brother!" said Bernie, chokingly.

"I am not, if I can help it."

"Irene, *can* you be my sister?" cried Bernie, slowly rising to that majesty of motion which would seem impossible in anything so slight. "Do you hate poor Harry?" she asked, in a low, mournful voice. "Because if you do, I will go and stay alone; I cannot bear it, indeed I cannot. To share the same room, the same bed, and feel that to one of us my poor boy is an outcast and an alien. O, Harry, Harry!" and, bending her head, Bernie burst into a passion of tears that shook her from crown to foot, intermingled with cries so piteous that they seemed almost to rend body and soul asunder.

"Bernie, you strange child," cried Irene, her voice hard with terror; "you will kill yourself. Be quiet; you frighten me almost to death. I must go and call mother."

"No, no," gasped Bernie, as Irene took a step towards the door; "it would break her heart as it does mine;" she added, after a strong effort at self-possession, "I *will* be quiet; I will never speak of Harry again, I promise you. O, if we could only go to some desert island, he and I, how I could love him and care for him! O! if we could both die, Jesus Christ would not refuse my poor boy a place among the angels."

It was curious to note the motherly caressing way in which she spoke of her brother, though he was nearly five years her senior. Irene's eyes were running over. She turned away to hide her emotion by putting things busily aside. Presently she spoke huskily,

"Don't worry any more, Bernie. I suppose I *was* harsh; of course, I don't feel right towards Harry; but I have suffered so, I can't help it."

"Think what *he* has suffered."

"Yes, I ought to; you may tell him I shall expect him to be here."

"O, but it must be a very earnest invitation," said Bernie, gravely.

"You little autocrat!" cried Irene, stamping her

foot, whilst amidst her tears a smile struggled.
"Shall I write him a note on double-gilt perfumed
paper, and tell him that for his special convenience
four bearers will be at his door at eight?"

"You know what I mean, you good, sweet, proud,
great queen!" cried Bernie, impulsively, throwing
her arms about Irene, who stooped to kiss her. "I
shall say that princess Irene sent her special edict,
and that if he does n't come, the princess and her
little maid of honor will be so gloomy and glum,
that all the court will wonder what has happened."

"Tell him anything you please. The witch,"
she added in an undertone as Bernie went off radiant on her mission of love. "I wonder what
strange power God has gifted her with? She turns
all hearts as if she held them in her hand. I wish
I could feel as she does towards Harry, but I am
afraid sometimes that I almost hate him. I do
hope he will not put himself in the way. I *cannot*
acknowledge him before Cecil Romaine."

Bernie entered the room of her brother noiselessly. A sun-gleam came with her, for the room was
dark. Not because of the want of daylight, but
the gloom of a human mind struggling with worse
than demons. Harry did not hear her. He was
on his knees beside the bed, and seemed to have
thrown himself there in utter agony. The Bible
was under his clasped hands; his forehead hidden

within the folded arms. Something nestled sweet and warm close to his brow; something stole over the broad shoulders; something cuddled down and felt for his cheek, and printed a holy kiss there.

The young man started, but he did not move. He smothered one sob, withdrew an arm and passed it over Bernie, pressing her close, close to his anguished heart.

" O ! Bernie," he cried, in a stifled voice, " when *you* are near, I feel I am not fighting this battle alone. You will have your reward, my darling, for caring for your poor, deserted brother, both here and hereafter."

" You sha'n't say that," cried Bernie, pressing her soft clinging fingers to his bearded lips. " My *dear* brother, the room is full of God's holy angels. I know it."

" There is *one* here, dearest," he said, smiling.

" If you will only believe, there are a great many here, only you cannot see them, as our dear Lord Christ did, for he was so holy and so good; and besides, they are His angels; but I am sure when we suffer, God sends them to us, the pure, sinless creatures! Now do n't you feel happier for the thought?"

" I ought to, Bernie," he said, with a sad smile. " But, oh ! darling, I sink so sometimes. I did not think it would be so hard to forget. I thought my religion would buoy me up infinitely above all my troubles; and when I am left dark, I am so afraid there is nothing in me that will answer to the requirements of my faith. If I *should* be left, Bernie! If in a moment of temptation " — he shuddered, and covered his face with his hands.

"Harry, Harry!" cried Bernie, "is heaven worth nothing?"

He looked up; the child-like face seemed transfigured. A great light shone in the almost inspired eyes.

"Isn't the glory that shall be revealed, enough to keep you from being faint-hearted here? Just think what a little while it is before the end. Ask Christ to dwell *in* you; then, surely, you can bear whatever comes."

" O, Bernie! nobody can comfort me with heavenly words as you can. I know it is wrong to feel as I do; wrong to wish we were poor again, so that I might go about unnoticed and unknown; but it is so bitter to meet men's eyes, and feel what it is they are telling. It seems sometimes as if I *cannot* bear it."

"And you were so happy once," said Bernie, sorrowfully. "They told me you were light-hearted and sang, and hardly knew that you were not at liberty. O, Harry! is that faith that buoyed you up so above all fear of imprisonment and persecution, is it gone? "

"Do n't think I have lost that sweet faith, Bernie. *I* had been lost long ago, if I had. With my temperament, I could not have borne the cold looks and chilling words that meet me so often. O, no! it has upheld me, and strengthened me; and it has been my own fault if I am less happy now than I was in that fearful place. But I will try not to indulge in this spirit of repining. Help me, Bernie, pray for me, child; you are nearer God than I am."

"Then you are going to be happy from this time," said Bernie, joyfully.

" I feel very much happier than I did, Bernie."

" Then I 'll tell you my errand."

" Well, what is it, sweet?"

" An invitation — a cordial invitation — special and urgent. Irene is to give a party, you know."

" I heard," he said, quietly.

" And you are to go."

" No, not for worlds," he replied, glooming again.

" O, yes you will; for if you do n't go, I sha'n't. And think of depriving them of my splendid presence!"

" You ask me too much, Bernie; it is enough to meet with these people when I am obliged to. I cannot torture myself afresh."

" I insist that you conquer this sensitive spirit, Harry; it is a great tyrant."

"Irene does not want me," said her brother, almost bitterly.

"Irene sent me to ask you; and, oh, I shall be so wretched if you are not there!"

"Has she asked aunt Chrissy?" queried Harry, brightening for the first time.

"I rather think not," said Bernie, laughing. "Poor aunty! she'd tell them to fold up the napkins, and be careful of the silver," she added, still merry. "Now promise me, you'll come, for my sake."

"No, Bernie; I may drop in for a few moments; but as to enduring three hours torment — that is too much to ask of me."

Bernie was obliged to be satisfied with this.

"I know what *I'd* like," she said, softly. "I'd like to make a feast for the poor, the maimed, the halt, and the blind, because they have no one to give them great parties; and I will, too," she added, clapping her hands, "if papa will let me. You'll come and *stay* at my party, wont you?"

"Yes, darling; I can safely promise that," he replied. "But it is time for us to go — and there is the bell for breakfast." She took his hand lovingly, and they went down together.

CHAPTER XIV.

GOING TO BE ROBBED.

A S the banker had foreseen, the little old gentleman's plans were soon put in active operation.
The aged minister, tremulous and infirm, but with
intellectual force unabated, found an asylum
where he was free from the petty cares of household drudgery, the annoyances of rude children,
and to which his talents made him sincerely welcome. He had his own little room for retirement,
in which were always to be found the best books,
and all the latest periodicals. In return for these,
to him unwonted luxuries, he was to bear down
upon the little old man's hard head, and uncom-
promising opinions, with all the Scriptural force he
could muster, and if possible, find an avenue to the
heart bolted against nothing but the admittance of
religious truths.

The kitchen, parlor, and two rooms on the same
floor were dedicated to Mr. Lyons, the minister,
and the two stated and one occasional servants,
who faithfully attended to the bodily wants of the
two old gentlemen. In the first room on the floor

above, lived a consumptive tailor, whose hollow
cough would have tired the nerves of any one less
benevolent than Mr. Lyons. It is needless to say
that he had his rent free, and that his kind old
landlord subjected numberless garments to his inspection, for the mending of which he paid him
liberally. In the room next to this, lived a German, who subsisted on the scanty wages afforded
him by the constant revolution of the unmusical
crank of a dilapidated and weather-beaten organ,
whose wheezy pipes suggested a continuous attack
of asthma and croup combined, but whose venerable age endeared it to the long-suffering, patient
proprietor. This man always carried with him a
sturdy, rosy-cheeked German girl, whose modesty
and sweet smile so inspired the old gentleman, that
he called in the owner of the organ one day, and
listened to a story, sad in its details, though un-
necessarily tedious, what with the man's slow
tongue and imperfect English. His left hand had
been terribly maimed in consequence of saving an
unfortunate woman from a conflagration in the city
of New York.

"De little girl, kind sir, ish de only little girl
what I ish got left from tree and mine poor vife,"
he concluded, mournfully.

"And do you make enough to keep you?" asked
Mr. Lyons.

The man shrugged his shoulders dolefully.

"Sometimes I pays; den, agen, I ish turned out, me and mine, with not'ing to eat. But Got in himmel care for poor German child," he added, resignedly, casting his eyes upward.

That did the business with this little old man, who could admire everybody's religion, though he could not believe any.

"Come and stay with me, friend," he said; "I am passionately fond of music, and we'll have a new organ one of these days, if it do n't cost too much. Then, when I want any of your airs, why, I can get them for nothing. If you behave yourself, you shall not have to pay a stiver for your room, except you earn it. And that fine girl of yours must go to school; it wont do for her to be wasting her talents in the street." And before the good German had quite time to be astonished, he was placed in a small and comfortable room, scantily but neatly furnished, and little black-eyed Gretchen was rubbing her eyes, and feeling very much like people in fairy stories.

In another room, a poor, homely dress-maker lived, whose often rheumatic pains, in joints and bones, caused a horrible fear that, before long, she should be obliged to go to that refuge for the friendless indigent, the poor house; and the dread of it almost made a maniac of her, which case,

coming to the ears of Mr. Lyons, through little
Bernie, he made her one of his extensive family.
And so up to the roof, where the very skylight
looked down in a series of benevolent shinings on
the white-headed old shoemaker, tapping at the
little old man's boots, pair seventh, and humming
to himself,

> "How long, dear Saviour, oh! how long,
>   Shall that bright hour delay?"

as he patted, and hummed, and stitched, singing
the old fugue tunes our fathers loved, in a cracked,
unearthly voice, and which were often caught up
of evenings by a queer little Methodist woman on
the same floor, who carried her pack daily, in a
small way, to support a helpless humpback. All
these people protested they had never been so
happy in their lives, and the mighty ear of our
Father was beseiged for blessings on the head of
that little, generous, glorious old man, who never
prayed for himself.

"And there he goes now — heaven's blessing
rest on him."

Yes, that was him in the queer, claret-colored
camlet cloak, edged with narrow brown fur; a
fur cap, with a huge visor drawn over his eyes,
and a big muffler or tippet folded round his throat.
Very briskly and cheerily he went on his way,
smiling to himself, and almost running into the
banker, who turned the corner in a hurry.

"I beg your pardon," he said, starting back and looking up like a mild kind of war-horse, of small stature.

"Not at all," returned the banker. "I wanted to see you. I will walk on with you a little while." And, suiting the action to the word, he continued up the street which he had just come down.

"And how does young Franklin get on?" asked Mr. Lyons of his friend, after other matters had been discussed.

"Tolerably well, I believe. Upon my word, I do n't know, though; I have n't thought about him much — have been so busy."

"Indeed," said the little old man, dryly; "that makes me want to ask a favor of you."

O! as many as you please," replied the banker, wondering what was coming next.

"Will you give yourself the trouble to see this young man among his fellow clerks, and take some little pains to commend him?"

"Indeed, sir, that is something I never do," said the merchant, inclined to fall back from his promise.

"But this is a peculiar case, Mr. Romaine," urged Mr. Lyons, earnestly; "and I was on my way to your place of business to see you about the matter. The poor, young fellow needs a word

of encouragement, now and then, in mercy to his
path of thorns. A good deed is often contagious.
The other clerks will take their cue from you, and
the poor boy will find friends."

"He certainly has enlisted a powerful ally in
you, Mr. Lyons," said the banker.

"I do feel for him, poor fellow," said the other,
in a voice almost broken with emotion. "He has
everything to contend with ; enemies at home, and
foes abroad, beside the humiliation that must necessarily accompany great sensitiveness of character. It was easier to feel happy in his long confinement, where nothing but the gray walls stared
at him, than to run the gauntlet of one little walk
from his house to the bank, now he is out of prison.
I can imagine all that he suffers, particularly as
his peculiar principles will not allow him to seek
consolation in the general amusements of the day,
or to drown memory in the pleasures of the cup."

"You make out a strong case, sir," returned the
banker ; "but, pray, what do you mean when you
refer to enemies at home? I thought that his
father — "

"I speak of his sister Irene," replied Mr. Lyons.
"She, contrary to all that womanly tenderness
with which her sex are proverbially invested,
treats him as an enemy."

"Irene — Cecil has become acquainted with her,

I think. I have seen her : a girl of really imperial presence ; a sort of royalist to the manor born. She means to queen it in society ; if I mistake not, she gives a fine party in a week or two. Cecil is going, and I suppose I shall drop in to pay my respects to this new millionaire. So she do n't deign to notice her unfortunate relative. It must be somewhat galling to her, too ; the young scapegrace has put a black mark on the family name that years will not efface."

"You talk like a man of the world," sighed Mr. Lyons, giving his coat an extra tug.

"And pray what are you, sir, if I may ask ? " retorted the banker.

"Well, a man of the world also ; but with a difference," replied Mr. Lyons, smiling. "I believe there are few human beings so hardened that an act of kindness is lost upon them ; and I believe, also, in the ape-like faculty of the human race, to do as their betters do. It will not injure *your* dignity, Mr. Romaine, to speak pleasantly to young Franklin, while it may be of incalculable benefit to him. You are a moneyed man, and as such, your power is almost omnipotent."

"You have a strong way of expressing it, sir, and I can 't say but you are right," said the banker. "I 'll bear it in mind ; good morning, sir."

That day young Franklin was electrified, and

his fellow clerks stared with wondering eyes when the rich banker appeared in their midst, and selecting young Harry from among them all, made him the bearer on an important mission. It need hardly be recorded here, that an impression was secured which resulted in a feeling of good will towards one whom they had consigned to a lower place in the social scale than that they commanded; though I fancy their own morals would not always have borne the strictest scrutiny.

Mr. Lyons returned to his hermitage, as he had christened the house, with a decidedly comfortable feeling in heart and body.

His room was cheerful, clean, sun-bright and warm.

The white-headed minister smiled a welcome. So did the fire; so did the clock.

" Pete has been waiting for you, sir, some time," he said, mildly.

Pete was the boy whose parents were in State Prison for " lifting ; " but who, under the little old man's guiding care, was subsiding into a respectable member of society, as far as he could command that important vehicle.

" And did Pete say what he wanted ? "

O, no; but judging from his actions, he has something quite overwhelming to communicate. He is on his round now, or rather his " beat," as he calls it, with the papers, but will be in by twelve. The little old man sat down, and as usual, fell into debate. His sparkling eyes brightened as he warmed. He had styled the venerable clergyman, "defender of the faith," and as such he listened to him with gravity. It was a small parliament of two, where heart and reason sat as umpires. With all the warmth of his nature he defended his pet theory : — Man lived forever by perpetual renewing; at some future time science would enable the human creature to destroy death.

"An earthly eternity would be a calamity so monstrous," cried the minister, "that I wonder *any* man can think of it with composure."

"Do you remember what Sappho said?" quietly asked the little old man :

"If it were a blessing to die, the immortal gods would experience it. The gods live forever; therefore, death is an evil."

"Very plausible reasoning, indeed," replied the minister; "and brilliant, for a heathen. But we who have only the one, true, eternal God, do not need to cheat ourselves with such sophistries. Listen a moment. I was just reading about this very argument.

The subject should be viewed by the unclouded intellect, guided by serene faith, in the light of a scientific knowledge."

"Bring your science to bear upon it as strongly as you please," he added, in a parenthesis, looking up from his paper.

" Death is revealed, first, as an organic necessity. Secondly, as the cessation of a given form of life in its completion. Thirdly, as a benignant law, an expression of the Creator's love. Fourthly, as the entrance to another and higher form of life. Death is a benignant necessity ; but the irregularity and pain associated with it are an inherited punishment."

"Very good, indeed ; go on," said Mr. Lyons, quietly, as, with an incredulous smile on his lips, he sat listening, running his slight fingers through his long gray locks.

" We have seen," continued the minister, resuming his paper, "that man often makes death an active experience — his will, as it is his fate. As Mirabeau sank, toward his end, he ordered friends to pour perfumes and roses on him, and to bring music. And so, with the air of a haughty conqueror, amidst the volcanic smoke and thunder of reeling France, his giant spirit went forth. The patriot lays his body on the altar of his country as a sacrifice. The philanthropist rejoices to spend himself without pay in a noble cause. Thousands of generous students have given their lives to science, and clasped death amidst their trophied

achievments.   Can you count the confessors who
have thought it bliss and glory to be martyrs for
truth and God?   I tell you " — and here in his
warmth the minister struck the table — " creatures capable of such deeds, *must* inherit an
eternity."

"Yes," spoke up the little old man, "an eterni·
ty in the grateful hearts of living men."

"But the greatest deeds, the sublimest actions
of men are many of them forgotten in the ceaseless
round of generations.   No, there must be another
place for their paradise ; a place where no decay
can come, no memory die.

Such transcendant souls step from their reject-
ed mansions," he continued, turning to his paper,
"through the blue gateway of the air, to the lucid
palace of the stars.   Any meaner allotment would
be discordant, and unbecoming their rank."

"Very flowery, very beautiful," exclaimed the
little old man, rubbing his hands.   "You call to
my recollection that scrap of poesy,

> ' Though I stoop
> Into a tremendous sea of cloud,
> It is but for a time.   I press God's lamp
> Close to my breast; its splendor, soon or late,
> Will pierce the gloom.   I shall emerge *somewhere.*' "

"Sir, you are a most inexplicable man," said
the minister, folding the paper from which he had
read.

"Why so?" asked Mr. Lyons.

"In your life, you are a practical Christian; in your belief — pray pardon me — you are worse than an infidel."

"Thank you; I'm glad you do n't mince matters, and I only hope that in time you may make me as good a Christian as yourself — if you can."

"O, do n't say that, sir," said the minister, gravely; "from my stand-point of fifty years experience, I can say as I never said before, it is all of Christ; I am nothing without Him. His spirit alone can change your heart."

"Then, why do n't it?"

"Jesus took a little child and set it in the midst of them on a certain occasion. Did he not in this teach that before honor, is humility."

"I see; you think I am too wise in my own conceit. Perhaps so; but have patience, good teacher. I will willingly give up all my prejudices, only show me something that shall be worth the exchange. But here comes master Pete. The lad seems to improve wonderfully."

Dressed in a suit of coarse gray, his seal-skin cap in hand, and one or two newspapers, too much demoralized by dirt to find purchasers, sticking out of his jacket-pocket, the hopeful youth came forward with a hungry, eager, excited air. His countenance was unnaturally flushed, and the muscles of his face kept motion with some active thought bursting for egress.

" Well, my boy, what is it ? "

" Please, sir, I wants to tell you something."

" Well, tell away ; it must be quite a secret."

" Please, sir, I'd like to tell you alone."

The old minister smiled, and good-naturedly sought his study.

" Please, Mr. Lyons, sir," he cried, vehemently, " you're a going to be robbed.   You're a going to be robbed, sir ! "

" What ! " exclaimed the little old man, starting back.

" Yes, sir," persisted the boy, breathlessly ; "it's true, sir, for I heard 'em a talking of it."

" Heard who ? " queried his listener, who was visibly agitated.

" I knows the men, sir, though I does n't know their names, except one, and him they calls the Duke ; a very hard sort of man he be, sir, in the way of drink, particular."

" How did you come to know ? "

" Me and Bill Striker was larkin, sir, and I went round the t'other side of the bales on Hobbs' wharf, sir, to hide ; and I could n't think where the voices come from, for there were a reg'lar wall of cotton bales all the way back.   But I heered 'em, sir, and they're coming here this very night.   One of 'em,

ses he, 'I a'n't a going to see my fambly starve,
and I can't git no work 'cause of a bad *caracter*.'
I guess he'd been in jail for a time, 'cordin to what
he said.   P'r'aps t'other one had, too.   And then
ses he, 'If nobody wont trust me, why, I'll have
the game's well as the name;' and so they planned
it.   I don't think the Duke wouldn't have had
nothing to do with it, on'y he's gen'ly half drunk,
and do n't know what he's about.   It a'n't like
him to do such dirty work."

Mr. Lyons was very silent.   He thrust his
hands behind him, beneath his coat-tails, and balanced himself on toe and heel, as he always did
under the influence of any weighty consideration.

"Poor devils!" at last he whispered, between
half closed lips.

"Sha'n't I go after the p'lice?" queried Pete.
who looked as if the commission would please
him hugely.

"No, sir," said the little old man, sharply.

The boy fell back a few paces.

"Are you going to let 'em rob you sir?" queried
the boy, with a half frightened face.

"They'll not rob me," said his benefactor, in a
brisk voice, that seemed waking cheerily up out of
a serious nap of contemplation.   "They'll not rob
me," he cried again, exultation in every tone.
"But I caution you to say nothing about the

matter. Leave me to manage it. I 'll bring the rascals to their senses."

" And you 'll not nab 'em, sir? " said the boy, lost in the labyrinths of his own exceeding great astonishment.

" Never you mind what I do. I can manage the business alone. All I ask of you, is to keep silence."

" But, sir, mebbe they 'll be armed to the teeth."

" So shall I, sir, so shall I. Now, go; but can I rely upon you to keep silence? "

" Have n't I done everything that you telled me? " asked the boy, with a proud consciousness of deserving merit.

After he had gone, Mr. Lyons had a long conference with his cook. Then, rubbing his hands, he walked back and forth, chuckling to himself, " we shall get along famously." In the course of the afternoon, he had the box labelled " nails " brought out into the room, in full sight.

CHAPTER XV.

A THICK snow fell before night set in. Already the streets had put out banners of fantastic designs, and the fleecy vapor printed cosy little pictures against flat red surfaces. It turned the men into walking statues, it shrouded posts, and hung pretty draperies around the street lanterns. Here and there, a line of crimson or yellow floated across the street from some pleasant household fire. Through gloom and gleam the ceaseless throng of pedestrians kept on its way, until, in the frosty air, a bell chimed the hour of ten.

The old minister had talked away the evening, oblivious of the cloud that rested on his listener's face, hiding the usual placid content with which he heard and commented. The huge clock loomed up in the background, ticking, or rather clacking away contentedly. Presently, in the midst of one of the minister's best periods, the little old man arose nervously, brought on his pitcher, sugar and tea-kettle.

162

The minister drew back quietly from the table.

"At least, I shall pray for you," he said, gently.

"Do, sir; pray for me always; and pray also for the benighted Christians of this favored land."

"What do you mean, sir?" queried the old minister, somewhat taken aback.

"I should have said, pray for dishonest Christians, if I may use such a contradiction in terms, who do not go down into the highways and hedges as your Christ commanded, and seek out the castaways. There are some who do so; but, alas, so few that their hands fall for very weariness. Sir, if this were done, then your religion would be a heaven. But no; perishing wealth, gorgeous churches, fashionable attire, and a humility that bends the knee to God, but will not hold out a helping hand to the outcast brother; these constitute to, too many by far, the emblems of Christianity."

"O! sir, let me entreat you, be yourself right. Remember what Christ has said: 'What is that to thee; follow *thou* me.' Vultures feed upon carrion."

"True, very true; I accept the reproof," said Mr. Lyons, meekly; "but I see things from my stand-point; you, from yours. I am on the search for a perfect Christian."

"You need search no farther than the pages of

the New Testament, sir," replied the old minister, sipping at the drink which his host had made.

Presently, the minister had gone, and Mr. Lyons was alone. Opening the door softly, he proceeded to help a servant bring in a table loaded with substantials and delicacies. Out in the kitchen, the fire was burning merrily. A huge pot of coffee boiled on the coals, a great kettle sputtered and foamed over the blaze. Then the servant spread a large cloth over the toothsome repast, and mended the fire.

The old clock rung out eleven, its metalic throat wheezing and coughing. The little old man put his light under a bushel, or, in other words, covered it with something that closed in its pleasant rays, and then set himself to watch alone and in the dark. Light and cheer were within a hand's reach; the old minister slept like a child. Nothing disturbed him. Pete, who had sight like an owl, was perched on the first landing, wrapped up in an old overcoat belonging to his generous friend, his eyes wide open with expectation, and a brave heart beating under his uncouth exterior.

Slowly and wearily passed another hour. Pete took cat-naps, and Mr. Lyons nodded now and then, rousing himself with a jerk, and at times giving up all expectation of trapping the thieves.

They were coming, however. They had started

from their rendezvous, the Duke between them, something the worse for strong drink, and now and then defiantly exclaiming, though in an undertone,

"*Who steals my purse, steals trash,*"

prolonging the last word between set teeth in a peculiarly savage style.

Why they had accepted this man as an accomplice, it is hard to say. Whether, because of his immense stature and muscular power, his familiarity with mock enactments of the kind, or because of his strength to seize and carry the booty they expected to get, cannot be conjectured. Certain it is, that a sort of undertow of rumor had gone forth that the little gentleman in the furred coat kept a box marked "nails," which was, in reality, filled with gold; that he had been a great Australian nabob, but to disguise the fact of his wealth, he lived obscurely, and in apparently unostentatious circumstances.

These men were armed, though not yet desperate villains. They had both served for a time in jail, one for petty larceny, the other for assault and battery. And yet they were not hardened men, for occasional frenzy, caused by intemperance, had mainly wrought their sorrow. The streets were hushed and deserted as the trio moved on, silent and thoughtful, towards the thoroughfare n which the "hermitage" was located. No watchman met them in their nocturnal tramp; nothing interposed to mar their scheme.

Silently and doggedly they neared the house. They had depended upon having a night-lantern, but the man who owned it failed them, and they had no money with which to purchase one. So they depended upon the lucifers that might by chance be found on the premises of their victim, and did not give up their plans.

Mr. Lyons had furnished his apartments with some strong bolts, one inside the front door, and another outside the one leading into his parlor, as he called it. The three found no great difficulty in effecting an entrance to the great, dark room, upon which little Pete slid softly down stairs and bolted them in. That was his part of the play, and very well it was done.

"All right, Jack," whispered one of the robbers, " now we must find a light."

"You shall have one, friends," said a cheery voice, and forthwith the light was produced, shining upon three glaring but discomfited faces.

" Don't use fire-arms, young men," said the odd little figure, now rising and taking from the brisk fire, that had almost burned itself away, the cover that had obscured its brilliancy. " You see, I expected you, and got all things in readiness. John, bring in the coffee," he added, in a louder voice.

The men had fallen back, and, one after another, tried the fastenings. To their consternation they were securely locked in. At that moment the door leading to the kitchen flew open, and the men, expecting to see a posse of police, fully armed, gave themselves up, as they fingered their weapons nervously. Instead of judgment, however, came mercy, in the form of a portly fellow, a dash of fear in his movements, bearing a great pot of smoking coffee, whose fragrance filled the apartments. The thieves were now seriously uncomfortable. The blood seemed to burn hot against their checks. The Duke folded his arms, drew his magnificent proportions to their most regal altitude, muttering under his breath—

> " Though justice be thy plea, consider this—
> That in the course of justice, none of us
> Should see salvation : We do pray for mercy;
> And that same prayer doth teach us all to render
> The deeds of mercy."

" Now, gentlemen," said the little old man, cheerily, " draw up to the table and whet your appetites. Come, come ; we are all friends, as I will prove to your satisfaction before we are through. Don't wait for ceremony ; I 've no doubt the sharp wind without has given you an appetite."

They came shuffling forward, almost helplessly, constraint in all their movements, confusion and shame apparent, though they tried in vain to put on a bravado which might be at least a sort of concealment of their real guilty feelings.

The Duke was the last. Mr. Lyons, looking up, met his eye; stood for a moment, startled and irresolute, his face quite blanched to a grayish white, as he exclaimed, leaning on the table to steady himself —

" Can it be possible ? "

The Duke seemed unwontedly affected. He trembled from head to foot; he gasped; he caught his breath, and made a quick, significant motion, shaking his head. It was sometime before the host of this strange company could compose himself sufficiently to do the honors of the table, and when he did, it was evident he was not the same man who had welcomed them with a by no means suspicious frankness.

They ate and drank, for they were hungry; and when they had satisfied the demands of appetite, he turned to them, and presenting the first one with a key, pointed significantly to the box marked " nails."

" O ! sir," cried the guilty wretch, " do n't torture me any more. Hungry as I was, the food almost choked me. Let us go, as we came, and I

promise you we sha'n't forget this." He wiped
the heavy drops of perspiration that stood thickly
on his forehead. He was a young man with a face
that did not indicate villainous propensities.

" My friend, I do n't wish to torture you," said
Mr. Lyons, quietly, mildly.   " Do as I wish you;
open the box, and draw from it the first thing you
touch. It is no infernal machine, I promise you,
but something that perhaps shall cause you to remember this night with gratitude, as long as you
live."

Thus reassured, the would-be robber took the
keys in his trembling fingers, and slowly opened
the box. The first thing that met his hand, he
grasped a — yellow envelope, nothing more. The
second man drew a similar package, and so did the
Duke, while, with compressed lips and a wild eye,
he stealthily read the face of his new-found benefactor.

" Now, my friends, see if there is sufficient for
your present wants," said the strange old gentleman, smiling.

They each drew from the package a hundred
dollar bill.

The one to whom he had first spoken burst into
tears. The other gazed at his, pale and speechless, while the Duke coolly folded his into a small
compass, and thrust it into his ragged trouser's
pocket, from which it speedily fell to the floor.

"Look here, my friend," said Mr. Lyons, picking it up, "is this the way you serve my gifts? But, stop! what is the matter with him?"

Well he might ask. The giant form reeled back, the face grew unearthly white, the dark eyes glazed as if death had passed his sealing fingers over them; and in another moment the man had fallen back, like one dead.

"He's been down among the shipping, and there's fever there," said the man they called Jack. "Perhaps it's taken him."

"We had better carry him off," said the other; "it's my opinion he's been sickening for some time."

"And where would you take him?"

"He's got no home," said Jack; "but now you've so kindly aided us, sir, when we meant to do you harm, I'll take him to my poor place, and my wife, who's as good as I am bad, will nurse him."

"I believe I'll keep him myself, men," said Mr. Lyons, opening a door near where he stood. "You two can perhaps carry him in here, and lay him on the lounge. I'll attend to him, and get him on the bed. He'll not be the first one I've doctored."

They took the great body between them, and bore him in gently.

"And now, men, I wont exact any promises

from you to-night, for he needs my assistance; but can I depend upon you to call here to-morrow?"

"We will come," they both answered; "and God bless you, sir," cried Jack, breaking down again. "You've saved us, sir; at least, you've saved me. I'll be an honest man, if I die for it."

"And I, too, sir," blubbered his companion — I swear—,"

"Stop; we'll wait till you're a little cooled down. It wont do to let rogues go, you know, without a decent respect for the law. I thought I would try to save you; but if one dollar of this money goes for drink, remember I have a hold on you, for I am not the only one that knows of this attempted robbery, which might have ended in murder. I want to see you both saved to your families, and I hope I shall not be disappointed. I said I should require no promise, but I will. I wish you to promise me that you will each of you, give that money into the hands of your wives. I will get you some business to do."

The men eagerly promised; and Mr. Lyons was left alone with his sick giant, whose terrible bass growling proclaimed that he had come out of his swoon.

CHAPTER XVI.

CHRISSY IN NOVEL SERVICE.

I HAVE not forgotten Chrissy. After her husband's funeral, the cottage was made over to her, and furnished by her brother-in-law. She would put on no crape or sable colors. " My heart is black, thát 's enough," she said, sorrowfully. " Besides, Joseph is better off, and should I show that I 'm sorry for that ? "

She went to her cottage grim and alone, and shut herself up for three weeks. Then, one fine day, she started out again, without a sign of mourning, save in her resolute, tearless eyes, and cheeks that had grown hollow.

Straight to certain authorities, who knew and respected her, did she go, and there seek for a position as a nurse for the sick. Not wholly as a hired nurse, she said; she was willing to give most of her services, and only wanted freedom to leave when she wished to avail herself of any other position. By dint of hard work, some coaxing, and showing an unmistakable fitness for the place, she at length succeeded, rented her cottage, and took her place in the sick wards.

The word hospital has grown terribly suggestive since the time of which I write. Then there were no trailing banners borne from bloody battle fields. Women seldom went to such work from homes of ease, leaving all they loved behind them, to care for the strange soldier boy, who, in his wild delirium, called in vain for his mother's cool hand to press an anguished brow.

No; from where we write, the walls of the gray hospital stand boldly outlined against the blue sky. Branching elms tower around it, cottages dot the green sward on every hand, and bright fields, budding with promise of a glorious harvest, sink and swell in dale or upland. Around our own cottage door the wind softly murmurs, and the red sunlight parches the ground, and makes the corn sprouts yellow; and calmness, quiet, peace and beauty whisper in all things — only those gray hospital walls bring a darker background to mind, as we people its interior, and think of the pain and voiceless suffering there. Many a young life is ending its thoughtless song or solemn psalm away from the home of its birth, the friends of its infancy.

The beardless boy, burning with fever, raves of his home, and catching the hand of nurse Chrissy, for she is there still, tells in words she cannot understand, the story of his love. Poor boy! the black-eyed girl on the banks of the Seine, curling her thick tresses before the little mirror, decking herself with roses, dreams not how her name is repeated in a foreign hospital, but sings, perchance, and laughs, and dances gaily, closing all her little speculations and pleasant plans with a —

"When Pierre comes home."

Pierre will never come home, gay, pretty maiden. His brow is growing whiter, his patient, dark eyes no longer turn with searching glances of the fever lunacy from mother to sister, and from sister to thee, as all, in fancy, stand beside him. He has babbled his last of "fader land," picked the last wild flower, drank the last cup of water from his beloved well, trod for the last time the green turf before his father's door. Nurse Chrissy wipes, oh, so tenderly, the moisture from his young brow, and waits for the last breath, so near — so awfully near!

"I knew you'd give me a home, George," Chrissy said, " of course I did; and have n't you, any way? But no; my heart is set on doing good to the sick. I have got so used to a l ead on my shoulder, and something to cling to me in all these years, that I — " she choked a little — " that I can't live without it. So I 've rented the cottage; that 'll be something coming in, you know. I can't seem to live there without poor Joseph, he took so much comfort when we were together there." Here she broke down and sobbed a little to herself. Then rising, with a loud ahem, and vigorous throat-scraping, she hurried away.

She had been at the hospital only a few months when the "Duke" was left upon the hands of Mr. Lyons. Finding that a run of fever was certain, he went immediately after Chrissy, and secured her services, so that for some weeks she was domiciled in the hermitage. There her powers found ample scope, and her almost unlimited strength its full exercise. The Duke was a host in himself, singing and raving by turns, starting up in bed after the most approved stage fashion, and pouring out the richest gems of lyrical art : sometimes a Hamlet, sometimes a Richard, sometimes a Macbeth ; until poor Chrissy cried out in despair that she wished Shakspeare had all the madmen he had made put under his special care. The poor woman had no appreciation of the fine arts, particularly when they were yelled in fragments by a great, wild-eyed giant, who beat her with the frenzied motions of his long, gaunt arms, until she was "black and blue in spots, from her crown to her heel," to use her own pathetic language. But with her solicitous nursing, the fever progressed favorably, and left him, after a two days' balancing in the scale between life and death, a weak, quiet, helpless, grateful man, subdued, and almost childish. Then nurse Chrissy found time to run up stairs and look after rheumatism and consumption, to make all manner of salves, healing drinks and nice gruel, and to be looked upon as rather a hurly burly, but on the whole a kind and guarding angel by the whole household.

"I never heard one run on as he did about his mother at times," said Chrissy, one evening, to the friends of her giant. Chrissy was knitting near the door of her big charge, who was sleeping soundly. The minister read the evening paper, while Mr. Lyons watched the steam go up from the indefatigable tea-kettle, as he rolled the lemons preparatory to making his usual evening beverage. When Chrissy said this, however, he lost the composure of his countenance. He started a little, and then grew strangely meditative.

"I wonder who he is?" pursued Chrissy, unknowing that her words gave pain. "He's had a good edication, I should think, and I know he's been a play-actor, for how he talked of right wings, and left wings, and wigs and robes. and the like nonsense. What did he mean about hulks, sir?" she asked, turning abruptly to Mr. Lyons.

"Hulks," muttered the latter, wincing; "why, did he say anything about hulks?"

"Often and often, sir; crying out that he would n't go to the hulks. Now, sir, what may that be?"

"Well, it used to be a prison ship, or ships," said her listener, uneasily, in a dry voice.

"Lud, sir, that splendid looking man could n't ever have been in such a place, do you think, sir?"

"You must ask him, Miss Chrissy. Doctor, will you have some lemonade?" His tone was strangely altered. The old clergyman started, and looked up in amaze.

"It's kind o' piteous to hear folks in fevers, the way they run on, sometimes," said Chrissy, still pursuing her theme. "They do n't know what they 're saying, poor souls. If I was you, Doctor, I 'd talk with him about spiritual things. It 's just the time to take him when he 's weak and tender."

"Yes, dissect him like a spring chicken," cried the little old man, in a cynical outburst. "Take advantage of his *weakness*, by all means. No wonder your sick bed conversions so seldom hold good. For the sake of decency, I beg you 'll convert me while I 'm strong and able-bodied; do n't wait till my mind has lost its balance to that extent that I forget what twice two makes. A very fitting offering that for your God."

"You forget that the intellect has but little to do with it," said the minister, deliberately sipping his harmless drink.

"Unfortunately, I ca n't believe that," cried the other, with hearty emphasis; "I ca n't conceive of a Christian idiot, although I have seen idiotic Christians. I confess — in fact, to tell you the truth, the whole thing seems a prodigious sham to me."

"Do n't talk like a heathen," said Chrissy, with some of her olden asperity, addressing her friend and employer; "for it 's my opinion you a' n't one, although you try to make some folks think so. If you 'd seen as many people die as I have, you would n't go on in that style, let me tell you. I say that dying Christians *prove* there 's a living God, and a heaven to go to; now, how are you going to prove 'em *false?* I tell you the ball is set to rolling that 'll run through all eternity, when a human life comes on the 'stage of being,' as *he* says, sometimes, in yonder. How do I know it? why, I 'm sure on 't," she continued, bringing her foot down with energy. "And *you* know it, in spite of your theories. Need n't tell me. I 've a common education, only reading, writin and 'rithmetic, as my poor teacher used to say. I never saw a Hebrew Bible, let alone read it, as you have, and other master languages; but with all my ignorance, you could n't convince me that my poor soul is n't immortal, if it *a'n't* worth much. Now do n't ask me *how* I know it, again. I do *know* it, and it would take more doubters than all Boston city holds, and all the world contains, to convince me that I 'm going to die like a dog or a cat."

"Perhaps they, too, have an immortality," suggested Mr. Lyons, dryly.

"Well, I a'n't no objections," she replied in her crisp way. "I 'm sure some brutes is more reasonable than men," which silenced the little old man for that night; but he put aside his glasses with a jingle, and slammed the door as he retired.

"Do n't you worry," said Chrissy to the latter, in her odd, short style; "when medicine does good, it always makes people cross. He 's nigher the kingdom than you or I think, perhaps."

CHAPTER XVII.

ALMOST AN ACCIDENT.

IRENE sat dreaming in her snug little boudoir. A few gems flashed upon her arms and bosom A glimmer of emerald light sparkled here and there among her dark tresses. Bernie hovered about her, clothed in pure white. She alone could put the finishing touches to the "queen's" toilet. Bernie, with her radiant head and shining eyes, seemed like some creation of olden artistic fingers, just stepped from an antique frame. This, because she wore a loose, gauzy mantle, to hide the inequalities in her poor, tender little frame.

"There, Iry, dear, I do n't think you *could* look more beautiful," she said, quietly.

"Thank you, Bernie; and you do justice to your dress of cloud," returned her sister.

"I! oh, do I? but I shall not come down to-night," replied Bernie.

"Not come down! Why, I thought you looked forward with so much pleasure, dear, to the party."

"Perhaps I did with too much," answered Bernie. "It was a novelty to me, you know; and I think it must have been partly on Harry's account, until I knew, to-night, that he is not to be with us."

"Are you sure?" cried Irene, with an expression of intense relief.

"Yes, Iry," answered Bernie, in a subdued voice, her face growing sad.

"Well, if he wont, he wont; I don't know why you should make yourself a recluse on his account. If he don't choose to enjoy himself, it's his own fault, of course."

"O, Iry!" and the great eyes, charged with soul-lightning, and moist with the heart's gentle fluid, were fixed full, reprovingly upon her.

"Well, what? You are talking without your lips, now. What do you mean?"

"O, Iry, you *know* you are glad!" cried Bernie, a passionate wail in her sweet voice.

"Pshaw!" Irene turned away pettishly. In the light of that pure face she dared not controvert her statement.

"Very well, Bernie, as you choose," she said, coldly, proudly. "I hope you will enjoy yourself alone."

"I don't think I shall, Iry; I don't believe I shall be happy a bit. Poor Harry!"

"Always poor Harry! Why, child, it's his

own fault, you know it is," cried Irene, half sullen now.

" *You* never asked him, Irene, you know; but I had better not say more. Perhaps we should both get angry. Even this little talk, *with the feeling*, has made my heart beat. Perhaps, sometime in the future, you will think differently of him; it may be you will love him yet, Irene, as much as mother and I do."

Irene turned away. She did not hope for such a consummation. If Harry had gone to the North Pole, she would have rejoiced. Bernie had stung her a little. Triumphant in all things else, a word, a look of reproof from Bernie set her wrong. She could not be wholly happy. An inspection of the rooms, however, quite banished her regrets. Here her taste shone pre-eminent. The house had been newly furnished, before their occupancy, as Bernie hinted in another part of my story, for a young married couple. The bridegroom's father had lavished thousands upon the decorations; nearly every room contained some masterpiece of art. The walls were tinted in cool, delicate colors, over which the blazing light threw a yellow glory. Pictures of richest tone, in which there were few neutral shades, met one at every turn. Rustic groups with plenty of emerald sward, yellow-vested peasants and red-frocked children, playing in careless happiness. Southern scenes in which the sunsets were gorgeous, the skies more than gorgeous, and the flowers and birds bright spots of flame on green that seemed paradisiacal. There was one storm-view, in which the cleaving lightning was caught and prisoned while holding open the heavens, letting its white splendor fall upon rifted tree and forests, bending to the sway of a mighty wind, that in its lurid splendor was something awful ; and yet it attracted more than many a softer picture. Then there were cupids in bronze, silver and marble ; angels, white-winged, as if plumed for heaven, and one statue of Silence, finger on lip, that seemed more divinely shaped than any creature of earth's moulding. There were orchards whose ripe fruitage goldened the atmosphere, and streams that almost chattered and foamed among the rocks and pebbly shoals, and moonlight deeper and sweeter than aught that has yet visited our mortal gardens. These had been the idols of the rich man who now sat in dumb agony beside the grave of his young wife, in fair Italia.

In the dining room, made beautiful by fruit-pieces, and pictures of stags, and hounds, and birds, the long tables had been furnished by a celebrated caterer, and words of mine cannot do justice to the rich compounds, the transparent jellies, mounds of ices sparkling with silvery frost work. It was like everything that emanated from Irene's perfect conceptions, singularly *re cherche*. Mr. Franklin, dressed with unusual care, sat in his great easy chair, in the back parlor. Luxury had not poured through his veins a healthier tide, or cured any of the pains he had inherited from a too close application to labor in his younger days. Still it had, perhaps, prolonged his life, suffering and feeble as it was. It had not, however, made him selfish. He took the bounties which God had bestowed, and with them lightened the burdens of the poor. No man suffered, if he knew it; and he was likely to know a great deal, for our Bernie's activity kept him well posted. Many a tear did those little cool white hands wipe away from "the least of these, my brethren." Many a sigh did she turn to glad smiles. She fluttered like a bird by cheerless hearths, and, as by magic, sprang up warm fires that sent a thrill through veins almost chilled. She whispered in the ear of the sick, and hard faces grew soft and human; she built little altars of perpetual gratitude in some hearts, that had shrivelled almost to nothingness.

How many, in that great day, shall rise up and call my angel Bernie blessed!

Mrs. Franklin was quietly thankful for all God's

mercies, receiving them as gently, as modestly, as
she had accepted the reverses and disappoint-
ments of life. Perhaps the great sorrow of their
family existence kept them both humble. As for
Irene, she had always seemed foreign to her mother's sphere, certainly, sufficient unto herself.
She was like what her father would have been,
had his career proved prosperous from the beginning. Irene seemed fitted for show and splendor.
There was little ideality in her nature, and no reverence at all. Splendid, even in her selfishness,
she needed no higher guidance. She had probably said her prayers from the beginning, but
only as a child draws a caricature on its slate, and
rubs it out again. There was nothing living,
nothing spiritual in her individuality. She could
not accept religion as many can. Her heart was
the hard marble, that must be struck, and bruised,
and chipped, and even broken, before the inner
life of the artist's thought stands forth an undying
miracle of art. It was still in the quarry, and no
mighty hand had yet disturbed its death-like serenity.

On that day, Harry Franklin had kept his room
since his return from the bank. He had no desire
to participate in the bustle of preparation, poor
fellow! He had promised himself a quiet evening
at the Willertons. There he was more truly at

home, than when under his father's roof. So he kissed Bernie, laughed at her tearful eyes with tears in his own, and sallied forth.

As he drew near the Colonel's residence, a carriage was coming from an opposite direction, and finally stopped at the door. The coachman descended from his perch, and opening the windows, spoke to the occupant. The sweetness of the answering voice sounded so much like Bernie's, that the young man lingered while the coachman ran up the steps of the Colonel's mansion. A boy at that moment turning a corner, flashed a lantern which he carried, full in the faces of the splendid steeds, who, instantly rearing, plunged forward and would have run, but for the agility of Harry, who, seizing them by the check rein, drew them back and held them, prancing and rearing though they were, till the driver came to his assistance. While thus he manfully exerted his strength, he saw a figure, all in white, half balanced upon the edge of the carriage door.

"Do n't attempt to jump, madam," he cried, in a terrified voice; but she seemed not to hear him. He let go his hold, rushed to the side of the carriage, and as she sprang forward, broke her fall, by receiving her whole weight against his chest. He staggered to the walk, for the horses had dragged the vehicle into the centre of the street,

and then found that his fair charge could not in
the least support herself, and that she was very
pale and faint.   Lifting her as gently as he could
from step to step, he threw open the door on
Alice, shawled and bonnetted, the Colonel coming
forward with her.

"Why, Harry, my boy! what does this mean?"
cried the Colonel.   "Miss Romaine, are you injured?   Lead her in; Madge will attend to her."

Harry, aside, told the story in a few words;
then hid himself in a little nook on the opposite
side of the parlor, that was lighted only by reflection from the hall lamp.

Cecil was more frightened than hurt, as she declared after a brief interval of rest.   She was pro-
fuse in her acknowledgments to her unknown preserver.

"The creatures sprang about so, I should certainly have been hurt," she said, "but for the gentleman who broke my fall.   Who was he?   You
all seemed to know him."

"One of your father's clerks," replied the
Colonel.

"And I know them all except"—she paused,
blushing a little—"it was then the brother of Irene
Franklin," she added, almost in a whisper.

"Yes; a right noble fellow he is, too," said the
Colonel, in which assurance he was backed by his

wife and Laura, who had made up their minds to fight for him, in a womanly way, if need be.

Cecil had called for Laura and the Colonel's wife. They had promised to accompany her to the party. For some reason, given and received with a smile, Mrs. Willerton remained at home. Her place was filled by the Colonel, who spoke in a low voice, as she followed him to the door:

"Mind you are, madam, and with the escort I have provided," the Colonel answered, in a sternly playful whisper.

"My dear madam," said Harry, emerging from his corner after they had gone, and ensconcing himself on the pretty sofa by the side of his best friend, as he loved to call her, "I have suspected within the last few moments, if you will pardon the egotism, that you remained at home on my account."

"Then you have suspected something very near the truth," was her gentle reply. "Stop, don't rise," she added, laying her hand on his arm with a detaining clasp; "and yet not quite the truth."

He glanced in her sweet, unfaded eyes — the purest violet in color — eyes not unlike Bernie's in spirit and expression.

"The truth is, my dear Harry, I have long been wanting to have a good talk with you, though this may not be the best time. I want to ask you if you remember the day when everything within and without you seemed bathed in a new light, an unfading glory?"

"Indeed, I do remember it"— his eyes sparkled with the soul's vitality — "I hope I shall never forget it."

"And have you always kept that Presence with you, my dear, since you came out of prison?"

Mrs. Willerton never minced words, calling it "that place," or any other but its true name.   She thought too lightly of earth's distinctions, its little greatnesses, for that.   Harry flinched somewhat, but he turned his earnest, handsome face towards her, as he replied,

"I have striven to, Mrs. Willerton, but sometimes it has been an effort.   O, the days have often been so dark!   How can I help saying to myself, as I catch men's eyes, ' they call me prison-bird?'"

"Ah! there comes self and pride — that same pride that keeps you to-night from your sister's festival."

"Pride, Mrs. Willerton! you mistake.   I have had all that quite crushed out of my heart."

"Is it your heart that says so?" echoed his mentor, softly, "or is it only the lips, that speak often words without meaning?"

The young man turned his gaze to the fire.   He dared not question his heart.

"How did you know I absented myself purposely from home to-night?" he asked.

"Through Bernie, poor darling. She was almost broken-hearted over it, and came as usual to me. I do believe I am the child's comforter."

"My dear madam, you are everybody's comforter," cried Harry, his eyes sparkling with sudden enthusiasm.

"That is quite too much like flattery," was her smiling rejoinder; "but shall I prove that you yet have something like that old unyielding pride left?"

"If you please," he answered, quite in the dark.

"Then I am going to ask your attendance with me at your sister's party to-night."

"Mrs. Willerton!" His chest heaved, he shrank back, deadly pale, without power of motion. She had risen, and stood stately and smiling.

"Ah! you are morally a coward, after all, besides being ungallant enough to refuse a lady's request," she said, still smiling.

"Yes — I am — I acknowledge — a poor, weak fool," he said, rising because she stood. "To go when Irene is so well satisfied with my absence? no, no. Besides, I thought you never attended such places."

"I seldom go, for my tastes lead me elsewhere," she quietly rejoined; "but I am going to-night, to teach you self-reliance, if I am a woman."

" O, — but — to go with *me!* " The hot blood
rushed to his temples.

" A gentleman, and my friend," she said, in her
calm, decided way. " Must I urge you to accompany me? "

He put his hands up in a deprecating way;
scarcely knowing what he did, he began walking
back and forth rapidly. His lips quivered, his
brow was corrugated, his motions were painfully
unsteady.

"I cannot, Mrs. Willerton, oh, I cannot! " he
cried, and fell back in his seat, bowing his head in
his clasped hands. " Think for a moment; you
do yourself injustice."

" Hush, Harry; I will not hear that. Suppose
I urge you, not for my sake, but for His? " She
pointed upward.

" My dear madam, that seems — indeed it does
seem almost irreverent."

" Perhaps so; but it is not. Every duty done
for Christ's sake is hallowed. I believe you are
inflicting a great harm upon your nature, an irrep-
arable wrong. Are you as ready to reprove and
commend as you were yonder, when out of darkness you burst into the light of heaven, triumphant
as a young eagle, whose wings bear it aloft for the
first time? You have a work to do; you will
never be blest or happy till you do it — till you
rise above this craven fear."

"Fear! madam, you mistake," said Harry, who had been sitting in a kind of stupor; "it is shame.'

"Then it is a false shame. You are living a blameless life. Men do trust and respect you. If they speak of your past, it is but to commend that which has risen new from its ashes. Nothing but a desire to work out your experience into the solid gold of doing good, will bring the balm of forgetfulness."

"Perhaps so," said the young man, moodily; "but spare me this once. Mrs. Willerton, I had rather hold my hand over that flame till it is burned to the bone, than appear at my sister's party to-night. There are some men there — oh, heaven! — and Irene—"

"As for Irene, you shall show that haughty, pitiless nature, that you can hold up your head in spite of her efforts to keep you down. If you will it, you can rise, step by step, to who knows what top of fame? I am not going to allow you to bury yourself any longer. Come, let us try and comfort little Bernie."

Harry, after a few heavily drawn breaths, turned his bright, pale face towards the gentle, pleading woman.

"You have conquered," he said. "I will trust something to my manhood."

"Thank you;" and Mrs. Willerton left the room,

soon returning, attired in a heavy brocaded silk, from flower to flower of which a sharp white sheen like moonlight seemed quivering and glancing. None knew better than Mrs. Willerton how to dress with magnificence, yet within the bounds of correct taste. To-night, of all nights, she wished to look her best.

Harry had suffered himself to forget the coming trial. And as he mused, he saw everywhere the lovely, frightened face of Cecil Romaine, enveloped in its cloud of fleece-white, as she stood under the mellow rays of the hall lamp.

Only to earn her esteem, he thought would be worth almost life. Yet how should he dare presume to speak to her as an equal?

" I am ready, and here is the carriage," said Mrs. Willerton. " You see how well I timed it."

Poor Harry! He felt like a culprit going to banishment, rather than a young, handsome gentleman, bound to a scene of festivity.

CHAPTER XVIII.

BERNIE A NEW GOSPEL.

AN endless maze of beauty, flitting hither and thither — bright eyes, bright jewels, bright smiles, all reflected in the panel mirrors let into the walls. A band discoursed the sweetest music, from an invisible nook in the conservatory; soft voices floated through the splendid rooms. The witching tones of vocal harmony made at times a pleasing variety. It was long past the hour of assembling when Mrs. Willerton entered the fairy-like throng, leaning on the arm of young Franklin, who, pale as death, but looking interestingly handsome, had nerved himself to the effort by a will that seemed to him almost superhuman. There was a sudden lull, so brief that none but those immediately around, noticed it.

"Just that sort of person you know," was whispered by several of Mrs. Willerton's admirers, for she was a woman well calculated to take the lead in whatever she aspired to do. Being rich and influential, in some things her word was law.

"Yes, Mrs. Willerton can do whatever she pleases."

Of course she could, and she was just the woman to do the most daring things, provided she was right, and duty called. The word meant something with her. She never let the poor, or rude but well-meaning people, into the back door. All who saw her were privileged alike; and no one was ever known to presume on her kindness. There was something in her face, her voice, her manner, that forbade that. Her life was marvellously wrought of the strong, sweet affections of the soul. Her face was not striking at first: pure, clear, gently attractive, there was a will in it; for all her sweetness, she looked like one that dared to contradict when subtlety or selfishness goaded her. Her name should have been Joan; a century or two ago, had it given birth to her, would have embalmed her memory for some deed of heroism, some sublime sacrifice — her life perhaps.

As it was, she came in smiling, leaning on Harry's arm; made the entire round, introducing her protege, and bearing him above the wave of prejudice with a grace and tact inimitable.

At last, Irene saw him. Consternation is a word all too weak to express the tumultuous rush of feeling that made her faint at heart. She had not dreamed of seeing him. Cecil Romaine was near.

She also had not seen his face in the early evening, for, as he stood in the Colonel's hall, his cap and fur collar concealed it. Now she turned a pleasant but curious glance from him to Irene.

"Mrs. Willerton is here — she said perhaps she might be ; but pray tell me, who is that very handsome, very distinguished looking young man?" she asked, directing Irene's attention that way.

The proud girl crimsoned. Every thing had gone on so swimingly, that she had gloried in her success. What need that this dark vision should blot the fair face of her serenity?

"O! with Mrs. Willerton?"

"Yes, dear ; he has just the countenance I should paint for a poet — an exquisite expression of melancholy. It struck me that I must have seen him before."

Just then Cecil cast her eyes upon Irene. The clouded brow, scarlet cheeks, and bitten lips were solution enough. She had divined, and it was her turn to grow crimson.

Meantime, little Bernie had flitted from chamber to hall for some reason that came impulsively upon her. Her eye caught sight of one beloved face. She clasped her hands, drew a deep breath of satisfaction, and cried with shining eyes, "yes, Harry *is* there." Cecil Romaine stood now by Mrs. Willerton. She had improved the opportunity of thanking her preserver, as she called him in her heart, and for a few moments Harry had forgotten everything else but her beautiful presence.

That little thrilling touch! He knew it above every other. Bernie's eyes almost dazzled him.

"Dear Harry," she said, "oh, I'm *so* glad! I've come to keep you company."

"Darling!" he whispered, his lips quivering a moment, as he held her hand tightly.

"And oh, Miss Cecil, this is my *dearest* brother, Harry! You must n't laugh at me; I'm always very foolish over him."

Cecil felt little like laughing at that moment; something like a sob swelled in her throat as she marked that pure face, bright with a love that seemed to hold something of the divine. She was mentally contrasting the difference in the sisters. Irene, as she caught sight of the group, seemed to herself to drop suddenly into a solitude."

"He has spoiled my evening," she murmured, with a curling lip. "Cecil pities him, and for *my* sake endures. I wish he had died in prison."

Bernie kept close to her brother, looking at the throng with far off glances, for her heart beat wildly with the delight of his presence. "As if any one dared!" she thought to herself, whenever she fancied one smiled at him, or sneered; and so, with such little defiant bursts of feeling, she held the object of her love unscathed.

"I wonder if Miss Cecil admires him," she whispered unconsciously; "she looks as if she did."

Yes, in truth, the fair, sweet daughter of the proud banker did look as if she admired Harry Franklin; she was talking with a charming variableness of face, now just flushed with the faint color of the arbutus, now rosy red.

At the farther end came in Mr. Lyons, nodding and smiling. His coat was blue, his buttons brass, his shoes were nearly covered with antique clasps of silver and precious stones. Bernie glided through the throng, a plain little bee, golden winged to be sure, but only plain in the midst of so many butterflies. He changed, as colorless crystal changes when red wine is poured in it. The gilt buttons on his odd coat did not shine more brightly than his eyes.

"My little lady!" he exclaimed, "I have been hungering and thirsting after you. Have you just come in? How do you enjoy yourself?"

"Finely," she replied; then added, "because Harry is here. Anywhere is pleasant you know, where he is, to me. But why have n't you been to see us? It 's three whole weeks, now."

"Because, dear child, I 've had sickness on my hands."

"Have *you* been sick?" she queried, with a look of affectionate interest. "If I had known that, I should certainly have come to help you but you see I go to school, now, and have so much to do, besides."

"And you really enjoy all this glitter and pride?" said Mr. Lyons to Bernie, who, seeing that her brother was earnestly engaged in conversation with Miss Cecil Romaine, seated herself quietly.

"Enjoy it? Not exactly. It confuses me a little, because there's so much hurry about it. I'll tell you — Harry and I think we should like to make a feast, a great feast, for — now who do you think?"

"For me, perhaps," laughed her fervent admirer, good humoredly.

"No; although you deserve it as much as any of these great or fashionable people here. No; but a feast for the poor, the maimed, the halt, and the blind. Don't you know our blessed Saviour said that we should feast such people, because they could not return it, as the rich can."

Those serious eyes, that low, musical voice, rich with faith, upset his cherished opinions more nearly than the good minister's labored argumentation. Such a nature as this *must* be the image of some transcendent good.

"If I can arrange it, and it will give you pleasure, *I* will make a feast for your poor," he said.

"O, will you? will you?" and the lambent fire

of her luminous eyes seemed to enter in and warm his heart to the core. She laid both clasped hands on his, and gazed at him with an eager, gratified smile.

"Yes, as soon as my great giant gets well," he said.

"Your great giant! Why, who is that, pray?" Her thoughts travelled to the mean store in that crowded thoroughfare, and the magnificent figure towering in the strength of genius — splendid even in the habiliments of the outcast.

"I never saw anybody like him," she murmured, her hands clasped tightly.

"Come out of your dream, little one, and tell me what it is," he said, bending close towards her.

"Did you ever see a man they call the Duke?" she asked.

"Why, that's my sick giant, birdie."

"It is!" A sparkle and a flush; then an instant calm succeeded. She let her folded hands unclasp gently, and fall at her side with a low whisper,

"I knew he'd be saved, someway."

"Where did *you* ever see him?" he asked, in amaze.

"O, sir, there was a time when I came very near death; when I had gone down, down under the black water. It was awful to see the great bales coming, crowding, pushing me; and I could

only stand and look, till they had no mercy.   O,
like great cruel hands, they flung me into the
water."   She caught her breath, lifted her arms
involuntarily as if to throw off the cold wet kisses
of the treacherous wave, and shuddered.

It was the first time she had ever spoken of her
sensations.   Now, as the recollection came vividly
back, she changed color.

" Then, from some place, mother could not tell
where, *he* came out, when she screamed for me,
and sprang into the water and found me sinking,
and — and saved my life.   Indeed, I have loved
him dearly, ever since," she added, looking up
with clear, candid eyes.   " I love him nearly as
much as I love Harry."

Mr. Lyons listened with marked astonishment.
There was a warm glow in his heart, as he recount-
ed this little history over to himself.

" So *he* did that, did he?   I never knew it before.   There 's something manly, something generous in him yet.   Poor fellow ! "

Bernie was musing with a strange, sweet smile.
Her eyes grew dusky with thought.   Was she not
creating a paradise for all repentant criminals?
Soaring above all the baser instincts inherent in
our common humanity, loving everything that
lived and bore resemblance to the eternal image of
God, no matter what its surroundings — penury,

disease, even crime; but loving these last with a
sublime pity, that could almost have given life to
redeem them, she moved upon her small stage,
followed by more blessings, more prayers, more
love, than ever entered her humble heart to imagine.

"*Blessed are the pure in heart.*"

Mr. Lyons still gazed with emotions that he did
not care to analyze. Every time he came within her
sphere, it seemed to him that there must somewhere
be a heaven. Her voice, rich with the heart's
sweet music, her smile, almost a transfiguration,
the azure of her eyes, were all, line upon line,
precept upon precept. This was the way the Holy
One led him, perhaps — him, whom the thunders
of Sinai or the threatenings of the great and awful
book of God might not have shaken. To him, she
was a little gospel. Earth did not seem immortal
in her; there was an outlook for the soul, a frail
casket, in some parts singularly beautiful; he
thought only of a fluttering bird, foreign to the
soil, that sang and plumed its bright little feathers,
yet turned a longing eye to the ripe airs of summer, that brought faint perfume of that rich world
he had left, to the gold and blue of Southern skies,
and longed for a far land, even while it warbled in
this.

And Bernie felt a sweet delicious rest — a rest

that came from prayer, and the consciousness that God heard her and answered her. For every night on her knees had those lips been fragrant with heart-breathings for all the world; but in especial for her brother, for regal, worldly Irene, and the unknown — the brave soul that had saved her life. Now she knew it would come, that better salvation, that great clinging to the hands of the Eternal, that trust in Him of whom the poor fluttering moths of an hour, called men, dare to speak lightly, while they deem it a pleasure to kneel before a crowned king, who, with all his honors thick upon him, is yet only dust; whose ashes may be dishonored to-morrow.

When I think of the magnificence of God's character, the lofty beauty that shines undimmed through ages upon ages in the being of Jesus Christ, King of kings and Emperor of emperors, when I feel through all the universe the power of his creative omnipotence, see His smile in the tints of splendor that gem the morning and the evening sky, I am overwhelmed with astonishment at the daring of poor humanity. I cannot understand how men can be ashamed of the Redeemer of the world. I cannot understand why they do not fly to him with the cry, Oh, thou great heart of Christ, that hast bled so freely for the salvation of men, gather me in thy sacred chambers, fold me away from the world.

CHAPTER XIX.

CHRISSY'S PATIENT.

A S he laid along the narrow bed, its whole length taken up, he was a study for a painter. Who can place upon canvas the absence of all colors with pigments? The heat and brightness of health, even of the meanest kind, were blanched out of his broad brow and massive features. His hands lay shadowy and blue upon the counterpane. The rich dyes that suffuse the veins, had changed into a thin, watery purple. The giant pulses were softened down into child-throbs, that sometimes could scarcely be felt. The hair, which had grown rankly through all his illness, lay heaped upon the pillows, thrown back from the waxen temples. The long lashes fell at times so slowly down over heavy eyes that were bold no longer, but soft, timid, beseeching as a woman's.

By his bed-side sat the minister, with his own Bible upon his knee.

What angel has ever been more steadfast by the side of him for whom heaven sent him to minister,

204

than that grand work of inspiration by the bed of death? There it comes, radiant with God's own smile; there, it patiently comforts the afflicted; there, it ministers to the dying.

"You like that psalm," said the clergyman, softly, shifting the book to the other knee, and taking off his spectacles, as he fixed his benevolent eyes on the face of the convalescent.

"I beg your pardon, I have been thinking of something else," said the sick man, his tones plaintive from absence of the sonorous qualities of strength and vigor.

"Well, that is candid, at least," was the reply, as the other moved back with a mortified air.

"I really am sorry," said the invalid, moving his hands, feebly; "but there are some thoughts which press down everything; some memories that swallow me up, soul and body; and when they come, I cannot fix my mind. The master of English poesy, says,

> "*A wretched soul, bruised with adversity,*
> *We bid be quiet when we hear it cry.*"

"And a greater than Shakspeare says," murmured the minister,

> "*The bruised reed will he not break, nor quench the burning flax.*"

"Aye," cried his listener, "but doubt comes in there":

" Our doubts are traitors,
And make us lose the good we oft might win,
By fearing to attempt."

" My dear man, I wish you were as familiar with the Bible as you are with Shakspeare," said the minister, sadly. " You would feel that the simplest words of Christ, ' Come unto me all who are weary and heavy laden, and I will give you rest,' are of more worth than all Shakspeare's golden words, and that they are, many of them golden, I will not attempt to deny."

The sick man looked at him vaguely. Leaning forward, his hands upon his knees, the mild meditative glance with which he usually regarded him changed to one of deepest solicitude. The minister asked, softly,

" Have you a mother, living? "

A low, sharp, inexpressibly bitter cry followed this query. The man's hands shook, and there was anguish in his eye.

" Leave me," he said, quiveringly. " You are cruel."

" Upon my honor," said the old minister, rising, almost terrified at the impression he made, " I did not intend to hurt your feelings."

" Leave me, *leave* me," cried the other, with a gesture of impatience turning his face to the wall.

Chrissy was over the fire, with arms red and bare to the elbows. She was cooking some savory little mess for her big patient.

" Well, dear me, and what is the matter?" she cried, as the minister stood regarding her in the utmost perplexity. He shook his head, sighing profoundly.

" Between the two of 'em," he muttered uneasily, " I hardly know what to do."

" Why, what *do* you mean ? "

" He, in there. I just spoke of his mother, and he got in the greatest way."

" There, now, ten to one you 've give him a relapse," said Chrissy, shortly ; and setting her pan on the hearth, she stole softly into the next room, and stood there as softly. The man had his head still hidden, but under the bed clothes his chest could be seen pulsating with deep drawn inspirations, while he sobbed to himself as piteously and continuously as a grieved child.

"I do n't know what you 've done to him ; I ca n't bear to see him go on so," the woman said, moving out again, her own voice broken. " I 've taken amazingly to him, and I know he 's got some deep trouble. There, I 'm glad of that," she cried ecstatically.

She had caught sight of the old gentleman, Mr. Lyons, alighting from a carriage at the door, and helping Bernie therefrom.

"There's that blessed child coming; *she'll* be a balm of Gilead, if nothing else wont," she added, soliloquizing. Bernie came in very seriously, kissed her aunt, gave her hand in a grave way to the minister, and seated herself like a miniature priest, come to hear confession and give absolution.

"Well, how's our big fellow by this time?" asked Mr. Lyons, cheerily.

"Not doing very well, I'm afraid," said nurse Chrissy, pulling down her sleeves, and turning her cap, which was wrong side before. "The fact is, your good man spoke to him about his mother, and set him off in such a turn."

"What! did he get cross and swear?" asked the other.

"O, no; worse than that. He took to crying like a baby, and is now, for what I know." Mr. Lyons looked very wise, and shook his head.

"Bernie has come to spend the rest of the day with us," he said, after a moment of thought. Then he went into the next room, came out again, saying he could do nothing with him.

"What is the matter?" Bernie asked. She had seated herself near the fire, and taken out her crochet needles. Her presence seemed to glorify the whole room.

"I do'nt know, dear. He's rather quiet now, but he wont speak."

" O, *I'll* make him speak," said Bernie, suspending her needles, her face lighting up, smiles glimmering over her dewy lips ; and placing her pretty work aside, with all the precision of a good lady of forty, she took counsel with herself, and marched straight to the room and the bed.

To some is vouchsafed the divine touch of healing. They do not know it, for the film of the world has dimmed those finer spirit perceptions which the Saviour gave to his disciples, saying, " Go heal the sick." But if ever such power lay in frail, tiny fingers, it surely must in those two loving hands of Bernie's. The instant that soft, flake-like pressure was communicated to the one exposed hand of the sick man, he turned, flash-like, and with a strength that seemed to nerve him all suddenly. He had wiped away the tears, but a mist yet hung upon his eyelids.

" I am come," cried, Bernie, cheerfully.

" Dear child ! " he said, tremulously, with a fervent thankfulness, turning nearer to her, and feebly taking both hands in his poor, slender fingers, " you are just the one I wanted."

" Well, I thought you would like to see me," said Bernie, drawing the chair close to the bed, and seating herself. " And, while I am here, remember you are to be very cheerful, because I feel more than usually blue to-day myself; that is, I did before I came. O, I am so glad, so *ve.y* glad you are better! I did not know it was you, or I should have been hero before. Do you want your pillow shaken?"

That odd little fussy manner of hers, as she essayed to move the great weight of his head, made him laugh outright.

Nurse Chrissy looked at Mr. Lyons, and nodded wisely.

"That's the first good medicine he's had for a month," she said, briskly. "Dear knows, I could n't get him cheerful; but there, that girl can do anything, and she'll talk the comfort into him, you see if she do n't. She's got more real piety in that little body then some whole churches have, I do believe. It's a wonder she a'i n't spoiled, everybody loves her so."

"Are you always happy, child?" asked the sick giant, yearningly.

"Always happy" — she thought a moment — "I believe I am always *contented*. Sometimes things cross me a little, and then I feel as everybody dces, I suppose. But if one only has plenty of hope, why, it seems as if one could endure all things, though they might not enjoy them."

"What! endure the memory of a past, whose records are written in guilt?" he asked abruptly; a question he would have scorned to put to any clergyman.

"I know it was very wrong," she said softly, "very wrong in you to take that poisonous stuff, and so degrade yourself, mind and body. But per-haps you were discouraged, and having no home to go to, and no one to love you and warn you as I love and warn my brother Harry, why, you gave way to temptation, and —"

"Bless your pure heart," cried the man, with a sort of groan; "is that what you think it is?" Bernie sat still for a moment, pale and startled.

"If I only *knew* something about you," she said, in a perplexed voice.

"Ah! child, how would you treat me, suppose I had been condemned by all the world, self-re-spect gone, manhood blasted, hope dead?"

"O! if that was it," she cried, almost gleefully, "I should know just what to do. I should forget all about it if you belonged to me, and treat you just as if nothing had ever happened, only, per-haps, a *trifle* tenderer."

"I think heaven sent you to comfort me," he said, a few moments after, during which there had been a strange revulsion in his feelings. "I think heaven, if it cares for me at all, knew just what I needed. Blessed saint! angel! which are you?"

"Why, I'm neither one or the other," replied Bernie, simply; "just a poor, weak girl, loving everybody, because, perhaps," and her eyes lifted softly, "I love Jesus Christ first of all."

The man reached for his handkerchief. It had slipped away when Bernie had attempted to arrange the pillows, and the tears, in his weakness, were crowding over his eyes. Bernie saw it. She caught the bit of linen from its hiding place, and herself wiped the scalding tears, at the same time touching his forehead, so pale, so shining, with her lips.

"God — bless — you," he articulated. "I did n't know anybody in this world cared enough for me to do that;" and then laid very still, trying to conquer, biting his lips, closing his eyes very tightly.

"And you saved my life," she said, almost reproachfully. "Did you think I had a heart of stone, not to be thankful — not to think of you — not to pray for you? O, if I had *quite* gone, that time! I ca n't bear to think of it, because there 's Harry and mother; and Steevie dead. Yes, I am thankful God sent you to do that good deed. Papa was very poor then — so poor, that he was in great straits sometimes; but perhaps you have never heard that we are rich, and able and willing to do all the good we can. And if you have no home, and wont be too proud to accept one from poor little me, until you grow strong and well again, why — "

"A nice little providence you are, to take things

ight out of my hands, Miss Benevolence," said a
jolly voice. "This big fellow belongs to me, let
me tell you, for the time being. Look at him
now; what a piece of flesh and blood for you!
Not to say that the flesh is much to speak of. The
world and the devil would have an easier conquest,
I guess, if the three were to take hold of him.
There, now, Bernie, don't look that way, child;
you know I'm an old heathen."

"I know you're no such thing," said Bernie,
retorting with spirit. "You're doing just what
Christ told us to do, with all your heart, only you
don't know it."

By this time, the Duke had grown quite calm,
and smiled pleasantly toward his benefactor.
Bernie was called out; his protector, bland and
benevolent, took his seat in her vacant chair,
crossed one knee over the other, and spread his
great, bright silk handkerchief a-top.

"I couldn't have spoken to you, sir; couldn't
have referred to the past, if that dear creature
hadn't come here to soften me."

"Well, well, don't worry yourself, Clarence;
it's so odd to call you that, too," he added, seeing
the start and wild look of the man. "You are
perfectly safe with me, however," he added. "For
your mother's sake " — his voice changed to a
whisper — "I would do more than I have done,
much more."

The man put out his long hand and clutched the palm of his kind friend.

"My mother" — he whispered huskily — "tell me — if she is — if she is " —

"There, there! you 'll work yourself into a fever again," returned the other, while his lip trembled violently. "You wish to ask me, Clarence, if she lives still? But you are not fit to hear — you — I mean — "

The thin, weak hand had fallen down, the eyes still gazed longingly, with a sideway, eager glance, but they were inexpressibly mournful.

"I need not have asked; she is dead," he murmured. "And with her departure, is gone the loving heart I wounded. Did she speak before she went" he cried, sepulchrally, "of the 'thankless child,' or the 'serpent's tooth?' Strange if she did not. O, my mother's face! my mother's face!"

He covered his eyes with his fingers.

"Was I thrust into this world to do evil, and only evil, continually? I have thought of that so often. *Are* some elected to be lost, that they begin in a maze, wander in a maze, and die in a maze? I shall have to ask that old man who reads the Bible so patiently. Sometimes a curse is worked out in the last of a doomed race. From my centre to the thinnest cuticle that covers my body, I seem sometimes doomed. What had I *not* to live for? O, my poor mother!"

"I shall call Bernie in, if you go on this way," said Mr. Lyons, who seemed utterly at a loss what to say.

"No, no; don't ask the child to see me now," he said, rapidly, "though her presence soothes me as nothing else can. I will be calm if you tell me about my mother," he said, a sudden quiet softening his voice. "She did not return to England?"

"No, my boy, she left us in Melbourne, after your father died; you knew he was dead, Clarence?"

The sick man's face flushed and darkened.

"Yes, yes, I know that. Never mind him," he cried, almost bitterly.

"Very well; after his death, she made preparations to go to England.

"'I want to find my boy,' she said, when I went over to help her, 'and if you will get my money changed, and speak a vessel for me, you will do me a great service.'"

"I remember how very kind you were to her," said the man, gratefully, "when I was a boy, and when my father — " he stopped suddenly, biting his lip.

"We will say nothing of him," responded Mr. Lyons, impatiently, a touch of color heightening the flush in either cheek. "He was his own worst enemy, and I never heard her give vent to an impatient word. As I was about saying, however, I had made up my mind that I would visit England myself, and so be of aid to her on the voyage and until she should be comfortably settled.

"While she was making her preparations, I chanced to be there once or twice, and I did not like the way she sat down every few moments, as if exhausted and faint. The red in her cheek went and came too rapidly, and caused me misgivings that I could not bear to give voice to.   Shall I go on?"

" Tell me every thing," said the sick man.

"I undertook the management of her business; sold off everything at a vendue, except some trifles valuable to her as mementoes of childhood, and tried to feel that the warning shadow of her fate would not mock me, if once she could breathe the breezes of the ocean. I can see her now—the white, patient face, the small lace cap, the little black square of silk folded around her neck.

" One night she sent for me. We were to start in the morning. Every thing had been arranged.

"'I believe I am foolish enough to feel a little ill,' she said. 'What do you think it is, the excitement, or have I really taken cold?'

" I felt her pulse; it was astonishingly rapid—so quick that it alarmed me. Her skin was parched and hot; her eyes unnatural in their dilation, their brilliance. My heart failed me; these were in that country almost as fatal as the signs of dissolution.

"'Shall I be able to go?' she asked; 'Everything is finished; my last trunk packed. O, doctor, say yes, for poor Clarence's sake!'

"I wish I could, was my reply. I will see by morning; and all that night I watched with her. I shall never forget it. She had taken lodgings with the widow of a former governor, or rather she had been made more like a welcome guest, and the room looked out on a garden of fruits and flowers. The night was one of broadest moonlight. The beauty of the southern sky, swiming in its sea of liquid splendor, seemed something supernatural. The great palms, their leaves rolling like silver clouds, stood up tawny and giant-like, gazing down upon earth's decay. They swayed, as if to some unseen pulse-beat, so regularly, so monotonously. The dusk woods in the distance were vibrant with insect life, but they all seemed as the echo of some slow funeral tune, chimed by white breasted campaneros.

"You seem to wonder. You did not know the old man could talk so fast," he added, marking the face before him, no longer quiet. "It is because I have written this down so fairly in the book of my memory, Clarence. I am there again. Beside

me stands a century plant, a passionate life throbbing through its veins, when all I love lies perishing. Ah, you did not expect that !   Certainly not.
You never heard my history.   Clarence, I knew
your mother when she was a little New-England
girl, and used to stain her innocent lips with straw-
berries.   I led her to school.   I kissed the tears
from her eyes if ever they came.   I was her protector, and would have died for her, even then.
And when she grew to womanhood—I a shy, quiet
youth, pursuing my studies in college; she a
beautiful, brilliant creature — too beautiful and
brilliant for her own good, poor darling !   I was all
the time nursing in my heart a great untold passion.

" She did not know it — perhaps she never knew
it.   She married a young Englishman, and so gave
the death blow to my love, to all hope — to every
good I had nursed in my soul.   Strange, how that
thing blighted me !   I am afraid body and mind,
dwarfed in consequence.   Well, I gave up my
country ; I went first to the West-Indies, then to
Australia, with a friend, young, but with no living
heart; and I was successful beyond my wildest
wishes.   Perhaps the gold poured in because I did
not care for it.   No matter.   Is it not very strange
that I met your mother there, a widow?   Again,
all earth seemed glorious ; again, it returned to

desolation, as beauty to ashes.   She was engaged
to a Colonel in the British army — your father.   I
read the man; besides, I had often heard from him
in my practice, and I trembled for her; but what
could I say?   Her mind was made up, and again I
lost her.   But this time I determined to watch
over her as a brother would.   You were born,
healthy and beautiful.   Year by year you grew
strong and vigorous, developing genius of no common order, promising to fond hearts everything.
To your father, you were a mere toy.   He liked
your brilliancy, taught you to swear, placed the
cup to your lips — but I forbear.   I had better
stop.   I agitate you too much."

"No, no; go on," said the sick man, sternly.

"This angered me.   I remonstrated, and made
him a bitter enemy."

"We will waive the interval.   Of that I know
nothing.   The last I remember of you, you called
at my office, fresh from school in England; you
were going back.   Well, well, let us not dwell on
the past.   Again, your mother was a widow; again,
my heart took courage and grew strong to win her.
It was not to be.   Death was the bridegroom ex-
pectant.   Tender and strong as was my love, heav-
en was stronger, tenderer, and wooed to win her.

"How strangely light broke over the fair earth
that day.   A shower came first, sharp and rattling;

I dared hardly glance at the face that had held my vision all night.   Yes, she was dying.   I knew it, although the rich flush still stained her cheeks, and spread a faint rose-tinge over her temples. I knew it by the unmistakable symptoms which I had learned through many watching nights.   Her eyes opened; the fire of decaying life burned there with a flickering radiance, making their intensity something awful."

" 'I feel strangely,' she said, 'is it the cold? Shut the door.   It snows, mother.'

" She thought herself in bleak New-England. Presently she came out of the vague, half-dream; she caught my eye.

" 'Sha'n't we be late?' she asked, attempting to stir.   Then she awoke all at once to full consciousness.

" 'O, I shall never go to England !' she sighed, drearily.   'I know all now — I was ill yesterday, to-day I am dying.'

" I soothed her as well as I could, for it seemed as if my own heart was breaking.

" 'I could die easily, gladly,' she said, after a short silence, 'if it were not for Clarence.   O, *will* a dying mother's prayers be answered?' I, having grown more than ever sceptical, could give her no assurance; but I stepped to the door and sent one of the servants for a minister."

"O, mother!" gasped the sick man; "to the last, did she not curse me?"

"No, but prayed till the lamp was out — prayed while her lips were stiff. I tell you, young man, if you do not live out your better nature after this, I shall be sure that there is neither a God, or an immortality. *She* had faith in God. 'My boy will be saved;' she said, more than once; and she made me promise that I would seek for you; that I would search all England, to find you; and, if I found you, entreat you, by all the love she bore you, to meet her in that heaven in which she believed.

"I did as she wished. I went to England; I travelled; I found people who had known you in the days of your prosperity. They said you bade fair to make the world ring with your name. But at the same time I heard other stories; I dare not say how true they were. Then, the last time — but no matter. I will not harrow up your feelings; but I know all. When I saw you here, on that night of the attempted robbery, your mother almost seemed beside me. Yes, for the first time, I felt a glimmering sensation that there was a

> " Divinity that shapes our ends,
> Rough hew them as we may,"

It seemed so wonderful above all wonders that *you*

should be brought straight here, when, for all I knew or thought, you might be at the antipodes. My resolve was made that first moment. I had not forgotten the softer lineaments that looked out from your features, dimmed and sodden as they were — the eyes, the mouth, the smile of your dead mother. And I shall constitute myself your protector, as I am your guardian. Let me feel your pulse; it is no higher than it was. I wish it might be; I do n't like this feebleness. Helloa! why, the dickens, he 's gone! Nurse Chrissy, come here like lightning. Bother your soup! 'tis n't that I want; do n't you see the man is as dead as a door nail? And I have the comfort of having been his executioner. A marvellously pretty doctor, I am! Here, hold up his head. Suppose he never comes to life, eh?"

CHAPTER XX.

CASH SHOWS AMBITION.

THE kind old man did indeed look but little less white than the still, stern face before him.

"We sha'n't have to put it under a cover, shall we, nurse Chrissy?" he cried, working away. "No, no, we'll hope better things; only he was so cruelly weak, and I such an old fool. Do n't cry, Bernie, he'll come again, I guess. We'll have many a good joke together. No heart? why, goodness gracious, the man's *all* heart, and I such a soft not to see it! You shall nurse him, Bernie; a little brisker, Mrs. Chrissy; there you are; lay on with all your might; rub his temples. He's full of vitality. Confound it, no signs yet. Bring the red pepper; I'll try a little back-woods dosing. Parson, do n't stand there in the way of his breathing. Here he is! That'll bring him! There, thank God! and catch me to be such a fool for one while. Now, Miss Bernie, go straight in there, and tell him he sha'n't see my face for a month. A plague take my silly sentimentality; I would n't have lost him for worlds."

223

"Stoop down here a moment," said Bernie, quietly.

He minded her; she whispered something in his ear. He grew quite red, smiled, and attempted to speak, but thought better of it; shook his finger at her, and vanished through the door.

"Now you may have some broth," said Chrissy, coming forward and placing the spoon to his lips.

"O, do let me feed him," cried Bernie. "I used to feed papa, when he had rheumatic fever."

Chrissy gave up to her in a moment, watching the feeble smile in his eyes.

"And Bernie, do you get him to laugh again; that's the medicine that cures quickest."

"I shall stay with him till he is better," said Bernie, with all the solicitude of a venerable and experienced nurse.

A singing voice greeted Mr. Lyons, close by, as he emerged into the larger room, wiping some suspicious moisture from his lashes. It was that of the little German girl, skipping up the stairs on her return from school. She was a bright-eyed, rosy-cheeked, industrious lassie, as quick with her books, as she was ready with her needle. Her father carried his new hand-organ alone, quite willing his girl should grow up a well-informed and useful young woman, instead of a street vagabond.

The news-boy had arrived at the dignity of a

junior clerk: a *very* junior, indeed, termed, in common parlance, "Cash;" but, under the little old man's supervision and the minister's catechism, he bade fair to become a respectable member of society. He took his meals with the servants in the kitchen of his benefactor, clothed himself, and laid something by, with the little compensation he received.

"Because, you see," he said with some importance, to Mr. Cardy, the cook and general purveyor for the house, "there's no knowing what I may grow to. Cashes *have* growed to pardners before now, and my biggest ambition is to become a pardner. Then, when mam and dad come out, and I have a house to put 'em into, fit for a king, jest let anybody whisper 'prison' to me!" and he flourished his fork with energy.

"I'm getting to read and write, too," he said, a moment after. "Just think! when I comed here, and washed up that harth out there with red paint, I could n't have told that cat stood for c-a-t; I was that ignorant. I tell you what it is, Cardy, that little old gent is a brick! Would n't I like to vote for him for president?

"I-f — y-o-u — c-h-e-w-s — t-o-b-a-c-c-o," said Cardy, who wore an old ship's cap, and was a very slow speaker.

"But I *do n't* choose tobacco," interrupted the

junior, with dignity. "That was one of my youthful follies, and I 've give up stumps. I passes 'em by, any number, on the street — Havanas — I can tell you, and there they lays, and I generally puts my foot on 'em, to keep other young fellows from temptation;" and Cash buttoned his coat over two slices of corned beef, quarter of an apple pie and a huge doughnut, and marched to "the store" with dignity.

Surely, good angels smiled approval on that little old man; and if the "spirits of the just made perfect," plead for sinners, many a prayer went up that his intellect might receive the light his heart had chosen to walk in.

That day a visitor called to pay his respects — a stout, good humored carpenter, who introduced himself as Tim Stebbins.

"I came to see about some men, sir, that wants employment. They said, both of 'em, that you 'd speak a good word for 'em. They do n't appear to be bad fellows, on'y I 'm told they 've got a hard name. They says as you gave 'em some money, and promised to stand by 'em. I 'd like to help 'em, if they 're capable; but, fact is, my wife — " he twirled his hat in his hands.

"Your wife objects, I suppose."

"Well, yes, she does. Things that she says gen'ly comes true. She 'most always has a little joke on me, if you can call it a little joke," and the man looked up with a grim smile. "She says, 'there now, Tim, I told you so.' And so you see, I like to foller her advice as near as practicable, because I do n't like such little jokes, no way."

"I did send the men to some employer, and stand ready to redeem my promise to them," said Mr. Lyons. "I think they will try to do their best. They have both been unfortunate, but that's no reason why they should n't make a living, or redeem themselves. I am willing to vouch for them to this extent. If you happen to lose anything by employing them, I'll make your loss good, no matter what the amount is. And that I'm ready to put on paper. I think I hold these men now. Give them plenty to do; you'll not have any trouble; and further " — was the man bewitched — Tim, the carpenter? for he had started up in his seat, and plunged forward without so much, as by your leave; and there he was, shaking Bernie's little hands up and down as if they had been two veritable pump handles.

"Bless my heart!" muttered Mr. Lyons, looking on in amaze.

"And who'd a thought, dear little Miss," — shake, shake — "of seein you here. Lord love you, I'm as pleased " — shake, shake — "as if J'd got a fortune."

" I 'm very glad," said Bernie, releasing her
hands with a sweet smile, and unconsciously rubbing the little white fingers, unused to such rough
ceremony.

" And how delighted my woman would be!
She 'd git right out of bed, sick as she is with the
rheumatiz. For you see, you made us, Miss Bernie, you just made us; fixed us right up; never
seen a dark day since.

" It was that young lady, sir, whom I made bold
to speak to, that raised us out of despair, as I
might say," he added, turning to his astonished
host, when Bernie went back to her patient. " I'll
never forgot it, and that 's what makes me willing
to do a good deed for others. For you see, jest
before Mr. Franklin come into his money, we was
all in the dumps, as it were; for my tool chist,
that cost me nigh fifty dollars, was burned up,
and I thrown right on the world without a penny.

" Well, sir, 't was Christmas morning, and blessed be Christmas! that she came, Miss Bernie; and
sir, she brought my woman and me one hundred
dollars in cash. Prosperity do n't harden some
people's hearts, sir; it did n't harden my old neighbor, for there 's no telling the good things he 's
done. And, bless you, only a week after, I got a
chance to buy out a good business with that hundred dollars, and two or three first rate jobs came

in, and I paid all up and went along swimmingly. So now I count myself well to do in the world, with money enough for my own wants, and some to spare for poorer folks; and if you're any kin, or only a friend to Miss Bernie, I'll take your word, sir, as quick as your bond; for I know when to show gratitude, sir, as well as the next one. I wont trouble you, sir, any longer. Good morning, sir," and Tim Stebbins walked out on air.

CHAPTER XXI.

THE BANKER AND HIS DAUGHTER.

IT was a comfortable looking room, large, well furnished, and exceedingly neat. The chairs and lounges were covered with dark crimson plush, he carpet was sombre brown and red; but here and there the effect was richly enlivened by a bit of color, a statue, a basket of roses, a vase of antique-crystal, a net-work of lilies woven in a dish of rare porcelain. The little chandelier in the centre of the room, flooded the whole of the large apartment, wrapped it in soft elysian light. Everywhere it looked as if the spirit of rest might dwell; rest and content clasping hands fondly, each sunny with the other's beauty. It was a quiet evening at home; at least Mr. Romaine hoped so, as he drew on his slippers and his gray and red dressing-gown. Descending to the drawing-room, as he called it, where Cecil had brought a little table and a cosy arm-chair opposite the glowing grate, there was no resisting the delicious home-feeling that prompted the banker to sink so easily into the arms of velvet-luxury.

"Well, dear," he said, looking over to her fondly, "no company to-night, eh?"

"No, papa, unless some chance visitor comes in."

"I had forgotten till this minute," said the banker: "Mr. Lyons is to call about that will-business."

"O! I'm glad of that, papa, because I'm greatly interested in him. I think he's an old darling."

"Ha, ha!" laughed the banker, "what an odd idea — an old darling."

"That's what Bernie Franklin calls him. Papa, is n't that a strange creature, that little Bernie; so small, yet a woman in years and ways, and a very child in innocence? Do you know, papa, I feel a kind of awe in her presence? She seems different from any of us. Don't you think there's a sanctity about her that one does not often meet with?"

"Well done, Cecil! so she has taken you captive, as well as the rest of us. I don't know but you're right, though. But it has often struck me that there's a similarity in the eyes, and in fact, the whole expression is like that in hers" — and his eye wandered to the portrait of a fair young girl opposite, so sweet, so winsome; and yet the spirit seemed looking out with a sad yearning.

"Like beautiful aunt Effie, whom I never knew. But was hers a sorrowful life?"

"I believe it was, from all I have been able to gather. I never fairly knew her, for I was quite a

child when she went away. And as I changed my
name when your uncle Romaine died, I have never
felt that she could take much interest in me."

"I had almost forgotten that Romaine was not
our own family name," said Cecil. "But, papa, is
aunt Effie living now?"

"No, my dear; I saw by an English paper six
years ago, that she was dead. Since then I have
tried to hear some tidings, but have never been
successful. As I said, however, there is something
in Bernie Franklin's face that always makes me
think of her."

"She seems very much devoted to — her brother,"
said Cecil, with a little hesitation. The banker
looked at his daughter carelessly. He thought
how very lovely she was; certainly, her face was
never so bright before. He did not for a moment
connect that vivid color with the subject-matter of
their conversation.

"Yes, I rather fancy Franklin has in her his
boldest and warmest champion. Poor fellow! he
has need of a few ardent friends, certainly."

"You think, papa, that he has entirely regained
his character, do you not?" Her face was turned
aside a moment. Perhaps she was studying the
scroll-work of a beautiful design that stood in
bronze upon a little stand near.

"O, yes, my dear; there's no doubt of that in

my mind. I'd trust him with uncounted gold. In fact, he's a sterling young man — but —"

" But, what, papa?" a fever flush came and went.

" There's a prejudice, my dear, that it will take long years to soften. He has gathered his experience from a sad soil."

" O! but papa, that ought to make him friends, I think. It is so hard to come upon the world, everybody should treat him kindly."

" Ah! you think so?" The banker spoke cooly, but with a furtive glance at her.

" Yes, indeed I do; and I could have thanked you the other night when you welcomed him so cordially, because, I'll tell you *why*, papa," with a rose color that spoke her sudden consciousness, " I did n't think his sister quite liked it that he was there. I judged so from something that dear little Bernie said. And then, dearest papa, if you had seen those horrid horses, and you know I am not a bit of a heroine. I could n't recover my self-possession at all. I know I should have fallen helpless, and perhaps the carriage would have run over me."

" It was very kind of the young man, certainly, and did not by any means lessen my esteem for him. But Cecil, though I would treat him with kindness and cordiality, I should not aspire to be on very intimate terms with one who is out of prison, you know."

"O, of course not," spoke Cecil, abstractedly, and the color faded slowly from her cheek.

At that moment footsteps were heard, and Mr. Lyons, in his camlet fur-edged cloak, entered smilingly. A quiet dignity graced his motions when in the company of ladies. The banker drew a seat near the glowing fire, so that when he sat down, Mr. Lyons nearly faced Cecil, whose back was to the picture, once before mentioned.

"A chilly, gusty night," he said, with a little air of uneasiness; "the wind fairly whirled me round the corner. I believe I'm sharp eight," and he looked at his watch.

"Just eight," said the banker, drawing his own repeater, slowly, slowly looking up; when, what should meet his eyes, but his visitor leaning forward, the palms of his hands upon his knees, his face pale, and brow contracted, devouring the picture upon the wall — the picture of the banker's sister — with eyes that were fixed and almost wild. Then passing his hand bewilderedly across his temples, he turned a glance of inquiry, and a startled expression towards Mr. Romaine, asking in sharp, condensed words,

"Who is that?"

"It is my sister's portrait. She is not living."

"So very like," he muttered.

"Effie was eleven years older than I when she was married," said the banker.

" Effie, good heavens! the same name;" and
again he glanced curiously towards Mr. Romaine,
Cecil all the time watching him, quite intent and
interested.

" Pardon me; she was the child, I think, of a
country minister in New Hampshire. The house
where she was born could scarcely be seen from
the road, so buried was it in vines and honeysuckles.
There was an orchard behind it, of fine Baldwin
apples, and peach-trees in the garden."

The banker smiled.

" Why, you must have known us," he said.

" Perhaps I did; but the name — the name puz-
zles me."

" I took my uncle's name, my mother's maiden
name, when I succeeded to his estates," said the
other.

" O! ah, that explains it," and Mr. Lyons fell
back breathless.

" Then you were the little curly-headed boy, her
brother," he said, after a short pause, during
which, various emotions had chased pallor and
color successively from his face. " It is hardly to
be wondered at that I seemed to have known you,
that you held a place in my heart. As for me, of
course you don't remember; I am nothing like
what I was. Beside, I have no especial reasons
for wishing to recall that time. If you are ready

for the business," he said, hastily, looking suddenly older than a moment before, going out of himself into a state of preoccupation that quite changed him.

"Certainly ; " and the banker sprang up.   " Cecil, love, you will not mind staying alone awhile.
I have some very important items to despatch,
with my friend's help."

" O, no, indeed, papa," she said, in her pleasant
way, and lifted a new magazine in one hand, her
ivory paper knife in the other, as the two retired.
Leaning back, she cut the fresh pages abstractedly,
stopping often and looking into the fire, then on
the page, then turning in a listless way to glance
at the portrait, to which the tremulous fire-flames
gave a smile of bewitchment.

" I wonder what he means," she murmured ;
" there 's some romance there ; he must have
known grandpa and all the dear old folks, I can
only dream of sometimes.   That beautiful country house ! I 'll go down there some day ; I have n't
been for years.   There 's a housekeeper there, as
gray as ashes, and she loves to talk of old times.
How splendid it used to be — the kitchen with its
white floor, and the sand, still damp with salt spray,
lying in great waves, as if the sea had drifted it
there.   There never was such sunshine, never, as
used to laugh in at those little old-fashioned win-

dows. Grandmamma was pale and quiet, but oh, her sweet smile! And the milk-pans on the green, shining like silver, and little Patsy with her short gown and blue check apron, going to milk the cows.

"The dear old house! I see it now, facing the river, and grandpa looking over his spectacles, in his long, brown camlet dressing-gown. Papa keeps that dressing-gown folded away; I saw it yesterday.

" How many times I 've thought of transplanting those rose-bushes that grew near the steps; but, poor things, they 'd die here, and they 'll flourish there, I suppose, till the old house crumbles.

" And this queer little man used to visit there, too. I wonder if he was one of aunt Effie's old beaus? I should n't be astonished if he was. What delightful times we had when I was a child, on the little lake, lilies of amber and snow lifting their pure heads at every touch of the oar. That must have been grandpa with me; they say he was a genial old man. I was such a little thing then, and still, I have not quite forgotten. We must go to the old house next summer; how different from this! and I must get more out of that old gray housekeeper, for she 'll die soon; and then papa talks so seldom of the past, that *that* too will die out of memory. How sweet the honey-suckles were last time I smelt them; they seemed like the very breath of fragrant summer."

She had ensconced herself more snugly, and began to reap interest from the printed pages before her, when John, the old house-servant, cried out at the farther end of the room, "Mr. Franklin, Miss," and vanished. Even at that moment, her cheek burned hotly, as she detected a smile on the lip of the old porter; but she arose in her seat, laid her book aside, and welcomed her visitor with feminine dignity.

"Miss Romaine" — he bowed somewhat constrainedly, as he always did where he feared he might be misunderstood, throwing forward his pride, as it were, to reconnoitre the ground upon which he intended to stand — "I have a message for your father. I was told that he was in."

"He is in, Mr. Franklin, but busily engaged at this moment; will you be seated, until he is at liberty? I presume that will be before a great while," she said at a venture.

"Thank you; I" — he was about to say, "will call again" - - but he checked himself. This warmth and comfort, contrasted with the cold without, tempted him. Besides, his message was important. It would not do to be delivered in a moment. It required an answer, for it referred to some misunderstandings that had recently occurred among the minor employees in the bank.

"I think I *will* stay awhile," he said, yielding to the bright fire, the glowing room, and not least, the sweet face of Cecil Romaine. So he sat down, gazing delightedly at a fragrant nosegay of hot-house flowers.

"You are fond of flowers, Mr. Franklin?"

"Fond, I have thought sometimes, I could almost worship them," he said, with that introverted smile, sad through constant consciousness. "There have been hours, Miss Romaine, when a little flower has kept my faith alive in seasons of depression." He did not add, "it was when I was in prison," but she instinctively inferred his meaning. "I do not often show these little fancies," he said, taking from some outer pocket a small book bound in velvet, which he proceeded to lay before her.

"O, Mr. Franklin," she said, with girlish enthusiasm, "did you paint these? Why, you are a genius. They are wonderful."

A series of flower-pictures : the trailing arbutus, its guardian angel, a shadowy, sweet and spiritual face bending over it ; a moss rose, a child, beautiful as a cherub, typical of innocence, and so on through the few leaves the book contained.

He saw a different picture : himself, bending over the task, wrapt, but pale—the colors furnished by little Benny, the jailor's son, a roguish, good-hearted little lad ; the flowers in a broken pitcher,

sent by Bernie or his mother. He had thought
more about that lately, more bravely, perhaps.
After every interview with the Willertons, he had
grown stronger for his life-battle.

"Yes, I had scant pleasure beyond that when I
was at work, Miss Romaine ; consequently, I threw
my whole soul in it. I think I have a talent," he
added, modestly ; "but, beyond making a picture
to please Bernie, who has her album full, I scarcely attend to it."

"I wish you would make me some," said the
fair girl, impulsively, regretting, the moment she
had spoken, however.

"With the greatest pleasure," he replied, his
pale face lighting up, his eyes glowing.

"Thank you ; " and then for a moment all conversation closed. Cecil thought of her father, and
feared she had not done quite right. Harry was
more at ease than usual, and did not stop to ask
himself the reason.

Presently he spied the pianoforte open. Cecil
interpreted his glance.

"Are you as fond of music as of flowers, Mr.
Franklin?" she asked.

"Perhaps. I often wish Bernie could play, she
intreprets music so readily. She has a sweet
voice, too, and sings like a little nightingale."

"Everything she does is beautiful, I think,"

said Cecil. The young man gave her a grateful glance, which was not lost on her, as she moved quietly toward the piano. It was rather strange; showed, perhaps, the direction Cecil's thoughts chanced to take, sometimes; the music standing there, still, was " *The Prisoner's Lament.*"

Cecil changed it dexterously, her face flushing a little, and began a lively Scotch air, which thoroughly inspirited her audience of one. Then she went on from grave to gay, from lively to sentimental, singing, as she always did, because she enjoyed it; never thinking of how this or that fashionable friend would sneer if they had seen her amusing a " prison bird," as a few of the high flown, brainless young men affected to call him.

Noble Cecil! so far beyond the prejudices of her set, though the daughter of an up-town banker, and entitled to an unlimited possession of aristocratic pride.

Meanwhile, Mr. Lyons was closeted with the banker. His office, as the latter called it, was a plain, small apartment, with heavy morocco-covered chairs standing round; a large, mahogany table, well furnished with stationery; a small grate, which sent out a delightful amount of heat, to the surprise of all who saw it, and a few shelves full of business-looking account books.

The banker had a letter spread open before him.

Mr. Lyons sat looking musingly, at what appeared to be the copy of a will, abstractedly brushing out the corners with his small, white hand. His face was wrinkled with anxiety; his lips tightly closed, yet vibrated to the tension of some perplexing thought under consideration.

"I spoke to you about a will which has come almost mysteriously in my possession," said the banker. "I need not go over the circumstances, I presume, as you are thoroughly acquainted with them already."

Mr. Lyons shook his head, to signify that he need not.

"I have a letter here which gives me some information about the young man who heirs this money — with reference to his former standing, I mean, and character. I find that the young man left England three years ago, was traced to this country, and then lost sight of for a year or two; but, guided by what little insight the letter gives me, I set some friends on the search, and they have just learned that a person answering the description given was in this city not long ago; that he was by profession an actor, and often gave minor exhibitions in bar-rooms and low places for the sake of grog, or a paltry consideration; but just as they thought they were sure of him, he disappeared suddenly and mysteriously from his accustomed haunts, and they have lost all trace of him."

Mr. Lyons made a sudden movement, began rubbing his forehead thoughtfully, in order to hide his face, which had certainly lost color; then sat and stared blankly at the will.

"There is at this moment a man in the house who knew him both here and in England — an English sailor, who was sent to me by one of my friends. I'll have him here." He rang the bell.

"Tell that sailor to come in here," he said, as the porter appeared. Presently, with a great affectation of humility, that sat oddly upon the burly, British independence of the son of Neptune, a short, stout man, whose bald head a-top made his forehead seem disproportionately high, bowed his appearance. Awkward and uncouth, his limbs fell into all manner of attitudes, and finally attained their climax, when he sat down on the small of his back, put his hands in his pockets, and lifted one knee over the other in such a way that his feet were higher than his head.

"Mr. Hadaway, I think you said," began the banker, nodding towards him.

"Which to say, my name are 'Adaway, sir," replied the man, changing his position by placing both hands on the edges of his chair, and stooping forward, his body resembling the letter U laid on its side.

"Did you know a man in England who was called the Duke, from some fancied resemblance to a nobleman?"

"Which to say, I did know such a man; an' further, which to say, I knew 'im both in the oold country and the new. Many's the time I've tipped a glass with 'im, your honor."

"Have you seen him lately in the city?"

"Which to say, your honor, not since my last passidge to Bermuda; but subsequently, afore that — not a week, your honor — which to say, I saw 'im at the wharf, and shook the parting 'and; which to say, the Juke and I was good friends, your honor, bein' as I'd knowed 'im in London, when he were considerable of a gentleman, an' never minded 'ow 'e spent 'is money; which to say, 'is Brutus was a sight to see. It's a 'ard fate 'as followed 'im, yer honor."

"What kind of a character did he bear in London?" queried the banker, while Mr. Lyons listened intently.

"Which to say, is haccording as folks views things. A reg'lar good one would ha' put 'im down as uncommon bad; which to say, a free and easy chap like I, might call 'im a good 'earted, but unfortinit character. He were quick to know when a friend's pockets was empty; and that easy, hanybody might 'a took 'im in. Which to say, 'is worst faults was drink, and cards, and frolic, which led 'im to join a lark, which shut 'im into a — a — private boardin' 'ouse, your honor," stammered the sailor, scratching up the few gray-brown locks behind his ears.

"Yes, I understand," said the banker, gravely. "The fact is, Mr. Hadaway, this young fellow has had a fortune left him, and we are hunting him up."

"Which to say, you do n't say so!" cried the sailor, electrified into a proper position, and staring like a man in a fit, surprise and pleasure mingled in his manly face.

"And we are very anxious to find him."

"A fortin'!" muttered the other, forgetting his usual preface. "Lud! Lud! the Juke a fortin'! Which to say, sir, 'e 'll spend it hall in a month," was the grave rejoinder.

"We 'll see to that when we 've found him," returned the banker, "and I shall be glad to engage you in the service. I think I can safely promise you twenty dollars if you bring me tidings of the man, and fifty if you produce the man himself."

"Which to say, is a wery respectable offer; hand I make bold to add that h'if h'anybody can find the Juke, it 's one about my size hand my initials."

"Very well; try your best. The money is ready for you if you succeed."

Mr. Lyons bit his lip again, and strove to look un-

concerned, as the sailor made his parting bow.
Two red spots burnt in his cheeks, and an air of
constraint, very foreign to his habitual manner,
would have betrayed his agitation to less experienced eyes.

"Have you employed a detective?" he asked.

"Not yet," the banker replied, "as they were
not so sure as they wished whether, as the man had
been amenable to British law, a clear title could be
made out."

Mr. Lyons fell to studying the will. The fortune was left by George Anson, Bart., to his nearest descendant in the male line — a grand-nephew,
Colonel Ashley Anson, of her Majesty's dragoons,
on foreign service, or his heirs in the male line,
etc., etc.

"Did you never hear of these people before —
this name?" he asked pointedly, looking keenly at
the banker's face.

"Never."

"Not through your sister? She went to England,
I believe."

"My dear sir, we never corresponded after the
death of our parents. I was so young when she
left us, that most likely, in time, I grew out of her
memory. We are none of us famous for our lite-
rary attainments, and nothing bores me so much as
to write a letter. Cecil will testify to that. She
is my private secretary on all such matters."

"Seventy thousand dollars! It's a nice little fortune," said Mr. Lyons.

"Yes, for a steady man; for a spendthrift scarcely anything. I am sorry that the young man bears a bad reputation. From all accounts, he was famous for splendid dissipation, and not above a propensity for low company. He has broken the laws of England, and not content with that, broke jail at the time three notorious burglars escaped, and I'm afraid he's liable to British clutches yet. His crime was poaching."

Mr. Lyons looked up, quite pallid now.

"I have an account of it in another room," said the banker, rising and leaving the office.

His visitor, left alone, threw his head back, and drew a long sigh.

"It's him! it's Clarence, by all that's good and great," he cried, bringing his hand heavily down upon the table; "but he must not be known. I must put my men on their guard — I must caution Bernie; he is Effie's son, and shall not be disgraced. I'll protect him with my life. Confound the money! I've got enough for both. Heaven grant that he reforms, and I'll stand by him to the last. Besides, he's this man's nephew, and I may use him in case a *coup d'etat* is needed to forward some matters which I plainly see are in progress. I'll keep dark, at all events, at present."

Mr. Romaine entered again, and placed a scrap
of paper in his hand, which, after its contents had
been read, he gummed inside the cover of a small
account book for preservation.

"I thought you met with so many of these people in your daily rounds," said the banker, "that
you might come across this fellow, who is, I judge,
pretty well put to it for the means of subsistence.
He is a great drunkard, and yet a man of fine talents.   In England, he was an actor of first class
abilities, and, but for his habits, might have become
renowned.   But there is still another reason why
I wish to find him.   I have a porter, an Englishman, who came within a year to America.   Hearing of this matter by accident, he requested my
attendance one day, and says he has a fine little
child at home, a girl that his wife took compassion
on — rescued her, in fact, from the work-house.
Her name is Effie Anson, and my porter says
that though they do n't want to part with the little
one, that she is the child of the very man we are
in search of, and that her mother was an actress,
which makes the thing seem true enough.   Now,
if that can be proved, you know it brings the
child forward to quite an important prominence;
and, on the whole, I 'm extremely interested in the
case."

"Worse and worse," thought Mr. Lyons, wincing; " so there's a child in the case, and wife, too, perhaps. It grows complicated."

" I should n't wonder if I can aid you considerably." said the latter, absently, as if still talking in a reverie. "At least, I'll keep my eyes and ears open. If you will give me the address of this old porter — that may be a matter of deception — I'll call and see what *I* can make out about it."

" Certainly ; I'll give you the address — there it is — seventy Vane-street, a poor street, down your way," added the banker, laughing.

" O, yes, I've cast my lot in with the poor," returned the other. " Bernie thinks I follow the injunctions of your religion better than some of you who are its professors," he added quietly.

" Well, you do, that's a fact," replied the banker, with unusual warmth. " You must have a peculiar aptitude for your work."

" The fact is, Mr. Romaine, it's all selfishness, from beginning to end," said the other, good humoredly. "I find it pays better, not exactly in cash, to be sure, to live in this way; but it keeps the spirits active and young, and the heart warm. It's not a bad sensation, sir, to feel that your neighbor is the better for your having known him, or to see the tears of gratitude well up to eyes that were hungry and tearless, before they knew you."

"Do n't doubt it, Mr. Lyons; and now we'll go into the other room. Cecil is playing, I think."

"You ought to be very happy in the possession of such a daughter," said Mr. Lyons, pushing the papers aside, and rising.

"I am, sir; Cecil has never given me a minute's trouble from her cradle. She has been motherless, now ten years; yet she is as affectionate and unspoiled as if constantly under the maternal watchfulness."

They had now opened the door at the farther end of the drawing-room. The banker looked curiously in the direction of the pianoforte. A young man of handsome proportions stood bending a little, absorbed perchance in the player, so intent that he did not hear footsteps. Suddenly he turned, and the banker gloomed. It was young Franklin.

"Why, Harry, my boy," exclaimed Mr. Lyons, his eyes twinkling.

Cecil arose confusedly, pushed back her music, returned to her seat by the fire, smiling a little, blushing a great deal. Harry was constrained for a moment; the advice of Mrs. Willerton occurred. He straightened himself, bowed politely, and then said —

"I called for Mr. Peabody," looking for the note. "He told me I was to bring him a reply. You were engaged on important business, your daughter told me, and I waited." That was all his apology, well told, gracefully delivered.

" Ah ! " The banker took the note in a frigid way, a good deal different from his usual manner, glanced it over; he excused himself, and left the room.

Presently he returned, gave a sealed paper to young Franklin, thanked him, and bowed his visitors out. Then he went to his seat near the fire; but Cecil had resumed her magazine — she was, or feigned to be, deep in the story, and the banker was silent, and very grave. Of what he was thinking, Cecil thought it best not to inquire, though she could not but divine it, cunningly as she had abstracted herself.

CHAPTER XXII.

BERNIE'S BEAUTIFUL PICTURES.

BERNIE was a genuine poet. All things seemed tinted with the happy coloring of her beautiful soul. Sometimes she rhapsodied; such tem-
peraments will; it is hard for them to hear or say
common-places. I knew such an one, whose nature was nearly ruined by being deprived of the
sunshine of sympathy. She was young and un-
comely. Her mouth was a trifle over large, and
her features were ordinary; but there was more
beauty in one thought of hers, than in whole books
written by some clever people. It was the story
of Pegassus bound. She was in a narrow place,
with narrow minds and narrow souls about her.
Her speeches were laughed at; nobody saw the
fineness and fire that played along her wit. She
was considered dangerous, and not to be trusted,
because she used the lavish coloring of words that
nature gave her. In the end, they had very nearly ground her down to their level; made a respectable mediocrity of her. But some good angel, in
the shape of a country school-master, with longings

beyond his means, picked her up out of the slough of despoi d, and sat her firmly in her own high place.   The consequence was, that if burning words, that go right to the heart, make people better for the reading of them, thousands of souls have been instructed and delighted through the efforts of that country school-master, whose wife the sweet poet, and rare woman, afterwards became.   So be gentle with these over wild exagger- ations, tone them down, but do not destroy them. They give life and beauty to the world.

Bernie sat on a low stool in front of the fire. One knee was crossed over the other, and her slight hands were folded a-top.   She looked thin- ner than ever, especially since her mother had loosened the net she wore at times, and the great, golden wreath of her tresses rolled over almost to the floor.   Mrs. Franklin was knitting; Irene, reading the fashions in a gorgeously illustrated magazine, now and then furtively glancing at, and perhaps envying the serenity of her saintly- browed sister.

" Now, Irene, you may laugh, and I dare say you will," the latter said, earnestly; " but remem- ber you have not seen him."

" Mother has," returned Irene, studying an angu- lar bonnet-shape, that seemed predisposed to con- sumption, in spite of its wealth of flowers and color.

"Yes, but my dear, remember it was at a time when I could distinguish almost nothing between anxiety and terror. I only recollect that he was monstrously tall."

"And *very* handsome, oh, you *must* remember, mother, although perhaps he did not look so then; but since he has been sick, his countenance has grown so spiritual!"

Irene laughed. It sounded a wicked little laugh to Bernie.

"Bernie, I do believe you were born to be the consoler of thieves and pickpockets," she said, lightly.

"Our Savior consoled a thief on the cross," said Bernie, with a sigh.

"Yes, I know you always have a reason. But I did n't mean to hurt your feelings, Bernie; I dare say your big giant is a perfectly splendid creature, and no doubt a Duke in disguise, as he is sometimes called in name."

"O, hush!" cried Bernie, with a frightened look. "Mr. Lyons begged us never to speak of him in *that* way, you know."

"Before people, of course not," said Irene; but among ourselves we might."

"Perhaps Bernie believes in the old proverb, that 'walls have ears,'" said Mrs. Franklin. At that moment the housekeeper came in to speak with Mrs. Franklin, who presently left the room with her.

"I do n't see why Mr. Lyons takes such an unaccountable interest in that man, said Irene, lounging more, and letting her book fall at her side.

"Of course he has good reasons; but, Irene, I wish *you* would go and see him."

"I!" cried Irene, with a grand look and toss of the head, "that would be a great joke. No, I thank you, it is n't at all to my taste."

"Well, if you did n't go to see him, you might at least, to see Mr. Lyons. I promise you, you 'd be amused; and, besides, we owe him some gratitude for his kindness."

"I do n't think so," said Irene, rocking herself lazily back and forth; "the money was left us by papa's uncle, and this little old fellow was merely the agent. I 've no doubt he paid himself well for it, too. How do we know about the genuineness of the will? Perhaps it was two hundred thousand pounds, and he has appropriated the other."

"O, Irene!" exclaimed Bernie, "how could such a thought ever come in your mind?"

"Well, it did," replied Irene, laughing. "The man is n't a saint; he do n't even profess to be a Christian; and his benevolent deeds are paid for out of other people's money. I did n't say it was so, only, how do we know?"

"Very low motives to accuse him of," said Bernie, gravely. "No; he's a great-hearted, great-souled, noble, magnificent little old man, and I wont hear him slandered."

"Why, Bernie, ca n't you take any fun?" asked Irene, picking up her magazine, which had slipped to the floor. "Actually, did I bring the tears? Why, you little goose! kiss and make up, and I 'll paint him as white as an angel, if it will please you."

"If you only could see, Irene, how much good he does, with your own eyes, as I have, I do n't think you 'd ever say a word," protested Bernie, though holding up her forehead to be kissed. "I 've been all over his house, his hospital, he calls it, and everything is so neat and clean, and the people love him so. He tends the sick ones, gives them medicines, and fire, and food, and there they have no care, but just to try and get well. And you ca n't think how they all love him!"

"Even your big giant, Bernie?"

"Yes, indeed; he, more than all, I should think, for I saw him one day with his arm round my little man's neck, as if he were thanking him for something, and could not do it as well in any other way."

"Your little man is so little, and your giant so

big," said Irene, " that I should think his one arm would cover him all up."

Bernie laughed at the conceit; laughed, till the shining bands of hair fairly danced in their splendid, luminous light.

" Well, then," she said, long afterwards, swaying back, and folding her slender hands over her head, " you might go there to please *me*. You 'll not always have me here to please, let me tell you."

" Why, where are you going, child?" queried Irene, stopping the motion of her chair.

Bernie laughed — low and rippling was the sound, full of prisoned melody — her eyes snapped it seemed for very delight; then she began to sing softly,

> " Heaven's my home,
> Heaven's my home."

" Why, of course heaven is everybody's home," said Irene, a trifle more of sternness in her voice; " that is," she added, "every Christian's home. But I confess that I do n't care about going there yet. I 'm not quite tired of earth and its delights."

" O, Iry, perhaps you do n't have so much to lead you there as I do. You can forget yourself, forget that you are mortal, because everybody bows down to you, and you are surrounded with everything heart can wish. It is n't so with me.

I'm crooked, though I seldom think of 't; if I do, it's only to believe I shall be straight enough up there; and I lie awake nights with that strange pain, and the fluttering of my heart, of which nothing relieves me, but the bright pictures of heaven, which God has given me the faculty to see. I lie and think, and hope, and pray, and imagine, till sometimes it seems as if I am taken out of myself, and begin to float up, up, toward heaven. I'm just as *sure* of it, Irene," she added, after a solemn pause, "as if I saw it, or that door opened into it."

"Sure of what?" asked Irene, in a hushed way.

"Why, of heaven. Do you know that Mr. Lyons do n't quite believe there is any? and, oh, I'm afraid, worse than that. Somebody told me he did n't believe there was anything but this life. O, Irene, it made me cry bitterly. It seemed as if I *must* bring angels down to convince him. At last, one day, when he had done a good thing, he said, 'Thank God!' That made me so happy! I whispered in his ear, 'they told me you did n't believe in HIM, but now I think you do;' and he did n't say a word. Silence gives consent, you know, so I have hope for him," she added, gravely.

"Bernie, you're an incurable Methodist," cried Irene, laughing at her gravity. "If you were only healthy and active, you would n't take such morbid views of life."

"Morbid!" cried Bernie, aghast, "Where 's the dictionary?   I suppose I 'm old enough to know, but I believe I do n't quite understand;" and away she ran, bringing back a small Webster in a moment, while her sister sat looking at her curiously.

"Morbid," she murmured, running her finger down the M's.   "Oh, here it is: diseased, sickly. Now, it is n't that," she added, with spirit; ":my *mind* is not diseased, I know.   Life is beautiful; I enjoy it every hour.   What do you think my teacher said to me, only yesterday?   'It seems to me, Miss Franklin, that you extract more sunshine out of life, than any other person I ever saw.' There, now; that for your theory!   I love life, because it is to be continued on, and on, and on forever.   But you *know*, Irene, you 're not certain of *this* part of life from one minute to another, and therefore, like that old, worn dress, that *I* think is the very nicest one I 've got, I prize it because it sets so loosely, though I know it must soon be thrown aside.   There 's a queer comparison for you."

"I should think so," said Irene, her eyes filling, she knew not why.

"And I was reading in the paper, yesterday, that children who thought and talked of religious things beyond their capacity, had better be running round out of doors and getting roses in their

cheeks, instead of preparing to go to heaven.
And, oh, Irene, I thought how many there were
who could n't do that; I, for instance, when I was
a child.   How many days and weeks I have laid
upon my bed!   It was not *my* fault, it was not
anybody's fault, for all the trouble came through
an accident that nobody could help only God, and
He did not choose.   I do n't like such things, and
I do n't believe people who write them, know just
what they are doing.   I wonder what they would
give us who *can 't* be active, in exchange for those
beautiful thoughts?   *I* would n't part with them —
no, not for perfect health.   If we can do more,
think more, feel more, enjoy more, without any of
earth's sufferings, up there, why should n't we
think about it, and live for it?   The same paper
laughed at a child's religion.   I think he, the
writer, or she, if it was a woman, forgot that
Christ told old men that they had got to become
like little children before they could please him."

"Well, Bernie, you are too religious, I think,
myself."

Bernie looked up, her eyes swimming in tears.

"Why, what *would* you have me do, Iry?" she
asked, plaintively.   "And what do you mean by
too religious.   *Can* any one be too good, too
happy?   Besides, it helps me bear my pain."

"Never mind me, Bernie, I shall never be like
you."

"No, indeed;" and Bernie sprang up, folding her slender arms about Irene, and kissed her. "No, you'll be better, and nobler, and more glorious than I, when you see and feel what I do. You'll come out such a splendid woman, Irene! I prophesy it."

For a few moments they clung together thus, till Irene found voice to say,

"Only don't speak of leaving us, Bernie, it hurts me."

"I sha'n't go till you're all ready to have me," said Bernie, in a low, soft voice; "perhaps not till you're married and have found something to love better than me."

A great choking sob swelled in Irene's throat; she was just beginning to appreciate the depth of the strong, tender soul, that dwelt in that frail body. She had never loved the little helpless sister more than now, perhaps never so much.

"But about this pain, Bernie; did you have it when I awoke and heard you whispering so, last night?"

"O, yes, I remember; I was repeating the words of my dear little hymn:

> "One sweetly solemn thought
> Comes to me o'er and o'er,
> Nearer my Father's throne, am I,
> Then 'ere I was before."

I said it all through, and by that time the pain was gone."

"Bernie, does mother know about it?"

"Yes, dear," replied the other, cheerfully; "but all the physiciáns have said that perhaps it will wear away, and so perhaps it will. It only comes once in a while, stays with me two or three nights, and then leaves me. Do you know what I call it? I always say, Here comes my messenger again."

"You should have a physician, dear. I believe something could be done."

"No, they all say the same thing. The little old man's medicine does me more good than anything else."

"And what is that?"

"Trying to live for others. But, really and truely, Iry, I do believe he is a physician. He has three boxes, all inlaid with silver, and made of a very costly kind of wood that grows in the tropics, and all filled with medicines and surgical instruments. I wish you could see his place, and particularly my big giant."

"I'll go and see them, Bernie, to-morrow, if you wish it."

"O, will you? Thank you, thank you." And pressing kiss after kiss upon her sister's cheek, she resumed her position upon the low seat before the fire, her face like an illuminated picture. Passing her brother's room not long after, she saw a light there, and called out "Good night."

"Look in one moment," he said, in a cheery voice.

She stopped, and stood there shaking her long locks playfully.

"That's all, dear; Good night. I was thinking up a picture, and wanted an inspiration."

The momentary loiter had done her good. Bernie had never seen her brother so cheerful, so animated before. "I'm sure he looks as if it was almost harvest time in his heart," she said; "he must be doing something that pleases him."

He was outlining the picture he intended to present to Cecil Romaine. Papers and colors, spread out for early use in the morning, flaked all the desk; ivory cups, culminated with carmines; heaven's blue gemmed saucers, and porcelain stands, bits of brown bistre, rich as a dove's breast, little waifs of color, born here and there of a touch, all proclaimed his artistic belongings. He was for the first time forgotten of himself. It appeared as if all his old life was beginning to grow away from him, and leave him a new creature. His very Bible was more precious that night, as he read the sacred promises that were doubly dear to him now.

All that lighting up of life, one fair face had accomplished.

O, vitality and beauty of earth, that can make even heaven's light seem whiter!

CHAPTER XXIII.

THE GIANT'S CONTRITION.

CHRISSY and the minister together succeeded at last. After manifold liftings, draggings, ejaculations and some laughter, the Duke was fairly bolstered up in the great easy chair for the first time. It was Chrissy's chair, sacred to the memory of her dead husband. She had sent for it because, she said, "Nowhere under the canopy was there another like it."

By a series of jerks, familiar to the experienced hands of nurse Chrissy, the Duke was pulled into a dressing-gown with a great many red spiders running over brown green vines. It was wonderfully becoming, however, in spite of its wealth of dyes, and almost long enough. The minister had contributed a unique study cap out of his little assortment of sacred trifles. It was quite a wonder of industry — a bit of embroidered sunshine — worked by a dear young girl, he said, twenty years before, and whose marvellous beauty had long been covered from human sight; a member of his congregation, whom everybody loved who knew her.

The gilt and crimson, and long tufted tassels transformed the invalid into a pale student, with beautiful eyes, of that melting brown, that seems, at times, a shadowy reflection of pure flame; at times, sleepy and tender as the eyes of a babe. Sickness adds new beauty to some faces — it did to his. As Bernie said, his countenance had grown spiritual. Some hallowed influence beyond him seemed to have transfused his features with the clearness and loveliness of innocence. He looked like one now who had never done harm in his life. Mr. Lyons loved that face. Was it not the mother-light and beauty that played over it?

The chair was wheeled out into the large, cheerful room, brightened just then with an April sunshine; and as he laid back his head thankfully, with a sigh of relief, he said, in a softened voice,

"It's all too good for me."

"I suppose you agree then with my old defender of the faith, that you 're a miserable sinner," said the latter, stooping down to the fire.

"I 've known that for years," was the quiet reply.

"Well, then, why do n't you try to get made over, according to his theory? Nothing *seems* easier."

"I wish to heaven I could; but the past, Mr. Lyons, the past can never be effaced."

"All you have to do, young man is to turn a leaf, paste it down, and begin new; so he says. If a thing is forgiven, I take it it's the same as blotted out. If I forgive a man a debt, I do n't expect him to pay me his money, do I?"

"Seeing as *he's* so comfortable," said nurse Chrissy, coming in bonneted and shawled, "I'll go over to sister Franklin's. Tell Cardy not to git his toast too brown, if I should n't be back in time; jest a *leetle* turned on both sides," and vanished.

The minister had gone out for a walk, so the two were alone.

"Are you well enough to talk?" asked Mr. Lyons, bringing up his easy chair on the other side of the invalid.

"Always well enough for that," was the reply, with a faint smile.

"Yes, but you had like to cost me a pretty penny a few days ago. I do n't care about your dying on my hands, particularly through my imprudence."

"There's no danger of my fainting now, doctor; besides, I've been thinking the matter over, and want to tell you about myself. I'm bad enough, but I'm almost as unfortunate as I am wicked. In the first place, you recollect my father?"

"Yes, very well: Colonel Anson."

"That is enough. You hinted the other day at

his habits. In spite of my mother's entreaty, he taught me to love wine and brandy, and every kind of liquor. Strange, as I now look back, his conduct for the *first* time seems reprehensible. I have had a sort of idea that children born in the station to which I belonged, were all thus educated. And the company I naturally fell into, strengthened the impression. At twenty-one, before I left college, I believe I was an inveterate drunkard; but I could drink immensely and not expose myself. My father wished me to be a soldier. I had a dislike to the profession of arms, but could not make up my mind as to my own aims in the future. I was too heedless for anything like the law, or any of the more serious callings; and my tastes all tended to the theatre. My voice is of unusual quality; it has been, I might almost say, my curse, for to its fine tones I attribute the brief success that ultimately ruinèd me. Of course, I could not long keep up my habits of extravagance. I gambled deeply; my father cleared my debts off twice, then anathematized me for following his own example, and ceased to remit. At last, I had become abandoned, to my reckless habits, I mean, and joining in one night with a poaching gang, from the mere love of adventure and the excitement of the thing, I was apprehended with one of the wild fellows, and nothing could save me. Yes, sir, for nearly a year I was imprisoned in the hulks; and that quite run me down."

"But you got your discharge," said the little old man, quietly.

"No, sir, I broke jail!" exclaimed the man, in a voice suddenly terrific from its concentration. "For months I lived, I hardly know how; it is humiliating even to me, to tell of that time; and now, sir, you know the character of the man you have saved. You cannot care for one so shameless; curse me, and let me go."

"Never;" and his host grew tall and stern as he arose; "never, Clarence, my boy; for your mother's sake, I will save you if I can. But you must tell me the truth, the whole truth, and nothing but the truth. Did you ever injure any one beside yourself?"

The man's eyes were fastened upon him; they were startlingly bright.

"Did I ever injure any one beside myself; how can you ask that question? Did a raking fire of artillery upon close ranks ever open without mowing down its fifties? I dare say there have been soft boys, and beardless, allured by my free and easy hospitality. I have taught games at cards to some who, till then, had a holy horror of all games of chance. Do you suppose I ever drank *one* glass without luring some soul to destruction? When I

get well, what am I going to do? I feel this burning appetite already."

"What is a man, if he cannot conquer his passions?" asked the other, with some contempt in his
voice.

"That will do for you to ask — you born in cold
New-England, not in the tropics; you, brought up
in rigid views of defiance to sin, and even temptation; not taught by a father to carouse while yet
in baby-frocks, and told that you were smart because you had the whole catalogue of blasphemy at
your tongue's end. And yet your question *is* per-
tinent. A man is *nothing*, if he cannot conquer
himself. I have made a thousand resolves on that
sick bed yonder. It does seem sometimes as if
there *must* be something grander in me than mere
human, lawless passions. I measure my stature;
I count over my capacities and talents; I stand
my soul up as if it were an image of flesh and
blood, and scan it narrowly to see if there be one
spot of whiteness on which I can hang a hope. I"
— and his voice took on that depth that startles
the hearer into admiration — "have even dared to
pray, since angel Bernie came. Do you know I
had nearly forgotten the Lord's prayer? Well,
she said it, and I repeated it after her, trembling.
The words seemed too holy for my polluted lips.
For, sir, as low as I have descended, I never *dared*

to question the truths of that revealed religion, which in some souls shines like a lamp in an alabaster vase. No, I have never gone down so far in an earthly sensuality, as to doubt that there was a God — a hereafter."

His listener winced repeatedly.

"Clarence, you have not told me all, yet," said the latter, after a pause; and fixing his eyes upon him with a look that was intended to be awfully severe, but lacked of the first ingredient in that expression, because of his constitutional benevolence, he asked, in solemn tones —

"Clarence, where is your wife?"

The man glanced up with an aspect that seemed like terror. His brow grew pale.

"My wife!" he exclaimed.

"Yes, Clarence, the poor thing whom probably you deserted; the poor soul who may have died in grief and destitution; perhaps of a broken heart, through your instrumentality. Where did you leave her, Clarence?"

The Duke still stared blankly, articulating only the words,

"My wife!"

"Yes, man; do you tremble that I know? Are you in reality the black-hearted wretch I thought you could *not* be? Clarence, am I so basely deceived in you?"

"Upon my honor, I cannot answer you," said the convalescent, drawing his gaunt frame up with an air of offended dignity. "I never had a wife."

"Do you pretend to tell me that?" cried Mr. Lyons, springing almost angrily from the chair.

"Are you insane?" echoed the other, cheek and eye blazing. "Low as I have descended, no man ever knew me to tell that which was false, Mr. Lyons. Do n't insult me, sir; for, remember there are some remnants of manhood left me; I am not quite a brute."

Matters were progressing unfavorably. Mr. Lyons had a quick temper; the Duke a fierce, ungovernable one. The former sprang from his place before the fire, whisked his hands under his coat tails, and began walking back and forth as fast as he could, to cool his excitement. The latter sat, following his motions with glances glaring and intensified, bending forward in momentary strength, his cheeks blazing, the straggling black hair covering his temples in masses, and clinging to his throat that was as white as a babe's.

"Do you mean to tell me, Clarence," at length said Mr. Lyons, planting himself again before his gigantic patient, "that you never had a wife?"

"No, sir, I do not," said the Duke, steadily. "I have told you twice; think what you please, only remember that my weakness saves you, and only that; for, upon my word, such reiteration, such an absurb declaration, question, or whatever you call it, almost obliterates my gratitude."

"And you persist that you never had a wife, when I myself have seen your child, and heard the whole story?" continued Mr. Lyons, more calmly. The Duke trembled now, from head to foot; it was with passion and weakness combined, not guilt, as Mr. Lyons suspected.

"Seen my child! are you an idiot, man? Heard the whole story!"

"*Angels and ministers of grace defend us!*"

"You will convince me soon that I am in an asylum for the insane. I have no child — I never had a child"— and he fell back exhausted and panting.

"What am I to think of you, sir, except as deep, designing, villainous. This little Effie Anson, whom I myself have seen to day"—

An instantaneous change flashed over the invalid's countenance, like the sudden sun-gleam over the surface of a clouded earth; he lifted himself, clutching both arms of his chair. "There, *now* I begin to understand you," he cried out heartily — "how did that child get here?"

"Ah! at last you acknowledge."

"Yes, yes," replied the other, with a weak laugh. "I know all about it now; it was very natural. Pray sit down; we were both of us in the dark — upon my word, I had forgotten —"

"Both wife and child," said the little old man, sarcastically. He had been so shocked that he could not on the instant recover his good nature.

"No, no; I tell you, my dear sir, for the last time, I have neither wife nor child. But poor little Effie, how in the world did she get here? The little one is an orphan, whom I intended in good faith to take care of. Her mother was a poor, consumptive creature — a costumer, who died when the child was six months old. Her father was killed, poor fellow, by a frightful accident; they were both connected with my profession, and I volunteered to keep the child from the poor-house — to pay a small sum weekly for her nursing and bringing up. I did it, too, till that unlucky trouble about the poaching business, and even then, left support enough for a year. The poor little creature was named by me after my mother, and I suppose in time, her own name was dropped; that's where the mistake occurred."

Mr. Lyons sat looking at him stupidly, with misty glasses. He took them off, his lips twitching, rubbed assiduously, then down dropped glasses and handkerchief. He caught his Hercules by both hands, exclaiming, "You wretched giant! — that's the second good deed that has come to my knowledge. I'm ashamed of myself — I'm an old ass. But never mind; it'll be all fair sailing now, henceforth and forever. You're my son, sir; yes, you're my son. Remember that's fixed, and we'll have to dress you like the gentleman you are, and change your name. Now suppose you take mine," he added, with quiet gusto; "it's not bad for a big fellow like you. As for my humble self, my name ought to be Lamb, I suppose, or Mutton," he added, meekly.

"I do n't know about it," replied the other. "I sha'n't make a very tame object of charity, I'm afraid. My feelings of self-respect are keener than they used to be; and if I start on a new track, I shall be my own helper, please God."

"All very right and proper; but, as it happens, I have burned your old clothes up. Now what are you going to do? The dressing-gown is a very comfortable affair, but not just the thing for the street, eh?"

"Then I suppose I must be an ' object,'" replied the other, with a faint smile; "at least, till I can repay you. As for the name, I'd as lief cast it off as not — I've disgraced it. I wish I could begin life a new man."

"You shall, sir, you shall!" cried his guardian, with enthusiasm, rubbing his hands. "I've got the whole plan laid out. I see it, I see it all! You're going to prove that you *can* be somebody, and then, sir, you will be a man of fortune,

take my word for it. Just talk as much as you
can with my old defender of the faith; and if I
stand in your way, why, bless me, I'll pound my
old head till I force a passage through, but what
I'll believe in *some* religion for your sake; I will,
indeed. Why, my dear boy, if your mother could
only see us now — us two together! It must have
been design; it couldn't have been chance. No,
no, it couldn't possibly have been chance."

"So far, so good," he muttered to himself, as he
sauntered to the window. "We wont tell him
about the little fortune, yet, or his new relations.
Some few preliminaries to settle first; but money
will do it, money will do it."

Suddenly he became possessed. Two or three
chairs out of place were whisked back, a little
breeze stirred by the turkey-wing with which he
brushed up the hearth, his coat pulled down, his
hair patted back, his blue goggles mounted, his
giant straightened by an emphatic nod and word,
everything jerked into apple-pie order, and then
the door-bell rang. It was not nurse Chrissy,
but —

CHAPTER XXIV.

WHAT CAME OF IT.

BERNIE, shining seraphically, and Irene, whose haughty brow had heretofore made him shiver.

"I never expected it," was on his lips, but he did n't say it. Instead, he received her with courtly politeness, though he felt, for the moment, that he would rather meet her under more auspicious circumstances : say, a spacious drawing-room, with velvet and gilt accompaniments. However, he welcomed her with cordiality, and offered her a chair near his patient.

Irene was introduced to the latter in this manner :

"A protege of mine, Miss Irene, with whom your sister is better acquainted than — any of us."

Now the cunning little Bernie had never laid bare to her sister's knowledge the fact of her preserver's previous bad habits. That scene in the grocer's shop was sacredly secret, and yet Irene, after the fashion of selfish natures, was prepared to see an inferior, gross, large, common-place person. Her surprise, when she met the full look of the man,

look the form of an emphatic stare, an impropriety of which she was seldom guilty ; for, in truth,
she was astounded — that gentlemanly, self-pos-
sessed, nobly handsome man, whose eyes revealed
a depth and power of expression as beautiful as re-
markable — languid, but in the presence of so
elegant a young lady, instinctively elegant too
He possessed all a gentleman's proclivities, though
the propensities that were grafted upon his very
nature had threatened to extinguish his manhood.

It had for some time been a rare thing for him to
be in the society of refinement and beauty, and not
feeling strong enough to despise himself, he displayed all his better qualities. Irene was fascinat-
ed ; nay, more, her proud heart, for the first time,
acknowledged that it could be stirred by a glance.
Bernie grew quite entranced by her sister's evident
surprise — she whose soul was swallowed up in the
effort to do this man good. He was her preserver,
and as such alone, held a most exalted place in her
memory, her imagination. And the purity of the
child-woman did not abash him. He dared to look
in her eyes, feeling that, with all his sins upon his
head, for the sake of his mother, he had never
wronged the simplest or most confiding woman, in
word, thought, or deed. There was *one* white
spot in his soul, after all, on which to hang a hope ;
for a man is well worth redemption who can make

a confession like that.   Bernie listened, looking
eagerly from him to her sister to note the effect;
her lips were wreathed in smiles, her cheeks rippling with dimples.   Her great eyes seemed all the
time saying, " Is n't he great? is n't he splendid?"
She would not think of the future ; the man *must
not* go back.   She *would* hold on to God's angels,
for Bernie had great delight in reading that sweet
promise among sweet promises : " Are they not
ministering angels, sent to minister for them who
shall be heirs of salvation?"

"Who *shall* be," she used to say, triumphantly,
pointing to the words ; " it do n't say who are, but
who *shall* be.   So there are angels about my poor
sick man, though he has been wicked, and God has
sent him this illness because I have asked for him.
He saved my life, now if I can only be instrumental in saving him, oh, what a glory it will be up
there ! "

"Up there " was pre-eminently the end and aim
of all Bernie's wishes.   Earth was bounded by her
narrow circle of duties ; heaven was the great
throne-room, the splendid audience-chamber, where
her humble recital was to be crowned with the
smiles and benediction of God.   The dear girl
never thought of pleasure in an abstract sense ;
her delight was in doing, thinking, acting, hoping.
At the same time there was nothing prudish or

unnatural about her, save, sometimes, a saintliness
that impressed the most unworldly.

Presently, another was added to the little group—
young Franklin. He had heard that Bernie was
on a visit to the old man's hermitage, not counting
to meet Irene, who was a little less constrained
than usual. The eyes of fashion were not upon
her just now.

To him Mr. Lyons introduced his friend as,

"My protege and namesake, Mr. Clarence Lyons."

Bernie started at this, and looked at her old
friend rather suspiciously. "He need n't tell *me*,"
she said to herself; "he's an angel, that's what he
      See how he tries to shield this poor man!"

"Who is he?" asked Clarence, when they had
all gone up to inspect the arrangements of "My
model hospital," as Mr. Lyons called it.

"He is Bernie's brother; and for your comfort
and encouragement, I will add he is but recently
out of prison."

"No, it's not possible," said the Duke, almost
fiercely.

"Yes, it is *quite* possible; and he will take his
stand in society again, too. I'm rot going to see
men kicked who are down. The world has had
its way long enough; I shall put in my humble
verdict against it."

"The world is older than you are," said his patient, taking an offered mixture with a wry face, and looking grimly at the empty spoon.

"Yes, and the mountain is older than the spade that levels it; but it has to come down in time, for all that. Society has been set against the criminal for this reason: there are more rogues out of jail than in. I am not going to plead for breakers of the law, by no means. But I have seen in my experience that many impulsive, good-hearted fellows in the main, caught in their first transgression, would, if pardoned, after the right kind of treatment, have made better citizens than those crafty, cold-blooded, cautious villains, who break every law in the decalogue with almost every breath they draw. Do you doubt now that if you overcome this love of drink, you would be an ornament to the world, you — six-footer?"

"The hulks knocked all that ambition out of me," said the young man, gloomily. "And think for what I was sentenced, and by whom? For shooting a rabbit, and by the landlords who can go out in broad daylight and shoot as many as they please. You can't convince me that I had not as good a right as they; and, therefore, I say it was for no *crime* that I was convicted. The shock-headed fellow who passed his judgment on my case, was more than half drunk, and evidently considered it

rare sport. I owe England one for that; if ever
a revolution breaks out, I'm on the side of the
poor poacher, remember that. If a man owns
an acre and three stones on it, it's all right; but
for the poor devil who has no farm, no garden,
no sport, unless it might be climbing a greased
pole, like a bear, for him there's the prison, without even the benefit of a jury. There, in the
midst of hardened criminals, he takes lessons in
real vice. The officers in charge knew how I felt;
I did n't scruple to air my opinions, and they made
me feel my degradation. They seemed to exult,
that, because I knew some things they did not, and
had been in better circumstances, they could tyran-
nize over me, and they did it to their heart's content. They worked to change man's very nature
for the worst, and, in truth, they did it too often.
Now, we all knew we were bad enough, with the
charges rung into eyes and ears every hour of the
day. We wanted consolation; we had to want.
We wished to find out whether there *were* any that
pitied us. That Christ felt compassion for us, was
dinned in our hearing often enough; but we wanted to see a little of it in his children. I could believe *you*, if you were a disciple of His, for the
way you received us that night. I felt it, though
I was as drunk as a fool, and knew hardly more
what I was doing than that sauce-pan knows it is

boiling, save a general consciousness that something wrong was going on, and you had forgiven it. That is what I call a Christian act, and the only mystery to me is that you never allow yourself to be called a Christian. What do *you* want to convert me to? "

" Why, a sober, temperate man, of course," said the other, poking the fire sturdily, and a little nonplussed.

" And you do n't think as the minister does. *You* think I can do it in and of myself, with all my inherent and educated tastes and passions against me? "

" Fudge ! " said his listener, harshly. " Was he to be taught by this heathen? "

" That 's no argument, retorted the other," quietly.

" I commend you to Mr. Callender," said Mr. Lyons, half exasperated. " Do what he tells you to do, and no doubt you 'll be all right."

" I prefer your teaching to his, since you have done me all the real good I have ever known," returned the giant, mildly, " unless you turn me over to Bernie Franklin."

" I 'll do it," said Mr. Lyons, lighting up, as he sprang to his feet. " She shall teach you. I 'll buy a catechism to-morrow."

CHAPTER XXV.

MY MODEL HOSPITAL.

MEANWHILE, Harry and Bernie, with Irene following, as a matter of course — not because she saw any deeper than the surface of things — walked over the house wherever it was practicable. The old organ grinder, who was too lame to go on his beat, laid aside his book (he had known better days and was something of a scholar), and gave them some gems from *Trovatore*, on his new hand-organ, which he displayed with many praises of the little old man. This was the only thing Irene really enjoyed, save that few moments talk with the invalid down stairs, who would have been flattered had he known the impression he had made. What did she, thoughtless and fashionable, care about sick old men who hobbled on crutches, or pale women, whose lives might each have made a separate romance? Here they were, poor, ill and destitute; that was all she noted.

Bernie, on the contrary, looked around with the eyes of her soul. Her voice was fragrant with love and good wishes. She saw here her special

charge from Christ, " my poor." In each decrepid
face an angel looked out to her, because, if they
were human, was not the angel in them already?
Yet to none of them would she minister as to that
invalid below, with gold-embroidered cap on his
black curls, and the bright dressing gown folded
over his wasted limbs. Harry was also interested
in him from the first; she was so glad of that.
Indeed, blessings brightened all her pathway; for
her brother seemed so much happier now than ever
he did before. Was it strange that the world
looked pleasant to her?

Harry and Irene went home, courteously declin-
ing Mr. Lyons polite invitation to supper.

" Will you leave her a little while?" Clarence
asked, holding Bernie by the hand, bestowing
upon her such glances of affectionate interest, that
Irene's cheek tinged with a momentary jealousy.

" How is it," she sighed to herself, " she attracts
everybody?"

If some one had replied,

" By simple goodness, only," Irene might have
sneered. As it was, she left the house with a
pang at her heart for which she could not account.

Mr. Lyons chuckled to himself, when he saw
Harry's happy face.

" I think I know that secret," he said to himself.
" Well, well, if it is so, I 've got a sword that I

can hang by a hair any time. Romaine is a proud man; it would kill him to know of any disgrace in his family."

Bernie staid. They were to send a carriage for her in the evening. Clarence made her sit down at his feet. He loved that face, and wanted to look at it, without its accompanying inequalities of form. His eye was artistic, and the purest sculpture would have seemed almost heavy beside the ethereal beauty of that countenance.

"I have been talking with Mr. Lyons," he said, "about a better life. How can I be good, Bernie?"

Her face flushed. Here was the very work beginning. She did not shrink into herself, but without vanity, or ostentation of any kind, she set herself about the task. The old minister, who was very learned, would have quoted from the Stoics, the Ionics, the Pythagoreans, until he came to the fountain-head. Bernie went there, at first. She took the Bible — an old, well-worn copy belonging to the minister — and she pointed out such sweet passages, or read them with such intonations of music, that tears came to the brilliant dark eyes regarding her so attentively.

"There! if ever I saw such goings on. Are you crazy to let that man set up to this time? I do believe everything would go to rack and ruin if it was n't for me. Here, Bernie, do untie this

knot," cried Chrissy, presenting her chin. "There,
now, Mr. Lyons, I should 'a thought *you'd* a
known better. You'll have him on your hands
again, as sure as you live;" and the nurse marched round, and commanded and drilled, till she had
her big patient, who was more exhausted than he
knew, comfortably tucked into bed, with Bernie
and a plate of toast at his side, which soon the
giant was quietly munching.

CHAPTER XXVI.

GETTING READY FOR CHRISTMAS.

A TWELVEMONTH had passed. Christmas was almost at hand. There had been no change in the house which the little old man had consecrated. The old clock still contributed its cheerful knowledge of the hours. Mr. Lyons had taken a sudden fancy to evergreens and holly branches. They strewed the chairs and tables, and great balls of twine stood here and there. Something better than mere pleasure made his face shine so. He had found a living faith. He knew what to say now, when blinded souls looked out of wild, haggard eyes, and asked for a medicine that only the open hands of Mercy could give. The old minister had retired. He was grown feeble in health, though still bright and clear in intellect. Quiet, mild and genial as ever, he gave small trouble to his benefactor; and Mrs. Chrissy, who was nurse of the establishment, now had her own way from the garret to the cellar, ruling her employer in the bargain.

It was evening. Three candles gave all neces-

sary light.   The tall clock, grown somewhat more
gutteral, broke the stillness with its accustomed
whuf, whuf.   Old Cardy still stood at his post in
the kitchen.   " Cash " had gone up one - more step
of the ladder of " pardnership."   Everything Mr.
Lyons had put his hand to had prospered.

Only Bernie had changed — not much — grown
strangely reticent, and more patiently beautiful ;
battling with pain, perhaps some other half-defined
and miserable ill, that no one else dreamed of.

Gentle, angel Bernie !   We shall know in the
world which is to come, why such spirits as hers
are marked for suffering, why the mere froth and
foam of earth sparkles and shines for many an
appreciative eye, and its pure diamonds glow only in
darkness.   Bernie's soul was troubled, not obscured.   Irene's was both.   Clarence Lyons had suddenly stepped out of obscurity, and dazzled the
world at once.   If his appetites were not changed, his will was.   He could hold them down now
with chains stronger than adamant.

God does not convert the intellect, the tastes,
the passions.   He converts the *heart*.   The others
yield to this great, central planet, so long as it
reflects God's love and power ; the desires gradually grow in harmony with it.   The tastes yield,
the passions lie down and obey, like lions, so
tamed that a little child might guide them.

The banker knew his history in part. With much quibbling, and some bribing, the money of the dead and gone Baronet was placed in Mr. Ly on's hands for safe keeping and investment, while the redeemed man, though nearer thirty than twenty, gave himself up to the study of the law. It was plain to be seen that some change had occurred — a mysterious, impalpable change — which, call it what we may, does give new impulses, new directions, new aims to the will, so helpless, or so tyrannical before.

Sceptics may growl, and weak devotees of the world smile in their super-disdainful way; but I know a man, who, without any peculiar or distressing providence, turned himself round, and from a hater of all good, a despiser of all virtue, a swearer and a mocker, became gentle, God-fearing, humble, holy. In his way of telling it, and mark you — the man was highly refined, educated and intellectual — he said he had experienced a change. Now, some of you extra good Pharisees, tell me what it meant? If his skin had been changed from black to white, you would have called it a miracle. The soul was most assuredly changed from black to white; was that no miracle?

At once, nothing of his past history being known, Clarence shone in good society. He was trusted, and he did not abuse that trust. Men met him sometimes, who could have kicked him once, with the greatest impunity. Now they no more remembered him in that stately man, than if he had come down new made out of the skies. Irene, alas, for proud Irene! She confessed to herself that at last she had found one who had thoroughly mastered her heart, and allowed herself, more than once, to be jealous of her poor, blessed, little sister. For Bernie was his idol. Her presence, as it were, absorbed him. As for her, she grew more transparent, more unearthly, day by day; strangely quiet when alone, singularly happy when he was by. She was willing to renounce all the world, every delight, and yet, at times — though very seldom — her heart swelled that she must. She was willing to bear the keen trial of her deformity, and yet she could not help asking herself, once in a very great while, if it would not be glorious to stand erect, with only nature's swells and curves?

Ah! well for her that she had long felt the great consolation. Well that her dreams of heaven did not grow dim.

Mr. Lyons suddenly threw down a heap of pine-branches. There was the carriage, and there were Bernie, Irene, and Clarence to help him. They had promised. He smiled, as he saw how gaily and confidingly Irene swept in with her manly

companion, Bernie lingering a little. Sometimes
the love of mischief predominated. He longed to
whisper one word in her ear, and set her puz-
zling over it; that word was "hulks." The little
old man hated pride, and Irene was its personifi-
cation, though she could descend at times into
the sphere of ordinary people.

"Here you are," he cried, gaily. "Now go to
work;" and he tossed the twine over, and pointed
to the evergreen.

"Bernie, you place them and I will tie," said
Clarence. Irene turned away angry, mortified,
though nobody knew it.

"This is Bernie's own pet plan," said Mr. Lyons, after a pause. "She suggested it one night,
at our brilliant party. Did n't you, pet? — a feast
for the blind, the halt, and the ugly."

"O, you know it is n't that," cried Bernie, looking up brightly, while her little snowy fingers
moved deftly in and out among the fragrant things.

"I expect we shall have *some* ugly ones, though,"
he replied. "There's Tom Dunkers, up stairs,
throws a bottle at my head every chance he can
get."

"That's because he's delirious."

"What are you about, Miss Franklin?" called
Clarence. He never addressed Irene as he did
Bernie. She would have given worlds if he had.

" Bring us some of those holly-branches, if you please."

Irene turned to obey, oh, how willingly; but started and grew pale as she met Bernie's glorious eyes shining out from under a beautiful wreath which Clarence had just made.

" I have crowned my queen," he said, gaily; then sang in a softer voice,

" Queen of my soul, Bernie, Bernie," laughing the while, and looking straight at Irene, who tried, with all her womanly power, to keep her cheek from whitening.

" There is your holly," she said.

" Shall I make *you* a crown?" he asked.   She could not have helped the answer, sharp and hot that sprung from her lips, had her life hung on the issue.

" Did you ask Bernie?"

Bernie crimsoned, and consciously put up her hand to snatch the wreath off, but Clarence arrested her.   It was the first time Irene had really stung her in that way; the first time for months her heart felt wounded.   The quivering lip and too bright eyes were concealed by bending over her work.   Then Irene went over to help Mr. Lyons.

" How disagreeable your sister can make herself," said Clarence, in a low voice, using the huge garden shears with a great snap. "I do n't like her sometimes."

" O, hush! you must, you *must* like her!" cried Bernie, almost passionately, the slow tears dropping like most precious diamonds, one by one, upon the evergreen.

"And why *must?* No, my little queen; I like — I *love* nobody but you."

Her eyes were lifted, a wild, startled but precious light in their depths.

" It is very sweet to hear you say that," she said, innocently; " it is very beautiful; but in this world, I must belong to nobody."

" Yes, you must, you shall, you *do* belong to me. You were the first to waken the soul that was sunk in such brutish slumbers. Do you suppose I forget that long journey you made through those filthy by-ways, to seek me out and throw your pure pearls before me? Do you suppose that for one single day I have lost the memory of that white face, looking out from its frame of sunny locks? And when, with patient lips and fingers, you led me along the glorious high-way of the better life, and I saw the fields 'n the golden shimmer of summer, though winter reigned, while the very trees appeared endowed with new vitality and almost intelligence, and hill and forest seemed instinct with praise and beauty, do you think that I do not associate you with all? O, child! rare and fair; precious, priceless! You are the gift of heaven to me, and I shall claim you."

"In heaven," whispered Bernie, veiling the splendor of her eyes, for never had that voice so charmed, so entirely enthralled and banished every recollection of pain and sorrow from her heart — that heart which was beating all too wildly at these earnest words.

"No; on earth, Bernie. I mean to ask your father to give you to me; and you shall be my one little diamond — my snow-drop — my white dove, untouched by any shade less pure. There, now I have told you in a very unromantic way, how much I love you. Shall you ever touch or see evergreen without thinking of it?"

She looked up, the old beseeching sorrow in her glance. Her heart was swelling with joy and grief; grief on Irene's account — joy unspeakable that she was so wholly appreciated, though she felt as truly as if an angel at her side had told her, that it could never be. Her messenger was closing up to the very doors of her existence. His hand already touched the easily lifted latch, that he might let her sweet life out. A passing pang, a prayer, and she was calm again. But not before two little words had dropped like agony from her lips:

"O, Irene!"

" Irene — why, darling, why do you speak so of her? Does she dislike me? I have thought so, sometimes. Does she say I have no right in you, whc made me what I am, because of the past? Are you afraid of Irene, little one ? "

" No, you do n't understand," cried Bernie, covering her hot face for a brief moment. " Irene dislike ! " suddenly conscious that she was betraying the heart and the tears she had seen, and interpret ed only too well, she became silent and passive.

" Irene does not dislike you, Clarence," she said, when he pressed the subject, speaking very softly.

" I hope not," he returned, with an ease that was perfectly natural, " because one wishes to be on good terms with ones sister." He looked up laughingly. Bernie, and Bernie alone, had read her sister's secret. She was the interpreter of that shy submissiveness that was so foreign to Irene's usual icy imperiousness. She knew what the long vigils meant, the sleepless nights, and her heart ached for Irene.

Clarence had often admired Irene, and it was marvellous that the petted beauty did not lay him " under spell." But he was very far from being a vain man, consequently he did not think that all who smiled upon him were dying for him. As he had hinted, the impression of Bernie's angel-face in the great old fashioned room, had never left him, no, not for an instant.   In some way he had connected it with the spiritual countenance of his mother ; it was the last thing he thought while consciousness remained ; the first thing when it returned after a carouse.   This feeling had deepened with time, and a more intimate knowledge of Bernie's lovable qualities.

Mr. Lyons was patiently festooning long lines of evergreen along the walls, under Irene's super-vision.   Clarence was talking to Bernie in a low voice ; all at once he was impelled to look toward Irene.   He caught her eyes fastened upon him. The movement caused her to drop her light bur-den, and the strain upon the string was so great that the frail drapery was detached.

" Miss Irene, if you do n't do better, I shall have to send Bernie over there," said Clarence, laughing, thinking the glance was purely accidental.

"Always Bernie," cried the girl in her heart, with a fierce pang.

" Now, Bernie, we 'll give our invitations out to-morrow," cried Mr. Lyons, surveying the work — " who shall it be ? "

" O, everybody ! " replied Bernie.

" Then we should have to hire the Common ; no, we must be more select.   We can accommodate a hundred, I should think, by setting dinner twice. I shall have to get a host to help me.   I 've spoken for a dozen turkeys, regular twenty-pounders, and as many loaves of plum-cake. Two bakers are in my secret, and one crockery-ware dealer. Mr. Tim Stebbins will be master of ceremonies in the carrying line ; you, sir Clarence, and Harry, I shall transform into waiters. Bernie and Miss Irene will be my ornaments in lieu of statuary, etc. All my sick people must have their portion carried up stairs. Nurse Chrissy will attend to that. I think, on the whole, it will be a merry Christmas.

CHAPTER XXVII.

A T last the decorations were completed. "A perfect bower," Bernie said, clapping her hands joyously.

Nothing could look prettier. The old clock peeped out under crowns and garlands; the girls had made mottoes for the entrance to the tables; the festoons and hangings were "executed in admirable style —" comment of Clarence; and the whole thing was "nice as a picture —" declaration of the little old man. When left alone, Mr. Lyons walked round — perhaps I should say danced — to notice the general effect. He appeared somewhat like a merry youth attired in his grandfather's clothes, so demonstrative and jubilant he was.

A knock at the door. Mr. Lyons admitted the banker, rather taken aback by his visit at this late hour. Mr. Romaine seemed unusually agitated; his manner was perturbed.

"I am glad to find you alone, Mr. Lyons," he said. "My man of business informed me that you wished a renewal of the lease."

"Yes, for a term of five years."

"Of course you can have it," said the banker, "and I have brought the necessary papers, which you will oblige me by signing."

He then threw the papers down so abruptly that Mr. Lyons looked up to see what was the matter.

"I am troubled to-night, Mr. Lyons. I wish to heaven I had never had a word to say to your protege, Franklin."

"Why! what has he done?" queried the other, so much discomposed that the pen trembled in his hold.

"He is mad enough, sir, to aspire to the affections of my daughter, Miss Romaine, sir," said the banker, curtly.

"Indeed!" was the rather cool reply, and the hand was steady again. "And does she like him?"

The banker started to his feet, white with passion.

"Do you, knowing me as well as you do, knowing my love and pride of family, ask that question, sir?"

"Certainly; if I remember, your father was a village clergyman and a good man, who, I am sure, never aspired to any extraordinary gentility."

"That is nothing to the point, sir. I stand on my own merits, not in the place of my dead father. I don't care how poor a man my Cecil marries, but, at least, his character must be spotless."

"In the eyes of the world," put in Mɪ Lyons.

"In *my* eyes, sir. I have not brought my child up, a lady of refinement and purity, to bestow her on one whose family escutcheon might be a convict's cell, or parti-colored dress."

"For shame, Mr. Romaine," said the old gentleman, indignantly, throwing down his pen. "I never expected, sir, to hear a gentleman of your standing use unmanly taunts."

"Is it not so?"

"At least, sir, knowing how I feel toward the family, you might come in a different spirit to me. You understand how much I esteem Harry Franklin — that I think there are few, very few, young men at all to be compared to him. A little milder way of stating the case would be quite as acceptable to me, as his friend, I assure you. In that form, you might possibly make an ally instead of an enemy."

"I am very ready to acknowledge my error," said the banker, seeing his mistake. "You must pardon much to a doting father, who would not, in any event, give up his only earthly treasure lightly."

"I dare say not; and now, I think we both feel better; let us consider the facts calmly. How long do you think young Franklin has admired your daughter?"

"That, I can hardly say. Such things often date

from the first acquaintance. I presume for nearly a year."

" And pray how did you discover this seriously misplaced affection? "

" By some very insignificant signs, I suppose you would say. At one time he presented her a package of books. He has been in the habit of sending choice bouquets; but as several young gentlemen have done that as a mere matter of compliment, I took no notice of it. Lately he gave her a very beautiful collection of pictures, colored by himself. I saw that the matter was going too far, and took the liberty of sending them back, for which, I suppose, the young fellow wont forgive me in a hurry."

" And now for the next question, which you must answer as candidly, Mr. Romaine, because much that is important hangs upon it. Do you think your daughter understands as you do that he aspires to her affections? "

The smile died out of the banker's face.

" She may," he replied, curtly. " Of course young ladies see these things much quicker than we men."

" And have you the slightest suspicion that she in any degree returns his affection? "

The banker pushed his chair back angrily.

" Tut, tut, now, Mr. Romaine," said the other,

quietly; "it would not lower the young lady in the esteem of any good person, if she was known to look with favorable eyes upon such a man as Harry Franklin. And I tell you again, you must be candid with me if you wish me to aid you."

"It makes no difference to me, sir, how my daughter regards him," said the banker, almost calmly, yet with a vague terror winding through the inequalities of his voice. "I tell you I would see her dead before her name should be merged in his. Think of the heritage to descend to innocent children. No, I would hang myself before I would accept a son out of prison."

"Softly, sir, again; you let your feelings carry you away. Why should we any of us heed the world's opinions, if we are contented with our condition? Provided I have enough to live above the necessity of asking alms from the world in the shape of flattery, position, or wealth, it may rate me as it pleases. My independence, thank heaven, is not to be shaken by anything short of Almighty Providence. I am sorry the young man has allowed his affections to be settled upon the young lady for — *both* their sakes," he added, with emphasis.

"What do you mean?" The banker looked up haggardly.

"I mean that I think the young people like each other; and the disappointment will be mutual. I have observed them together more than once. Perhaps, however, the matter will stop where it is. I will see Harry at all events, and counsel him how to act. He always takes my advice, poor fellow!"

" I wish you would; it would add to the many favors you have kindly done. Tell him there is no hope — no hope whatever; place before him the disadvantages it would entail upon her, to call it by no severer name; plead with him Lyons; if he loves her, he will see the propriety of abandoning such a mad scheme."

" I will do my best for him," replied his friend, cooly — a dubious assertion that might be taken as for or against the interest of his friend; but, at the same time, there was a twinkle in his eye, and a smile on his lips, that would have afforded a well wisher of young Franklin not a little satisfaction.

Meantime, a scene no less full of interest, was at that moment transpiring at the house of the banker. Cecil had sat for an hour as her father left her, her thoughts strangely occupied. She was not proud in the sense her father was. And if she had been, I doubt if she would have banished these same thoughts. Self-interest, ambition, neither of these were worth so much to her as the heart. She had studied the character of Mr. Franklin more than that of any young man of her acquaintance; led first to do so through pity. His moral excellences delighted as well as gratified her. His person was unexceptionable; but the mind was his lasting beauty. She had measured him in all situations. In the house of God, reverent and worshipping; in his Sabbath class, indefatigable; in society, modest, yet at times brilliant. One by one he had overcome even the prejudices of her set. Everybody called Franklin a noble young fellow. He bought no one's esteem. He did not seek to forget himself in conviviality, or by plunging into the pleasures rightly called vices. Thus was laid a broad basis for the foundation of solid happiness. Before she knew it, she was interested in him for his own sake. Her father's evident liking for him misled her, and she awoke fully to the bitter truth, when the banker told her that henceforth she must be as a stranger, where the whole love and strength of her heart were given.

That night at the supper table he had said it, half wild at her silence and the tears that brimmed her eyes, though she would not let them fall. And yet she was so noble it may be doubted whether she suffered as much for herself as for him. Pity for herself was passive and inert at first — she was reviewing the sad epochs of his life. How she would have brightened his pathway, and, like a loyal woman who gives herself as a sacrifice for her country, sacrificed everything for his happi-

ness, being all in all to him, at his fireside, queen
and wife combined — a broad defence and encouragement. Ah, was it never to be?—that sacred
tabernacle of home, where,

" The world forgetting, by the world forgot,"

they two could defy all the shafts of fortune, should
she prove unkind ; or to themselves be all of world
and society they wished. She did not dream of
seeing Harry that night, and it was with feelings
of alarm, hope and pleasure combined, that she
heard his name announced. He came forward with
the embarrassment of one who knows not how to
express the depth of his feelings, and yet betrayed
it in every look and gesture.

For awhile he talked quietly ; then his voice
trembled as he spoke of his returned pictures.
Cecil had known nothing of this. It was her father's act without warrant ; he had done it upon his
own responsibility.

" I did not send back your little gift," she said,
with warmth, yet with modesty. " I have always
treasured it."

" It was the last one," he responded. She blush-
ed, but said nothing, seeing how the matter stood,
that her father had judged for her. From her lips
he should bear no blame. She had been over san-
guine — there was indeed no hope from him.

Harry pleaded his cause as we might expect he would; resigned, in a degree, to what he foresaw would follow. As he grew eloquent, Cecil trembled. He did not stint the darker shades of coloring as he spoke of his own unworthiness. She listened, hardly conscious of listening. She was, strange as it may seem, seeing all these things with her father's eyes. To her they boded no dismay; but to him she knew they would be barriers insurmountable. As the yellow leaves drift to and fro in the sharp wind of December, so all things at times seemed whirling and eddying around her in the trouble and confusion of her spirit. That she felt, she dared not express, for she had never defied her father in her life, even in thought. Every moment her love strengthened, her estimation increased, as she listened to his low, frank utterance; but what must she say? That she was indifferent, she could not; that she loved him, she dared not.

When he grew silent, there was a weary, hopeless look stamped on his brow, as if he would say — "There, I am now ready to be offered up." She hid her face, could not speak, could not even give faint hope. He saw how it stood; bent his head down upon his clasped hands, lifted his face again, whiter but more patient.

"I should have expected this," he said, slowly;

"perhaps I did look for it, but would not confess it even to myself. But it shall not quite unman me. I am used to bearing burdens; so much so, that perhaps I could not walk in the straight path without them. Forgive me, Miss Romaine, for troubling you. I will dream no more of earthly happiness. Perhaps heaven is good in withdrawing all my props."

It was a hard trial for one so gentle as Miss Romaine. The look and manner touched her to the heart.

"You must not think of me as I fear you do," she said, in a changed voice, her own lips dry and colorless. It is not for anything in the past that I cannot, must not, encourage this matter on my own part. If—if my father"—she struggled to go on, but could not.

"I understand you, Miss Cecil, and I ought not to blame him. Your future is too precious—a matter of too much moment to him, to decide in my favor, even if his heart and his conscience approved. There are some things worse than death to a sensitive man—this is one of them. I have calculated all possible chances, and am prepared for—failure."

The hopeless voice, the drooping eye, the quivering lip, all spoke his utter despondency, in spite of his vaunted heroism. He arose to go; he nerved himself to calmness; he held out his hand.

"We part to-night, perhaps forever," he said, with pale lips. "I only ask you to remember me as one, who, whatever have been his faults, has striven most earnestly to be of some use in the world, and will *still* strive, with God's help, though working under the cloud, and the burden of a spotted life. Good-bye!"

She could not say it. In spite of herself-command, a quick, dry sob broke from her lips —

"You shall at least," she cried, passionately, "carry away with you, wherever you go, this consolation, that not only will I not forget you, but that no other can be to me what you have been."

"Noble Cecil!" he cried, in a voice nearly choked with emotion. He seized the hand she extended, pressed it to his lips, and covered it with kisses.

Cecil stood where he had left her, silent and white as a statue, till she heard her father's footsteps. Then she started, ran noiselessly down the room, and disappeared.

CHAPTER XXVIII.

IRENE'S battles with herself were desperate indeed. She stood alone, isolated from God and man. She would sooner have gone down into the tomb and communed with the dead, than have humbled herself to confession and contrition. And yet, how was she humbled. Her love was idolaatry — unmasked, unappreciated, save by the sister who would willingly have given her life for her, if it had been in her own power. Even, as it was, Bernie had prayed for this, always adding with an angel's meekness, " Thy will be done."

And yet at times Irene hated her. Such emotions, such passions are beyond the power of description.

Is there one terrible hour in the life of humanity when, as old legends have it, all the powers of darkness combine to crush out every vital spark of celestial fire, and leave the soul groping in darkness that shall never be reillumined — a moment in which the angel of our destiny entreats in vain, and if, alas, baffled, turns away in solemn sadness, too awful for tears, while the irrevocable deed is

309

done? If so, that time came to Irene; the time of temptation; would it be also of salvation?

Terrified at the depth and strength of Ler own emotions, Irene strove at times to fly from herself; even to despise herself. She compromised with good resolves. She embraced Bernie more tenderly, after one of her whirlwinds of secret accusation, and devoted her spare moments with the gentlest apparent solicitude to the interests of her sister. But one chance word, the entrance of Clarence, a quick expression of delight, would change the whole current of her feelings to the deadliest hate. Then a torrent of passion, all the more violent for its concealment, would dash against the heart so poorly disciplined, so frail in its best resolves, and she would go by herself to struggle into calmness. To her, there was no " up there," as to Bernie. She groped among the clouds of passion, and saw never the sunshine of truth, of purity, that purity, I mean, which sees no guile because it knows none.

One night, sleep had quite forsaken her pillow. Unable to rest, unwilling to hear the soft, regular breathing of her sister, Irene arose, threw on her dressing gown, lighted the gas, and began pacing the room, keeping back the half hysterical sobs that struggled up from her bosom. Angry with herself, impious towards God, jealousy, engendering hate, surging from every avenue of her heart against the sweet name and presence of her sister, her state was pitiable indeed. Like a spirit, she wandered through the rich and costly adornments of her room, her heavy locks escaped from their confinement and gleaming on her shoulders, the mirror reflecting a wild, haggard face, destitute of all human compassion, her hands locked as if despair held the key, the wail of the lost in her low, harsh sobbing sighs.

She threw herself in her dressing-chair, flung her arms over its side, buried her head in them, and gave way to unrestrained weeping. The noise wakened Bernie, who, stretching herself softly forward, saw the desperation in her attitude, and grew frightened.

"O! Iry, dear, are you ill?" she cried, throbbing from head to feet with solicitude and terror.

Irene was icy calm in a moment. She lifted her head, a mocking laugh on her lips.

"Am I getting to be a sleep-walker, do you think?" she asked, in an altered voice.

"I'm afraid you're in trouble, darling; come and tell me." She held out her arms as if they would fain take all the sorrow into her own gentle bosom.

"Trouble!" cried Irene, quickly, "what made you think that, child? What do you watch me so

for? What reason have you, pray, for harping
on that string, trouble? If I am a little nervous,
or my head aches occasionally, I do n't know as
it 's so very serious a matter as to occasion you so
much needless anxiety. Go to sleep."

"I ca n't, Iry; I believe I 'm not very well."
Her lip quivered, as placing one hand over her
heart, she seemed striving to still its rapid pulses.
I will not say that Irene wished it might be stilled
forever. It is hard to define or even imagine that
impetuous, selfish, rash emotion that in its heat
and depth, dares almost any fate so that success
may crown its wishes.

"Nonsense ; you are always complaining."
But the words had not left her lips before she
started to her feet; Bernie was sinking back, whiter and whiter.

"What shall I give you, Bernie? I was cruel;
you are very ill. Oh, Bernie, tell me quick."

In her fright, she caught up one of two vials that
stood on the *etegere*. It held a colorless liquid.
This she had lifted, and with a hand by no means
steady, dropped from its contents, into a little
silver tankard, from which her sister always took
her medicine. Suddenly, something arrested her
hand: a word on the label, printed in red letters.
She became transfixed. A fearful look, rigid,
ghastly, crossed her face, as in mid-air the vial

was still suspended.   Her lips purple and parted,
her eyes distended, filled with the horror of a half-
divined purpose, a nearly completed deed of
death.   Thus she stood : her chest rising and falling in irregular panting breaths.   Then the vial
came down on the marble of the *etegere;* she carried the tankard, her fingers shaking as with palsy,
to the bedside, her eyes fixed, her lips drawn in.

Bernie was waiting.   The innocent one raised
her feeble hand and grasped the awful draught.
An instant of hesitation — caused by weakness — it
was at her lips, slowly upturned ; when, with a
shriek scarcely human, Irene dashed it across the
bed and its contents were lost.   Bernie glanced
up ; the deadly weakness was passing away.   Was
her sister mad ?   Was that her sister, indeed, with
the great black circles under her eyes ?

" O ! Bernie — I — I happened to think," gasped Irene, breathless, her lips still rigid, " it was —
the — the lotion — I dropped in your cup.   Great
heaven ! I should have been your murderer ; " and
she fell heavily forward, gasping and sobbing
among the pillows.

Bernie's gentle hand was upon her head in a moment, Bernie's caressing voice in her dulled ear.

" You did n't know, darling, you were so frightened.   I should have done it myself, perhaps.
Do n't cry ; it is all over now, and no harm come ;
do n't cry, dear."

Ah! little she knew the cause of those heavy, tearless sobs; little she knew of the horrible intent that had so nearly been fulfilled; little she knew that her brilliant, beautiful sister was evermore, hereafter, to be goaded by the remembrance of that intentional sin. And humbled — yes, humbled, as nothing else could have humbled such a nature. Never again would hatred fasten its pangs in that proud heart; never again would she dare to trust herself. Oh! could it be that in that heart she had ever cherished the shadow of such a desire? No, no; and yet it must have been, or why did the fiend tempt her so nearly, even till the deadly poison was close upon the lips of that beautiful life? Her shudderings, her self accusations, her wild petitions for pardon, need not here be reiterated. It was no simulated tenderness that ever after pressed timid lips upon the brow she had so nearly consigned to the grave. She accepted her lot with a meekness that was almost child-like. She distrusted, nay almost hated herself, when the dark cloud of that night's memory swept across her vision. She went with a broken heart to Him who saw and saved her from the tempter.

CHAPTER XXIX.

BERNIE'S SYMPATHY.

THE Colonel was at home; Mrs. Willerton would be in soon; would he wait? and the servant led the way to the snuggery.

Harry entered, sat down uneasily, apologising, for the Colonel laid aside a book as he came forward.

"Do n't say a word; glad to see you. But how is it? are you really going off?"

"That is my present intention, sir," said Harry.

"I do n't like it, I do n't like it at all;" and the Colonel shook his head. "Madge told me all about it. I'm quite angry, sir, quite angry."

Harry tried to smile.

He did not succeed, however; and the Colonel seeing that some mystery underlaid his sudden desire, grew silent.

"I'll tell you what, Harry," he said, after a few moments of thought, "I'll send out a venture by you. In that case, you might just possibly make your fortune. Besides, I have some good friends in Barbadoes, whose well-stocked plantations will

315

do your eyes good to see. There's Captain De Laury, one of the most, genial old fellows you ever met in your life, and whose pretty twin daughters must have finished their education in England, by this very time. You shall have letters to him. Then, there's Lance Terry, a judge by now, I suppose, though he used to be my small red-haired chum at college. You'll like him, hugely, and all his family, particularly his wife, who used to be a school-girl sweetheart of mine. O, but if you're bent on carrying that lack-a-daisical face with you, I advise you to take passage for Japan, where they don't understand physiognomy."

Again Harry tried to smile, but the poor contortion was only a ghost after all. It was a bore to sit still there, waiting for Mrs. Willerton, so he said he would call again, and left the house.

The Colonel was very pathetic over this visit when his wife came home.

"And I say, Madge," he cried out, "I've just thought of it. Our poor young fellow likes Cecil Romaine, I'll wager the scar on my cheek. (He knew nobody could take up that wager). And so he's going away where he'll be worse off than ever. Why don't he stay here and just fight for her, as I did for you?"

"But, dear, remember," said his wife, with a touching pathos in her voice.

"O, yes; he's out of prison!" sighed the old Colonel. "Jove! do n't I wish that girl was my daughter?"

"Would you give her to him?" asked Mrs. Willerton.

"Would I?" roared the Colonel, springing to his feet; "would I kiss you thus, if I did n't love you? Yes, would I, and thank God that my child had found an honest man. Honest, clear through; none of your mock gentlemen, who, if tried, might not come out of the furnace as pure as he has. I do n't care for the prison; the question is, is he better or worse for it? I say, he's the better, as many another poor fellow would be if he only felt there was a chance for him, if he could only lean on some helping hand.

"Barker — you know Barker of the Western land business — says he to me, yesterday, speaking of somebody he had helped, 'I let him have a hundred, and now he's down again.' Let him have another hundred," said I.

"'Why, you might be helping some people all the time,' said he.

"Of course, said I, that's what we're put here for. You and I, Barker, must work on Scripture rule, which says we must forgive seventy and seven times. So I say, help your brother seventy and seven times; the money is all out at interest;

that's what I call carrying your pure gold to heaven with you. I hate that cold philosophy which consigns a man to oblivion because he is unfortunate. Besides, I'd a great deal rather invest in humanity, even if I lose, than in selfish pleasures. Hit him, there, my dear, hit him hard; for he's tremendous on game-suppers, and other slightly expensive little matters, on which he spends thousands in a year."

"Speaking of suppers, reminds me that Mr. Lyons is going to give a party on Christmas day," said Mrs. Willerton.

"A party! what, down there?"

"Yes, my dear; humoring a little notion of Bernie's — a feast for the poor."

"A glorious little old man, that Mr. Lyons, my dear," said the Colonel. "Notes for us, eh? Certainly, I'll go, certainly."

Clarence was master of ceremonies. A red ribbon crossed his broad chest. He had never been so happy. It was, he declared, the first real holiday of his life — his jubilee of freedom.

Bernie had been given *carte blanche*, and succeeded in gathering a motley group. Humanly speaking, it was not a choice collection — that gathering from the by-ways and the hedges of society; but some of the souls that dwelt side by side with

dwarfed limbs or perverted intellects, were perhaps pearls in God's great cluster. We cannot
see as the angels do, or our eyes would open
wider with incredulity than they have been in the
habit of doing. We are most of us Pharisees
when among the poor and degraded.

The good carpenter, Tim Stebbins, worked with
a will and a flushed face.

Among the bowed down, the aged, the infirm, a
little child flitted like a sunbeam; a little English
child, with cheeks like the rosy side of a Baldwin
apple. She came with the old porter of the bank,
and seemed to claim Clarence as her especial con-
ductor, clinging to him with her fat, pink hands,
and thereby finding favor in the eyes of both Bernie and her sister. A very bright little creature
she was, always laughing; the embodiment of happiness and health.

Bernie, for almost the first time in her life,
seemed restless and careworn. She flitted round
among her poor, receiving blessings from all, audi-
ble and unspoken; but she did not eat herself, in
spite of many a playful threat from Clarence that
he should send her home.

Perhaps, if the truth had been told, she would
gladly have gone. Harry was there: he had accompanied Irene as soon as the people were fairly
seated at their dinner. She alone interpreted the

cloud upon her brother's brow; she alone guessed at the unhappy audience he had had with Cecil Romaine.

There were merry tunes from the old German organ-grinder, and a song of long ago by the little shoemaker, who stood upon a chair in order that his face might be seen by the crowd. "Cash," with a few grins and awkward scrapes, delivered a neat speech, and was applauded vehemently. Clarence recited a beautiful poem, which, if not understood, was at least listened to with respectful attention. Then they drank healths all round with spiced lemonade, and were very jolly. After that came the presents, each person receiving some appropriate gift; and the day ended, as days well spent will always end, in deep, calm, sober enjoyment.

Bernie returned home, dejected and pale. Irene had dressed, and gone already to some bright gathering, accompanied, as they supposed, by Harry.

"I declare, I've a great mind not to go, after all," said Clarence, throwing his fine length along one of the lounges; "I'm as tired as a dog, begging your pardon."

Bernie had also seated herself, wrapped round as usual by her fleecy, Shetland scarf, in one of the easy chairs. She laid back wearied and drooping.

At this speech she roused herself a little.

" O, yes, Clarence, you promised Irene," she said.

" She knows I 'd a great deal rather stay here with you," retorted Clarence, spreading the large pillows comfortably, and closing his eyes.

" But you promised her."

" Yes, that 's rather awkward, I know ; but can 't I plead indisposition ? I 'm horribly tired."

" But you 're well enough."

" Perhaps ; at any rate, I 'll nap it a few moments, if you 'll overlook the impoliteness." He smiled as he caught her eye.

Bernie smiled, too — a radiant smile it was, all to herself, for Clarence could not see her. It was one of her moments of inspiration, voiceless but fleeting ; a celestial peace, that sometimes the dying feel as they near heaven, descended upon her soul. The light was turned down ; the bright walls and the brighter pictures reddened and paled in the soft, warm atmosphere. Bernie looked around. Her eyes lingered on the manly brow of Clarence, and deepened and grew more beautiful as they gazed.

" I shall at least have one star in my crown of rejoicing," she whispered softly — " one angel in heaven, who was led thither by this weak hand. And if heaven accept the sacrifice which perhaps I am about to offer, then Irene will at last, after the sharp sorrow is gone, be happy."

She was startled by quick footsteps. Her father never walked like that. Bernie was scarcely visible in the dim light, half hidden by the great easy-chair. Her brother did not see her until he had taken several strides to and fro, passing quite near. She could not speak, for that something terrible that whitened his face so palsied her tongue that she could only gaze and tremble. Still walking hurriedly, abstractedly, he caught sight of Clarence, whom he thought asleep, but who was watching him intently.

"Ah, you're not gone, then," he exclaimed, stopping abruptly.

"And you, Harry," said Bernie, softly; "I thought you went with Irene."

"I did," returned the young man, the pallor of his face changing to a burning red.

"But I excused myself on our arrival, supposing that *you* would certainly be there, as you promised," turning to Clarence.

"And what did you come home for, in this unceremonious way?" asked the other, rising from the couch slowly, as he spoke.

"I — I was ill," replied young Franklin, putting his hand to his forehead.

"O, that's it; then of course I'll go, if Irene

expects me." He arose, unwillingness visible in every motion. Standing a moment before the fire, he looked down on Bernie. Never had she seemed half so lovely.

"You are a spirit," he cried out, smiling; "there's no flesh and blood about you. Sometimes I'm afraid you'll melt away before my eyes."

"Perhaps I shall," she returned, quietly.

"No, no; I shall hold you with the force of my strong will — weave of it a matchless silken web, as Vivian did for Merlin, so that you can never go away from me unless I wish it. That time will only come when I am ready to take wing also. By the way, what a tremendous angel I shall make!"

"You mustn't jest about such things," said Bernie, gravely.

"Of course not; I'am not joking. If, in that world invisible to us, we keep our stature, surely I shall be a spirit strongly framed and fashioned, while you will be such a wee, light, airy thing. But time flies, and if I must, I must. Good-bye, Bernie."

He stooped and touched her forehead lightly with his lips; a faint crimson spread over its pure white surface.

"As for you, young man, if your head is n't right, the best thing you can do, is to take my place upon yonder lounge. You will find the pillows placed just in the particular angle that in ures a snooze. Good night."

Bernie's eyes followed him half proudly, half tenderly; then she turned to Harry, who stood with folded arms, before a superb painting of Mary, the mother of Christ, touched perhaps by the sorrowful benediction in her sweet face.

"Harry, you are in trouble again," she said.

"I'm always in trouble, Bernie."

"Not always, dear. I havn't seen your face clouded like that for a twelvemonth. Tell me — you know I can sometimes help you a little."

He still maintained his position before the picture; his chest swelled once or twice with strongly subdued sobs, and his whole frame trembled. Presently turning, yearning for sympathy, he threw himself on the floor beside her, and hid his face on her knee. She passed her hand lightly over the curling masses of hair, sometimes tossing a lock aside, or twining it around her fingers, wondering what she should say.

"Bernie, I shall have to give it up at last; there's no manhood in me, I'm afraid," he said

"I wont believe you," she responded. "To me, you have seemed more than grand; for you know, greater is he who ruleth his spirit, than he that taketh a city. And only think, dear, what you have had to contend with! Besides, have you not won esteem from everybody?"

"Esteem," he murmured bitterly; "at least the *show* of it," he added, in a quick, fierce whisper.

"No, not that, but true esteem. I do n't believe there's a man who really knows my own dear brother, but respects him;" and she laid her cheek lovingly against his forehead. A deep sigh was the only answer just then. By-and-by he said, wearily, "No, no, I am to be under a cloud all my life."

"And if you are," cried Bernie, lifting her head, as if in her little self she defied the whole army of shadows with which he was battling, "what is this poor, short, dream of a life? Harry, you know as well as I do, that it is nothing. It is very pleasant to have the good opinion of the world — perhaps to be bowed down to, and held in high esteem; but what Christ was — a suffering, houseless wanderer — bearing all manner of evil falsely, let me be, before I begin to murmur of the ingratitude or injustice of the world that crucified Him. I do n't mean to be harsh, you know, dearest, but oh! I wish I could lift you for a little while from your dark surroundings."

"Bernie, you are good, and pure, and right, as you always are; yes, you *are* — let me say it; and I, no doubt, am committing sin with every breath I draw; for I am repining, with all *His* goodness in full view. But perhaps I ought to make a clean breast of it; you will know how to pity me a little, when I tell you — that — that I have lost all I cared for, in this life. You must have known how I felt towards Cecil Romaine. Well Bernie, dearest, the pleasant dream is over. I have been made to feel that I am not a fitting match for the proud banker's only daughter."

"Did *she* say that?" asked Bernie, still stroking his hair, and gazing into the flickering firelight.

"O, no; she was goodness itself. She pitied me."

"She loves you," whispered Bernie, putting her lips close to his ear.

"I have thought so," he murmured, tremulously.

"I know it, dear," persisted Bernie.

"But of what avail, if she does?" he asked, bitterly. "She will never fly in the face of her father's displeasure."

"Would you have her?" whispered his sister.

"No; not for one so worth —"

"You shall not say it," cried Bernie, placing her hand at his lips again. She was thinking what she could possibly do to help him. Her face brightened.

"I believe Mr. Lyons could aid you in some way; why do n't you go to him?"

"I did," replied the young man, with a shiver.

"And what did he say?"

"Advised me to forget her, like the old bachelor he is."

"O, Harry! did he? Then there *is* no hope," wailed Bernie.

"Of course there is none; and as I ca n't forget unless I tear my heart out, I shall do the next thing that is possible."

"And that?" cried Bernie, breathlessly.

"Is to leave the country at once. I have already arranged for it."

"Harry, you do n't mean so." There was absolute terror in her voice.

"I do mean it, darling — I must."

"Leave us! go from here — from all who *do* care for you; from your home and country? Harry, not till I am gone. I could not bear it, indeed I could not." Her face fell on his bowed head; her tears rained on his forehead. He felt the pulses of her slender frame throb through his own, and, gathered her in his arms, soothing, or striving to soothe her.

"My own Bernie, my darling Bernie!" he cried, himself moved to tears, "what can I do? You would not surely have me stay where I must meet *her*, and feel that I am regarded as an interloper — a pardoned reprobate? For, you see now I *must* give up my place in the bank, and no light excuse will warrant that. You will be calmer when you think of it, and see the necessity for such a step."

"I ca n't let you go, Harry; or, if you must, I shall go with you."

"No, Bernie, darling, that would be preposterous," said her brother, aghast. "You are not strong and well; I could n't take you from your cosy nest to share such a fate."

"Harry, you must not go," cried Bernie, still sobbing.

"Well, well, dear, we wont talk about it now. Thank God that I still have one friend who loves me as you do. Cheer up, dear, or I shall not forgive myself for making you so wretched."

Bernie brightened a little, but could not get over the shock. Holding her brother's hand tightly, she reasoned with him, still trembling in view of his banishment. It seemed to her worse than death for him to go forth from all good influences that had been quietly evolving his higher virtues, and winding him about their hearts, even till Irene confessed her injustice toward him, and yet her heart told her she could not blame him. To lose so much where he had staked all; to love so sweet a creature, and forfeit her possession, was more than she could think upon with calm nerves.

"Harry, in some way, God will bring even this about," she said, after a long silence. "If you have faith, great faith, go to him, feel that he is your nearest Friend, for he has said he is not a

God afar off. I will pray too, with all my might, and mind, and strength. Wait a little while before you decide to leave us, and see what God will do for you. There, you are smiling; oh! I do love to see you smile."

"Just as you said 'wait a little,' such a singular happiness penetrated my heart! It was as if a voice spoke and said, 'Have I led you all this way, and can you not trust me?'"

CHAPTER XXX.

THE HEART OF MR. LYONS.

A MOST welcome visitor appeared. None other than Mr. Lyons, claret coat, furs, and all. Bernie forgot her weakness, and hovered about him till he was comfortably seated. The sight of his face always did her good; and as for him, he declared that Bernie was his twin soul, and that it was only through a freak of Dame Nature that she was born so late.

" Company spoils me," he said, folding his arms, and sinking down complacently. "I do n't know but I 'm getting to be a bit luxurious, too. Whenever I go from here, I 'm inclined to buy a new carpet."

" And that reminds me of old Mrs. Darby," cried Bernie, " one of my dear, poor women. I found her out by what seemed like the veriest accident; I do n't know but she would have starved sooner than told of her sufferings voluntarily. After I had stocked her small closet, I begged her to tell me if there was anything else she wanted; but she would n't, though I knew by her manner that there

was some one thing that would be acceptable. At
last, she said one day, when I was trying to make
her more comfortable,

"'O, Miss, a bit, the *least* bit, of old carpet, just
big enough to put under my feet when I gets up,
and handy to move when I goes about.' Do you
know, that minute, I wanted to laugh, and to cry'
too? for the tears were actually in her poor, faded
eyes, almost as if she were pleading for a life.

"Why, you dear soul," said I, "you shall have
enough to go from your bed to the fire-place ;
and I got it — thick, warm carpeting, and a nice
little lamb's wool mat.   When I gave her that, she
just rocked herself to and fro, and cried till I
was frightened, she sobbed so."

"'I ca n't do nothing to pay you back,' she said ;
'but just as soon as I get up *there*, I 'll tell my
Lord.' Why, Harry ! why, Mr. Lyons ! well, I
believe we are all crying over my poor old
woman ; " and Bernie wiped her eyes, shining with
both smiles and tears.   Then, turning to Mr. Lyons, with an air of the greatest *naivete*, she exclaimed,

" Have n't we had a splendid day ? "

" Splendid ! " replied Mr. Lyons.   " As for the
people, I think they enjoyed it hugely. To tell
the truth, though, I was glad to pack them off,
after I had packed them full. I shall leave the

gathering of the fragments till to-morrow; then
we know what to do with them, eh, Bernie?"

"Yes, indeed," she answered.

"Clarence is off to a Christmas party, I suppose,
with Miss Irene."

"Yes," with a half sigh.

"And Mr. Harry preferred to stay at home and
mope, and worry his patient sister."

"And keep me company, rather," cried Bernie.

"And get you to moping too, if I had n't come
in, you mean." Mr. Lyons rose up and went across
the room, came back and threw himself in his chair
again.

Presently, weird, beautiful, witching strains of
music came floating down as from an invisible choir
of instruments. At first, faint wafts of harmony;
then, little, tricksy, airy rounds, the very mischief
of music embodied, winnowed the atmosphere,
while all were intent, breathless.

"How it startled me," said Bernie; "but I know
what it is. So you came here to-night with a
pocket-full of music. O, listen! it is like the
voices of the angels."

"How do you know?" asked Mr. Lyons.

"Because it seems to me that I have heard them
in my dreams."

"It's a Christmas present for you Bernie, but
you may thank Clarence for suggesting it."

"I do thank him, and you, too. How kind in you to remember me!"

"O, of course; my kindness is proverbial you know, particularly as I retain something of that old leaven, still — pleasing others because it pleases me."

"To be sure it pleases you. How can one do a pleasant thing and not experience pleasure. But you do n't do it *now* entirely for that reason."

"Bless your heart, no; thanks to you and that kind Power that has borne with me so long, I have a higher motive now. I may not talk of my religion much, Bernie; it 's not my way. Besides, I 'm very young, if you consider, and can only stammer out my praises and my thanksgivings; but I 'm a new man, Bernie, all made over, as it were. Indeed, as much as I have derided the term, I do think, dear child, that I 've got a new heart; for the old one seldom thought of its mercies, and went to rest, and got up again, like the heart of a heathen; but the new one no sooner wakes in the early morning than it looks straight to heaven with gratitude for the mercy that kept it all right and straight while the wonderful machinery rested. And at night, it thinks up so much to be thankful for, that it 's really a very foolish old heart, sometimes, and fairly breaks down and goes to crying like a baby. In fact, it gets a sound scolding from its keeper, now and then, but it does n't seem to mind it much, but goes and does it all over again."

Bernie laughed heartily at this, and so did Harry.

"I suppose Clarence could give you the very same experience," continued the old gentleman, cheerfully. "Clarence is a noble fellow, and he is rising in the world — is going to make a big reputation, and crowd the elbows of some of these aspiring lawyers. By the way, he made an application, the other day, that I laugh at even now, every time I think of it. It 's a little fact in history which you have no doubt read, and which I have n't thought of since I was a boy, till he pictured it out so capitally. A Swedish ambassador, by name Otto Christof, attempted to make a speech in his own language, which he had learned by heart, before Louis XIV. Well, the poor fellow appears, his suite around him in the usual order, when, lo, and behold! not a word of his speech can he bring to mind. A queer position for the handsomest gentleman of his time, surrounded by all the notables of the court; what should he do?

"A bright thought occurs. Not one whit disconcerted, he recites part of the Swedish catechism, with a grave face and appropriate gestures. Think of the emotions of his suite! their covert glances, their efforts to keep up a studied decorum, especially when king Louis listened with the utmost gravity, doubtless thinking every other word a compliment to his august majesty. What a scene! How irresistibly ludicrous! It is one of those things that need the pencil of a Hogarth to be fitly illustrated."

Harry heard all this abstractedly. He still stood leaning against the mantel, his arms folded, his lips trembling with words that could not be spoken; an inexpressible sorrow in his whole attitude. Hitherto, Mr. Lyons had not noticed him. Now the fairy little brass band in the distance struck up, after the briefest silence, the *Dead March in Saul*. Small as was the instrument, every note of that grandest of solemn airs pulsed through the room with a vibration that reminded one of the wondrous, sepulchral under-note of prisoned thunder; for therein could be heard the distant volley of the artillery, as dead heroes were lowered to their last resting-places, and the pomp and circumstance of death in war seemed to glide through the room, and make the air heavy with clouds of grief.

The old man shut his eyes and listened. Harry bent his head a little, and pressed his pale lips tightly together. Bernie, breathless and trembling, leaned forward, her soft eyes lifted and dewy. Then, when it was still again, she whispered,

" And music, what is it? and where does it dwell?
I sink and I mount with its cadence and swell;
While touched to my heart with its sweet thrilling strain,
Till pleasure, till pleasure is turning to pain."

"We shall know all those things up there," she said, reverently.

"And *why* we must endure," repeated Harry.

"When, if we only had the power, we might make everything *so* straight, and fair, and charming," chimed in Mr. Lyons, without looking up. "That is, for *our own* particular benefit."

"How selfish it would make us !" said Bernie.

"It might have that tendency," rejoined the old man, rubbing his hands slowly. "For instance, if I had possessed my particular will and desire, perhaps I should have become so entirely wrapped up in self as to make my own ends and purposes the leading care of my life; instead of which, having suffered soundly, the prize for which I would have given the world, and my soul into the bargain I fear, being thrice within my reach and thrice lost, I was forced to accept something else in its stead, and here I am to-night, all the better for my struggles; at least, I hope so," he added, with unwonted meekness.

"Excuse me, dear sir," said Bernie, in a very gentle voice, "but I have often wondered why you never married."

"That is easily told, Bernie. Somebody else married the woman I wanted, and now she is in heaven; yes, I believe that, thank God! I was wretchedly disappointed, my dear. I never submitted, never, till the dust I loved was laid away in darkness; and even then I turned proudly from God, and walked in my own way. If Mr. Harry, over there, is n't careful, he 'll become just such a crooked stick as I am."

"Poor Harry!" sighed Bernie.

"Nonsense! I sha n't let you pity him. If he is in the fog now, that's no reason the sun is never going to shine. You should have seen me; for I confess there was pluck in me, little as I was. I packed up and was off; catch me sitting down and 'sighing like a furnace.'"

"O, Mr. Lyons! do n't say that," cried Bernie, drawing her breath hard. "Do n't tell him to go off."

"Travel would improve the boy, you silly little woman; besides that, it might better his prospects. There are other eyes besides yours that would grow dim, I fancy; and fond fathers are apt to give in when there are pale cheeks about them."

Harry brightened perceptibly. "I believe Bernie *must* let me go," he said.

"Of course she must. I know she is not so selfish as to keep you on her own account."

Bernie was nettled; she did not like the whole-sale way in which Mr. Lyons disposed of the matter. She had a vague idea that he might make it all right if he would. He, on his part, wanted to see if there was metal in the "boy," as he called him; he was fond of trying experiments. Presently he took Bernie's wrist in his fingers.

"You have sat up late enough, my little lady," he said. "As your medical adviser, I counsel you to retire."

"Promise me you wont urge Harry to travel," she pleaded.

"Certainly I will not; he must act himself in the matter," he said, and Bernie left them together.

CHAPTER XXXI.

A GREAT SURPRISE.

IT'S an applatic strike, sir, they said."

"But who is it?" queried Mr. Lyons, as Pete peered through the crowd.

"It's the rich banker, as comes to your place sometimes."

Mr. Lyons waited to hear no more, but moved impatiently forward, forcing aside those who stood in his way. He had met the throng in a crowded street. Pete, hurrying to the shop with a bundle, had also paused to see what was the matter. Mr. Romaine, quite insensible, was being lifted by two or three strong men.

"Bring him in this store," said Mr. Lyons, pointing to an establishment whose windows were filled with costly pictures and frames. The beetle-browed proprietor frowned. "Some fellows had fits every day — he didn't want them brought there." But when he found out that the passive intruder was Mr. Romaine, the rich banker, he smiled complacently. Had it chanced to be some poor soul, with humiliated and beggared garments, he would have hustled him off·to the hospital with little oɪ no ceremony, as soon as the fit left him. Whereas, in this particular case, he wheeled out a handsome lounge from some room conveniently near, and himself assisted in placing the banker comfortably upon it.

Death, in passing, brushed him with his wing, and left him faint and helpless.

"Mr. Lyons, I am glad you were near," he said, as soon as he could speak. "I felt myself going, and tried to get out of the street. It's an awful sensation — the world spinning away from one. Be kind enough to call a carriage. I must get home without Cecil knowing it; it would frighten her."

"I'll attend to all that," said Mr. Lyons, and he did.

Cecil knew nothing about it, until he had been comfortably in bed an hour or two. Illness succeeded; nothing alarming, however, necessary, his attendant physician said, for the depletion of his system. He awoke one morning, calm and clear headed. His first words were:

"I'm very grateful to you, Mr. Lyons."

"Doctor, if you please," responded the other, with dignity.

"Are you really a medical man?"

"You'd think so, if you saw my diploma," was the grave reply.

"Well, doctor, you are an enigma, any way; but I'm just as grateful. Shall I pull through, do you think?" he added, anxiously.

"Yes, you'll pull through almost any thing with that constitution of yours. But I can tell you, that you will have to carry a careful hand in future. No more late suppers, no more stimulants, or, I'll insure you another fit in three months."

"I'll do whatever you wish me to, doctor," said the banker, resignedly.

"You will, will you?" asked the old man, looking up briskly.

"Anything in *reason*, doctor," replied the banker, pointedly.

"I'll ask you something in a week," was the smiling rejoinder.

In a week the banker sat by his window, thankful for the luxury of an upright position without pain. Mr. Lyons, now familiarly called "doctor" by his patient, sat opposite, his keen gray eyes shining under the mild blue radiance of his spectacles. The banker's hands were thin and white, his temples hollow, his lips colorless, yet he was rapidly convalescing. Someway, conversation turned upon the day of the fit.

"It was a curious sensation," murmured Mr. Romaine, softly. "When I regained my consciousness, I smelt the honeysuckles that grew on the old parsonage wall. Do you remember them? Never were odors half as sweet, but it was very singular."

"A reminder that you should not forget the humble walks of your life," said Dr. Lyons. "I went on a pilgrimage there, last summer. With what emotions I walked up that long trodden path to the little brown door. Three cabbage-roses flaunted in their waning glory under the parlor window. I gathered them, I am not ashamed to say, with moist eyes, and their spicy aroma weaves many a story of the past, when like a child I take the poor dried things out, and open the book in my heart."

"O! yes, I think you told me you were familiar with all those matters."

"Yes, and up that path have I led you by the hand more than once. You probably forget the shy, sensitive young man, who played ball with you sometimes, or cut you hickory sticks for canes."

"I seem to remember," said the banker, slowly.

"It was heaven to me — that little spot in front of the orchard. A radiance and freshness that belong only to youth, come over me at the very mention of it. The look out upon the river, the river itself, with its glinting groups of white lilies; it was not that, however, that made it the Mecca of my adoration. Your father loved me; but I wanted another love, which I never had."

"Ah! I begin to comprehend," cried the banker; "you loved my sister."

"Madly, for I had nothing else to love. I was a sceptic from constitution — and knew no God. When I lost her, there was neither peace or joy for me. I pity every disappointed soul, remembering the bitter anguish of that period. When I was there the parsonage was to let. No minister has staid there as long as your father. I went to the sexton's and got the key. What associations overwhelmed me as I opened the door and entered the broad, cool entry. The furniture was almost the same; the pictures still remained as they were then. But little new garnishing had been added. I could almost see the good old man, your father, smiling, as he always did, on whoever came. It might be Gentry, the rich farmer — it might be ragged old Black, the wood-sawyer, or some child strayed from its home. I verily believe, Ponto, the dog, knew and loved that smile. How serene the old pastor was! how humble, yet how great! They say his acquirements were something wonderful in science and the arts, as well as the wisdom that directs to the head and fountain of all. I know now why he was so divinely submissive; he lived very far above our common sphere. Nothing could disturb his serenity, because he saw nothing worth struggling for in all the empty distinctions and ambitions of this world."

" He was a noble old man," said the banker, his lip trembling a little.

" Noble, hardly expresses it; there was something angelic about him. I believe he would have gone into the very Gethsemane of every human heart, and taken upon him all its agony, and placed to his own lips every cup of bitterness, if it had been possible. And yet he did not talk much. The daily example of his life were his weapons of opportunity, of reproof, of instruction. Were you with him when he died?"

The banker nodded; he was too full of emotion to speak.

" It was a glorious death, I doubt not. And if you had passed on the other day, what a happy meeting there would have been!"

" O! doctor, how you place my worldliness before me! I am very dark in such matters. I scarcely think of them. Yet you do right. I am ashamed that I have not been a worthier son of such a father. God helping me, I'll be a better man if I get up from this illness."

" There is a little more probing to be done," said the other, gently; " the wound is not quite clear yet."

" Go on, but have pity," responded the banker.

" The pity I feel just now is for others," the doctor said, softly; " suppose Harry Franklin—"

"That will do, doctor," returned the banker, sharply, with a motion of dissent.

"No, it will not do. Do n't you see you stand in the way of your daughter's happiness? Look at her narrowly when next you see her. She will avoid your eye ; something in her nature tells her that you are her enemy. Her manners are more languid now ; her cheek is pale, and her eyes grow heavier every day. You may smile, you may say she will get over it. Perhaps, after a mental crucifixion, which it is agony to think of. And she may never get over it. It is not a thing to laugh lightly off. It may be a drop of bitterness that will spoil the cup of your happiness, Mr. Romaine."

" I will take care of that," said the banker, wincing.

" There is a higher power that will take care of it, also," said his visitor, quietly. "I now wish to allude to one thing more ; something that possibly you may think of vital importance. You are already acquainted with a portion of the history of Clarence Lyons. You know that I have the care of his property ; that he has taken my name."

" Yes." The banker listened now with a fresh interest.

" But there is something you did not know. Of his career of dissipation, you are aware ; there is no need that I dwell upon it. He is now a gentleman, both physically and morally. I think I have heard you say that you never heard the name of your sister's second husband."

"I never did," said the banker, nervously. "What in the world has that to do with it? Her death was announced under her maiden name."

"Yes, because, for some years before her death she went by her old name. No matter why. She had good reasons. But she did marry again—a gentleman (so called,) in the British army — Colonel Ashly Anson."

The banker clutched his arm—stared stupidly, the color faded from his face.

"Married—Colonel—Ashly—Anson," he cried, the drops of perspiration standing on his forehead. "Great heaven! then — he — Clarence — "

"Is your sister's only child," replied the doctor, gravely, finishing the sentence.

The banker sank back, panting, exhausted, stricken down as with a mortal blow.

"If you had not been willing to wreck the happiness of two young hearts, you should never have known this," said the old man, watching his patient with all the interest of a practiced physician. "But we must even cut off limbs sometimes."

"I want proof," cried Mr. Romaine, sharply.

"Which I can give you this moment," said the other, diving for his pocket-book.

"No, no," cried the banker, catching his hand, "there is no need; of course I take your word. But I am sadly discomposed. Leave me now, if you please. I wish to think over this thing."

"Before I go from the house, shall I send your daughter in?" asked the doctor, significantly.

"Never mind that, Lyons; one do n't like to be forced; it makes one strain at the curb. I 'm too much confused.

"Bear in mind it is her happiness I seek. Young Franklin is booked for the next voyage of the *Laura*. She sails to-morrow."

The banker frowned, turned his head to the window with resolute lips. At the opposite window a sad face looked out. It was that of a young creature recently widowed. Perhaps the anguish in her eyes softened his heart.

"Tell her to come," said the father, his voice unconsciously tender.

Cecil went softly in, not long after. Her father had thrown himself upon the bed, quite exhausted. His eyes were closed; she bent down, and pressed a soft, fluttering kiss on his pale forehead. His eyes flew open.

"Cecil," he said, gently, "are you unhappy, my child?"

Her lips moved, but there was no reply. Her head bent lower — it was to hide a few falling tears.

"If you really love young Franklin," he went on, forcing himself to be calm, "I will stand no longer in your way. Tell me, candidly." Her head fell on the pillow, close to his face, as she sobbed a faint response.

"Because," he continued, after a momentary pause, "I am thinking somewhat seriously — of — of taking him into the business. There, child, go — you have my consent to marry him — and — and leave your old father." He gave way at last — bit his lips and faltered.

" I will not be selfish, my child."

This he said, as one arm stole round his neck and she kissed his cheek. She started from her recumbent position, and looked anxiously in his eyes. She had noticed the sad tones of his voice — his evident repulsion.

"Not without your full and free consent, dear father," she said, firmly. "I never yet offended you — I never will."

His lip quivered. This time he brought her face down to him, and kissed her tenderly.

"You never did, my darling, you never did. And for all this devotion I was willing to sacrifice you ! No, Cecil, I am no longer angry at your choice. The boy has earned you, nobly. Forgive me for my coldness, my harshness. I thought it was for your good ; but the world is no longer all in all to me."

After that there was a private meeting of four: the banker, his daughter, the new-found nephew and cousin, and the little doctor. Standing before the picture of his mother's innocent girlhood, Clarence reviewed his life and renewed his vows.

CHAPTER XXXII.

A DOUBLE WEDDING.

I'M not to be turned from my purpose," cried Clarence, walking back and forth, a slumbering passion in his voice. "You say she will, in all probability, never rise from her bed again, but that she may live months, perhaps years."

This was on the same day that the banker held an interview with Cecil in his sick room. The doctor had encountered Clarence on his way home. Bernie had been very ill; a slight paralysis threatened her active usefulness, if not her life.

"Yes; perhaps I should not have said even that; she cannot live years. I see no reason why she may not continue several months."

"Then I must, I *must* have the right to watch over her; you would snatch from me this exquisite happiness? I love Bernie with a love as pure as an angel's. I must be *everything* to her, now. Do not speak, doctor, unless to sanction my wish. I tell you, I'm not to be turned from my fixed purpose."

"Softly, Clarence," said Mr. Lyons, perplexed, thoughtful; "you are such a volcano of impetuosity, that your lava fairly scorches me at a distance. I have n't said a word against it. If Bernie is willing, why, so am I. But there is Irene — I am a little astonished "—

"Irene is a good girl; I think more of her than I did. She is growing like Bernie; but Bernie is all the world to me, and I shall be miserable unless I have the right to call her mine. I know I must part with her sooner or later — I know she must die — but I will be father, mother, sister, everything to her all in one; and when she is gone, it will be such a sweet pleasure to think how I have lightened her way to the tomb."

"Well, well, we will see what the others say," and Mr. Lyons took up his hat to accompany his restless *protoge* to the Franklins. Bernie was engaged. She had sent for Cecil Romaine, Irene said, quietly, and Cecil was with her.

A softly shaded atmosphere, the fragrance of violets and the dream-like harmony of the little music-box greeted Cecil, as she glided into Bernie's room. Bernie hardly seemed ill, except for the languor of her movements and the etherial beauty of her face. She greeted Cecil with a smile.

"Sit down, by me, dear," she said. "You see I am laid by."

"Only for a little while, I hope," said Cecil, pleasantly.

"O, yes — I say it with perfect cheerfulness — but I never shall rise again in my own strength. Papa and Harry lift me from place to place; and I am a great deal happier, so helpless, than I ever thought I should be. But I sent for you"— she caught Cecil's hand — "because I cannot bear that Harry should go."

Cecil turned pale.

"O, my dear friend, if you knew him as I do — if you knew what a noble heart he has — how humble, and yet how great he is! And above all, if you knew how much he loves you! None of us can keep him but you — we are all powerless. And O, Cecil, he will leave to-morrow — it frightens me to think of it."

"What do you wish me to do, dearest?" asked Cecil, struggling with her tears.

"Keep him here, keep him here, that is all I ask. Don't let him go with a divided heart, and a heavy sorrow that is like no other. Plead with your father — I know he loves you; plead for my poor boy — I know *you* love *him*. Tell him only to encourage him a little, to put the marriage off for years, if he will, but not to send him away broken-hearted."

Tears in her eyes, blushes on her cheeks, Cecil

knelt down and whispered to the little figure, whose face, on the instant, grew seraphic.

"Then God *has* answered my prayers again," she said, with solemn joy. "I was almost afraid, for He has always been so good, it seemed like trespassing, to ask so *many* favors. O, my darling! my darling! what *can* I say? I am so thankful! If I could only fly up stairs to Harry. I *may* send for him, darling *do* say I may send for him."

"You shall, if you like, dear," said Cecil, quietly. She could not refuse her anything with those patient eyes imploring.

The little cord was pulled by Bernie's own hand, and a servant despatched for Harry, who did not know Cecil was in the house. He stopped his packing, laid by his keys, brushed back his disordered hair, and hurried down stairs. On his entrance, only his heart told him whose was the figure there, for Cecil did not turn round.

"O, Harry! you're not to go; everything is ordered just right. Kneel down here, you blessed, blessed brother. Come, take her, and give me a sister."

Harry still stood flushing, shivering, fearing and hoping, in a breath.

"Is it not true, Cecil? See, he does not believe me. Is it not true? He wont kneel down! Tell him, Cecil."

"It *is* true," whispered Cecil, looking up. "I shall never know how to be exactly proper, I suppose," she added, modestly, her face flushed, her eyes down cast. "But, certainly, it is no impropriety to say that my father takes back the rash words he said; and I hope Bernie and I can induce you to stay."

He caught her hand, his whole face brightened; he needed not to speak. As for Bernie, nothing, not even death, could now disturb her happiness. Only when, a few moments after, Mr. Lyons came, and seating himself by her, talked in a low voice, then she trembled, then she wept. Then, in soft whispers, she talked with her old friend, ending by saying,

"I will think of it. Tell him all I have said; then, if he *will*, why, I shall not say no; because it will be only for a little while, and it will be so sweet to call him *such* a friend."

So it was all settled.

That night, Irene listened with pale cheeks to the conversation of her father and mother, which turned upon two weddings. Suffering had softened her character. Could she ever forget that night? Much thought, and Bernie's holy example, had gone far toward eradicating the seeds of pride which seemed an inherent gift. Subdued, pale, and unwontedly humble, she accepted her own suffering, and with a smile that was heroic, wished her sister joy.

The double wedding was impressive. Clarence knelt, an image of radiant happiness, unselfish, tender, by the side of Bernie, who, in her robes of spotless white, with orange blossoms in her glittering tresses, and the bridal veil floating to the floor, looked almost celestial — too beautiful, by far, as indeed she was, for any earthly destiny.

The Colonel and Mrs. Willerton were present with Laura, who did not accompany her husband on his last voyage.

Mr. Lyons, now the Doctor, restrained his tears with difficulty, as his old "defender of the faith" performed the ceremony. At its close, he saluted Irene, went up to Bernie, knelt down, and imprinted a long, fervent kiss upon her forehead. Then, taking the aged clergyman by the hand, he said,

"I wish publicly to express my thanks to this good man and kind friend, for his patience with my waywardness, and the priceless example which he always set before me. And now it is time that you should all know who I am.

"To you, sir," he continued, addressing himself to Mr. Franklin, "I came as a stranger. Happening to see, on one occasion, when there was a great mortality in the town where I was living, myself reported as dead, the scheme which I have since worked out flashed through my brain. I was immensely rich, childless, alone in the world, and I did not want to buy love or esteem. I determined to place nearly half my fortune in your hands, and then to be guided by circumstances. I have not been disappointed in the son of my only brother. He has proved himself pure gold by ministering to the necessities of those who could not help themselves. As you have accepted me, coming to you as I did, a stranger, will you receive me into your heart and home, as one who loves you for the sake of nature's holy ties?"

What a joyous hour then ensued! How everybody thronged around him, some in tears, some with laughter! What embracings! what deep, unalloyed, almost angelic joy! Even the banker sobbed as he, too, threw his arms about his old friend.

Dr. Lyons turned to Harry, who seemed indeed to have overcome the last obstacle in the way of his success.

"My boy," he said, "I have great pleasure in wishing you joy. I have yearned over you when you knew it not. I have tried to help you up the path of prosperity, because I saw that you deserved it. I congratulate you on your attainments, and am empowered to say, by Mr. Romaine, that you are henceforth an active partner in the banking-house of Romaine & Co."

Harry was overcome; but it would not do to be seen in tears on his wedding night, (I dare not say how many he had stealthily wiped away,) so he swallowed them as best he could, thanking his friend and helper with speechless thanks.

"This is a great night for Zacheus Franklin," cried the little old man, running back and forth with wonderful celerity, carrying loaded plates to Bernie, who, with her sweet smile, thanked him for everything, but took nothing.

She beckoned to him. He was there at her side in a flash, almost.

"I only wanted to call you uncle — dear uncle!" she repeated, taking his hands.

"If you will let me exact a kiss for every time you say it," he whispered.

"You will kiss me a great many times then," she said, laughing.

Chrissy was there, but as she was, to use her own words, "struck with a Spanish mildew," her acts and sayings are not worth recording.

And now to close up these last pages. To say farewell to sweet Bernie, the bride of a few suffering, yet joyful weeks, to leave the dear little doctor, doing good to his utmost capacity every day, and almost every hour, to shake hands with Irene, just as the fine points in her character are being developed by a hand that never disfigures, I do feel a reluctance which words cannot express. And yet it must be done. There is no need of saying that Pete was the doctor's ward to some purpose, and that showing an aptitude for learning, he developed into a first class student; or that Harry Franklin lives yet, honored among men, showing the fruits of forbearance with the erring; or that the Colonel and Mrs. Willerton are passing into a serene old age; in a word, that all the dear friends of my story, including Irene — who long after her sister's death became the wife of Clarence, with a full knowledge of his past life — are yet happy and beloved.

If I have succeeded in comforting any heart that suffers through guilt, if I have induced any to look with something better than curiosity upon those who are put beyond the pale of the pure and virtuous, if I shall inspire any of the rich and prosperous to go about doing good for Christ's sake, then I shall not have written in vain —

"OUT OF PRISON."